The Commandment

Anna Kittrell

The Commandment

Contact Information: titleadmin@pelicanbookgroup.com

Cover Art by *Nicola Martinez*

Prism is a division of Pelican Ventures, LLC
www.pelicanbookgroup.com PO Box 1738 *Aztec, NM * 87410
The Triangle Prism logo is a trademark of Pelican Ventures, LLC

Publishing History
First Prism Edition, 2018
Paperback Edition ISBN 978-1-5223-9782-3
Electronic Edition ISBN 978-1-5223-9781-6
Published in the United States of America

Dedication

To Inez. Thank you for hiding His word away in my heart.

1

"It's late September, not the middle of July," Briar's mother said, blotting her forehead as she clipped down the walkway toward the car. "Seems Mother Nature didn't get the memo."

"Can I drive?" Briar jogged to the driver's side.

"We've already discussed this. You're not allowed behind the wheel until that thing comes off your leg." Her mother nodded toward the clunky black box strapped around Briar's ankle.

The infamous ankle monitor—aka life destroyer. Briar's electronic prison guard since age seven.

"But that's so ridiculous. What am I going to do, pick up a bunch of other unlevels and start a crusade? Come on, please? Only to the clinic. They'll never know."

"Don't argue. Get in." Her mother aimed the key fob at the car.

"You know, Mom, if you owned a cuffphone, like the rest of the population, you wouldn't need that old fob. The car would sense you coming and the door would pop open on its own."

Briar drudged around to the passenger side and climbed in, the headachy, sweet scent of floral air freshener hitting her between the eyes.

Her mom slid behind the wheel and clicked her seatbelt. "Buckle up," she said, double-glancing at her daughter. "What on earth is that on your head?"

"You noticed?" Briar pulled the seatbelt over her shoulder and snapped it, catching a section of long blue hair in the clasp. "I was chatting with Mouse online, trying to cheer him up." She plucked the wig from her head, freed the strands from the buckle, and pushed the wig into her bag, causing her furry keychain to fall out onto her lap.

"He was sad about losing his dad."

The little boy's face had crumpled as he'd told her he wanted his dad back. She'd known how to make him feel better but had swallowed the comforting Bible verse on her tongue—one of many passages her grandmother had taught her as a child—and put on the silly wig instead. Blue hair was acceptable. Reciting Scripture would get her arrested. Sharing Christian faith was illegal by law of The Commandment. The crime carried an even stiffer penalty than skipping a SAP injection or disabling a fleshcard.

Not that either of those things meant anything to Briar. Her body repeatedly rejected the Serum to Accelerate Progressivism, meaning she had no need for the under-the-skin device that kept track of SAP levels in the brain. Her body's intolerance of SAP was the reason she couldn't take a walk around the neighborhood, or drive—or do anything that made life worth living.

Her mom flicked her gaze to the little stuffed lamb dangling from the metal ring. "For goodness sake, Briar, need I remind you that you have graduated from high school? You are far too old for stuffed animals and playing dress up." She glanced over her shoulder and backed from the driveway, her mouth a tight pucker. "It's time for you to grow up." She snatched her oversized sunglasses from the dash and shoved them onto her face.

"Not good advice to give someone majoring in child psychology, Mom. I actually want to be able to relate to the kids I'll be working with face-to-face each day." She picked up the stuffed toy handmade by her grandmother and shined its button eyes on her t-shirt. "Make that face-to-screen, in my case," she muttered.

"Stop complaining. Your high school diploma is every bit as good as the ones received on that Greenfield High commencement platform—earned yours a full six months before the rest of the class, I might add. And your degree will be as commendable as those earned on the Greenfield College campus. Besides, don't jump the gun. I have a good feeling about today." Her mother gave half a dozen small nods. "Today may be the day we've been waiting for. Your brain might respond to the serum, and you'll be free of that clunker around your ankle forever. Have a little faith."

"Last time I checked, my faith is what the OLG was trying to get rid of."

Operation Level Ground maintained a no-tolerance policy when it came to Christianity, and everyone knew it. The organization had long ago integrated the United States Postal Service, and now they owned cyberspace. OLG surveilled every email, video stream, blog, social media site, text message, phone call, and all other means of electronic communication known to man, to ensure nothing slipped past.

"Don't get smart with me." Her mother slid a hand from the wheel and pulled her sunglasses to the tip of her nose, throwing Briar a sharp look over the frames.

Briar smirked and tucked the lamb keychain into her bag. She lowered her gaze to the black box on her ankle. If by some chance her brain did accept the SAP injection, she'd be loose of the ankle monitor; but in turn, a fleshcard would be implanted in the back of her left hand to make sure her SAP level never dropped below the mandated amount. She shuddered. The thought of a chip being shoved under her skin set her nerves on edge.

The beep of an alarm filled the car. Briar glanced at the red light flashing on the ankle monitor and released a frustrated sigh. Her mom had forgotten to inform the OLG of her trip to the clinic.

"Dig the receiver out of my purse and text your appointment information to OLG headquarters." Her mother pushed the designer bag toward her.

Dig. Definitely the right word. Briar poked around in the overstuffed purse, finally pulling out a phone—the wrong one. She needed the government issued receiver, not her mom's personal cell. Why her mother insisted on holding onto that rigid old dumbphone instead of getting a cuffphone like the rest of modern civilization was beyond her. Briar tossed the thing back inside and then fondled it three more times before fishing out the right device.

"Booster?" she asked, keying in her I.D. number.

"No. Recheck," her mom answered.

Briar texted "recheck" to the headquarters' pre-programmed number. In a few seconds, the phone chimed. "That's the code." She unhooked her seatbelt, leaned down, and entered the digits into the ankle monitor's keypad. A twenty-minute timer appeared on the screen, the blue numbers immediately counting down the seconds.

"Hope we don't have any driving issues," she muttered, re-clasping the seatbelt. "You'd better hurry. Five o'clock traffic is about to hit."

"We've been doing this since you were seven. You know the timer automatically adjusts to traffic conditions. Sometimes I swear you try rattling me for fun."

Briar pressed her lips together, fighting a grin.

Nineteen minutes later, her mother pulled into the parking lot of Greenfield Medical Center. "There's a good one." Briar pointed through the windshield at a space near the front of the building.

Her mother eased the car between the yellow lines and killed the engine. "Right on time," she said, glancing at Briar's zeroed-out ankle monitor.

They exited the vehicle and walked up the sidewalk to the automatic glass doors. "Find us a couple of seats. I'll get you checked in."

Briar scanned the waiting room, settling on a pair of padded chairs against the far wall. After a moment, her mother joined her.

"At least they're not terribly busy today." She sat and began rifling through her purse. "Now where is that lipstick? I tucked a brand new tube in this morning."

"Your lips are fine," Briar said. "Red, as always. Like you've recently devoured a cherry popsicle—or a small animal. Why don't you have them tattooed?"

"No, thank you," her mother said, continuing to ransack her bag.

"Briar Lee." A pretty woman in blue scrubs that Briar recognized as Nurse Sheila held open the door that led to the exam rooms.

Giving up the hunt for lipstick, Briar's mother

stood and walked with her.

Briar uncurled the cuffphone from around her forearm. "Hold this for me until I'm finished?"

Her mother took the device and tossed it into her purse.

Briar cringed. "Couldn't you snap it on your arm? Now it's lost forever."

Her mother shook her head. "Nope. Thing's like a vice. Makes me claustrophobic."

A younger woman with yellow scrubs and a dark, messy-on-purpose bun met them in the small corridor.

"Briar," Nurse Sheila said, "this is Megan." She's interning at the clinic. I invited her to observe your procedure, unless you or your mother object."

"Fine with me." Briar smiled and shrugged.

"Of course, it's fine," her mother said as Nurse Sheila led them into a room containing an exam table and two chairs.

Familiar with the routine, Briar hopped onto the table as her mother chose the nearest chair. "Guess we came at a good time. That's the shortest stint we've ever experienced in the waiting room." She inhaled the disinfectant scented air, glad to rid her sinuses of Mom's cherry blossom car deodorizer.

"Yes. The past few weeks have been pretty slow," the nurse said, unlocking a drawer and removing a small key from one of the compartments. "Before that, it was chaos. August was a blur of parents rushing in to get their kids' SAP boosters before school started. Things have pretty well settled down—thank goodness."

Briar held up her foot to the nurse, who unlocked the monitor and typed a code onto the keypad.

"Do you have the receiver?" she asked, lowering

Briar's foot before positioning the monitor on the counter next to a device port.

"Briar?" Her mother raised an eyebrow.

"I put it back in your purse."

"For Pete's sake." Her mother dove into the bag again, shaking her head. She excavated the device and the nurse settled it onto the dock.

Megan the intern stepped to the counter, her curious gaze on the ankle monitor. "Can I look it over? I've never seen one of the old models."

Briar tried to ignore the invisible kick to her gut. What Megan was saying—without actually saying it—was that SAP was very well received by the human body. Normal people responded to the serum at birth. Very rarely did a child remain unresponsive by the age of two. To remain unresponsive, or *unlevel,* as OLG liked to call it, into almost-adulthood was nearly unheard of—entirely unheard of in Greenfield, Oklahoma. Yet there she sat on the exam table.

Sheila nodded at Megan. "Bit of a relic, isn't it?"

Megan picked up the bracelet and turned it over in her hand. "Heavy. I've never held one over a couple years old. How long have you worn it?"

"Ten years. I got it when I was seven, soon after The Commandment was instated. My brain didn't respond to SAP. Still doesn't. You probably already knew that part."

"The OLG headquarters are alerted if the monitor travels outside the electronic receiver's range." Sheila pointed to the device on the dock. "The radius is a hundred and fifty feet, about half a football field." She opened a metal cabinet filled with neatly folded hospital gowns and chose a light blue one from the shelf labeled "medium." She handed the gown to Briar.

"In other words, Briar and her mother are very close." She winked and patted Briar's arm.

Briar rolled her eyes and mouthed the words, "too close."

"I saw that," her mother said. "Lucky for you I feel the same way."

Megan clunked the bracelet onto the counter next to the GPS receiver. "No fleshcard?"

"I'm SAP-less, remember?" Briar answered, unfolding the gown.

"Fleshcards measure the amount of serum in the body, and are implanted when the patient is leveled." Sheila cut in. "Briar's brain doesn't respond to SAP injections—she's never been leveled. A fleshcard can't monitor what isn't there to begin with, so it would be useless." She turned to Briar. "We'll give you some privacy so that you can slip into that fashion-statement of a dress. I'll be back in a couple minutes to escort you to the cellar."

Briar rubbed her hands together. "The *cellar,*" she said in an evil whisper. "I can hardly wait."

~*~

Briar pulled off her disposable slippers and stepped barefoot onto the cold floor of the cellar—a glass-enclosed booth, deriving its nickname from the cyclonical scan that took place inside. She pulled the protective goggles from around her neck, placing them on her eyes.

"Actual or virtual view?" Paul the technician asked over the booth's intercom.

"I'm trying to decide." Briar chewed the inside of her cheek. Did she want to stare through the goggles at a string of funny cat videos or watch the multicolored sensors swirl around her body at a zillion miles-per-hour? "Actual, please."

Today she'd watch the lightshow. Being trapped in the core of a glowing tornado would be a fun skit to play out for Mouse and some of the other kids she video chatted with. Never know, one of them might undergo the procedure someday, and her experience could help them face their fear. She, of course, wasn't frightened or even the least bit uncomfortable, having been through the same process over a dozen times.

"I'm going to fire it up. Stand still, please." The technician's voice came through the speaker.

"Can you play the windstorm track? The one that sounds like a tornado?"

Paul chuckled over the speaker. "Only for you."

"Thanks."

She planted her feet on the stainless-steel floor, smiling as the sound of rushing wind filled the booth. She could picture raindrops slapping against the panes of surrounding glass. Lights of green, red, blue, and every shade in between, swirled around her toes and then moved upward, faster and faster as it bathed her body in a whirling kaleidoscope of color that lingered around her head.

Mouse would love this.

After a few moments, the cellar door popped open and Nurse Sheila escorted her back to the exam room to change clothes. The nurse waited outside the door then ushered her to the consultation office for what Briar referred to as the "after party" with Dr. Parker. She walked to the polished wood table and slipped into the large chair across from her mother.

"The doctor will be in shortly," Sheila said, closing

the door.

Her mother frowned and snapped her gaze up from her black coffee. "For heaven sake, Briar."

"My stomach's growling, so sue me. I'm hungry. It's not like I can help it." She rubbed her middle.

"Soon as this is over, we'll get some lunch. Drink some coffee to hold you over." Her mom lifted her Styrofoam cup in a mock toast and took a sip.

Briar slid from the chair and walked to the coffee station on the far wall. She poured a packet of hot chocolate mix into a disposable cup and added hot water from the coffee maker. "I wonder where they hide the cookies?" she asked, balancing on tiptoe to open a cupboard.

"Sit down." Her mom smacked a palm to the table to show she meant business.

At the sound of the doorknob turning, Briar slammed the cabinet shut and shuffled to the table, careful not to spill her drink.

A thirtyish man in pressed jeans and a long-sleeved navy-blue shirt walked into the room. "Good morning." He glanced at his watch and winced. "Make that good afternoon. I'm John Hartley, Dr. Bingham's physician's assistant." He stepped to the table and stretched out his hand to Briar's mother. "You must be Mrs. Lee. And you must be Briar." After shaking hands, he pulled out the chair at the head of the table and sat.

"PA?" Mrs. Lee frowned.

"PA-C, actually. I've already passed the Board."

"And who is Dr. Bingham? Briar sees Dr. Parker."

"Dr. Parker couldn't be here today. I assure you, I'm well informed of Briar's...unique case history. I've studied her file at length." He reached into his breast pocket and rolled a small, iridescent cube to the table as if it were dice. "I have the results of her scan, and am prepared to discuss the outcome with both of you." He tugged up his sleeve and tapped his cuffphone screen. From the cube, a virtual file folder emerged and hovered eyelevel above the table. A crease formed between his brows as he swiped through the flickering pages. "Mrs. Lee, the results are very concerning."

"Let me guess. Her results are the same as the past twenty scans. Despite the injections she's received every six months for the past ten years, Briar is unreceptive to the serum. Am I right? Those tiny thorn-shaped whatchamacallits, the 'God-zones' in the temporal lobes of her brain are still lit up like holiday trees, and no amount of SAP in the world will extinguish them. Is that about the gist of it, Mr. PA don't-forget-the-C? Same song, same dance. Sign off on her chart, give her the injection, and we'll return in six months."

"The scan did reveal Briar's Agathi are functional, as you assumed, Mrs. Lee. However, today the situation is more complicated than it's been in the past. Due to Briar's age, there will be no further injections. By order of The Commandment, the day Briar turns eighteen—" With his thumb and middle finger, he enlarged the type on the virtual document. "On October sixteenth, three weeks from now, she will report to the Alternative Research Center in Fleetwood, Montana for extended treatment. ARC officials will provide transportation by private jet to the facility." He swiped to a new document and pulled a stylus pen from his pocket. "I need for each of you to sign this acknowledgement."

Briar's swallow of hot chocolate backed up her

esophagus. The ARC? The Cadillac of treatment centers? He wasn't serious. Of course not. Mom managed to aggravate him, and he was bluffing.

Her mother shoved back from the table and stood. "Stick that acknowledgement in your Agathi, Mr. Smarter-Than-Thou. We're not signing anything. I demand to speak with Dr. Parker, immediately!"

"I already explained, Mrs. Lee, Dr. Parker isn't avail—"

"Go get me a real doctor, before I go marching up and down the hallways and find one myself," Her mother cut in.

A muscle twitched in the man's jaw as he tapped his cuffphone and dropped the stylus pen and unlit cube back into his pocket. "I'll interrupt Dr. Bingham." He turned from the table.

"Yes, you run along and do that." Briar's mother lowered into the chair and rested her forehead in her hand. She cut her gaze up to her daughter's. "I won't let them take you to that godforsaken place."

Briar reached over the table and took her mother's hand. "It'll be OK. Dr. Bingham will talk to Dr. Parker and get this all straightened out."

"Darn right it'll get straightened out." She slid her hand from Briar's and pulled her purse to her lap. "Where'd I put those blasted tissues?" A tear splashed to the table as she plowed through her belongings. She finally came up with a wrinkled wad of paper.

"Whole thing's ridiculous. Locking you up like some wild animal," she said, dabbing her lower lids. "*The ARC*—right. Over my dead body. What do they think? That because you can't absorb SAP, you'll suddenly start preaching like a religious zealot and contaminate everyone in society? Even if you did start spouting out Scripture—which you *wouldn't*—where would be the harm in it? All the rest of us have SAP in our brains to keep us from absorbing religion. Got this nifty little chip shoved under my skin to make sure of it." She slapped the back of her hand, indicating her fleshcard. "Everyone—*everyone*—is immune to Christianity except those already locked away in the ARC."

Briar sighed. "I'm aware, Mom, but it's a huge rule. I'm worried about you challenging The Commandment. I'm nervous about going away, too. But I'm also a little excited. Maybe it'll only be for a week or two. I might respond to whatever treatment the ARC offers. Adult therapy is probably more advanced. More radical. Isn't it worth a try? Honestly Mom, I'm sick to death of the injections. They're useless."

Not to mention she could actually leave home for the first time in forever. Maybe even make a friend or two in the facility. Comrades who were experiencing what she was going through. A tiny spark of excitement zipped up her spine.

A man wearing a white lab coat and a stethoscope entered the room with the smug-looking PA-C in tow.

"I'm Dr. Bingham." He nodded curtly at Briar and her mother then took his turn sitting at the head of the table. "You've met my assistant. Do you feel your questions or concerns were not properly addressed?"

The assistant physician set the cube on the table in front of Dr. Bingham and glanced at her mother. He cleared his throat and selected a chair to the right of Briar.

"That's putting it mildly. Where on Mother Nature's green earth is Dr. Parker?"

Dr. Bingham wove his fingers together and leaned forward on his elbows. "Dr. Parker is not at this facility anymore. He suffered a stroke four months ago, and is no longer practicing medicine. Currently, he is residing at a rehabilitation hospital on the east coast."

Briar heard her mother's throat click as she swallowed. "OK. That answers one of my questions. Here's another one—what exactly is wrong with my daughter? We've been told over and over again that her Agathi are functional. Big deal. I can glance at those bright red splotches on her electronic imaging printout and tell you that. My question is *why* are they working? Never once has anyone on staff—including Dr. Parker—been able to give us the reason."

Briar slowly stirred what was left of her now cold hot chocolate. She knew the reason. Her Agathi continued to thrive because her grandmother had prayed that the serum wouldn't work. For the first seven years of Briar's life, her grandmother had taught her about God. Right up until the night Granna Grace had died peacefully in her sleep—three days before the loving woman was to receive her SAP injection by order of The Commandment.

Granna Grace had prayed for that, too.

Since Briar's brain was unfazed by SAP, the memories of her grandmother's biblical teachings were alive and well, tucked snugly away in her temporal lobes between what Dr. Parker referred to as her "hippocampus" and her "substantia nigra." In that tiny sliver of brain the OLG was so obsessed with.

Not only were her memories of Christianity still there, they became increasingly vivid as she aged. Many times, in childhood, she'd heard her grandmother pray aloud for God to use her to bring about change. She'd heard Granna Grace ask God to protect her grandchild as Briar carried out His will.

No doubt about it, Briar's serum-resistant Agathi were all Granna Grace's fault.

And God's.

2

Using the cube and his cuffphone, Dr. Bingham retrieved Briar's medical file. "Mrs. Lee, I don't truthfully know what is causing Briar's resistance to the serum. Neither did Dr. Parker. But the reality of the situation is that we have run out of options. By order of The Commandment, the next step in Briar's treatment is admittance to the ARC. She will remain there until leveling is completed and adequate changes are achieved within her brain. SAP acceptance and renewal of the mind is not only the OLG's goal for your daughter, it's the law."

"So, I've heard. Doctor Wanna-be over there told me the same thing." She jerked a thumb toward the PA-C who inhaled slowly through flared nostrils.

"Dr. Bingham, does that chart floating in front of your face tell you who Briar's daddy was? My late husband was a chief researcher in the field of leveling. His name was Windsor Lee—that should ring a bell. His research is the very foundation leveling was built on. Before Windsor Lee, there was no Operation Level Ground. You presume to tell me that you would dishonor my husband's countless hours of research—not to mention his memory—by imprisoning his only child at that abomination you call the ARC?"

"Mrs. Lee, I'm well aware of who your husband was. Indeed, he was a brilliant man, renowned not only for his leveling research, but his contributions in many other areas as well. The OLG holds Windsor Lee in the highest regards. His work is universally respected and appreciated."

"It should be. It's what killed him."

Briar's heart froze. The image of her father's lifeless body flashed behind her eyes. Nine months ago, he'd ended his life by swallowing an entire bottle of painkillers. He hadn't even left a note, only the words "I'm sorry" scrawled on the bathroom mirror with a bar of soap.

She was glad Granna Grace hadn't been around to witness what happened to her only child—the son she'd tried so hard to teach of Christ's love, mercy, and grace. Briar's father hadn't been interested in the Spirit of God. Study of the human brain required all his time and energy—and there was never enough of either.

Briar's mother dabbed the frayed tissue beneath her eyes again. "My husband and Dr. Parker had an agreement. My daughter will not go to the ARC. Not as long as I have breath in my lungs." She leaned slightly forward. "I'm aware of what goes on in that place, Doctor," she said in a determined whisper. "If you go through with this nonsense, everybody else will be aware too. I have documentation, and plenty of it. Restricted reports, videotaped patient and staff interviews, hidden camera footage, audio recordings. And before you get some wild hair about burning down my house to destroy the evidence, I'll have you know it's everywhere—cyberspace, bank vaults, locked in the wall safes of friends and relatives. You're right about my husband being a brilliant man, Doctor. He covered every base to ensure what you are attempting to do would never happen. No daughter of Windsor Lee will ever set foot in the ARC." She balled the tissue in her fist. "Or you'll regret it."

Briar stared at her mother. Had the woman gone

crazy? Hidden camera footage, secret documents? It was the ARC they were discussing, not Dr. Frankenstein's laboratory. Her mother was behaving as if Briar was being carted away to an asylum that conducted illegal science experiments, not the health spa meets affirmative-healing facility Briar saw advertised. She watched all the commercials—mini documentaries of cured patients happily reuniting with family members upon release. As far as treatment centers went, the ARC was practically the Asklepieion.

Dr. Bingham frowned down at the table and repeatedly tapped his stylus against the surface, as if his mind were somewhere else. Finally, before the silence became unbearable, he spoke. "Mrs. Lee, Briar, excuse me for a few moments." He rose and motioned for the PA to go with him.

"Mom. What's with all the ARC bashing? Secret video footage? You make it sound like a chamber of horrors. I've never heard anything like that about the ARC before."

"That's because it was top secret. Now that your father's gone, there's no point in keeping it hushed up. That place is right out of a science fiction novel. The quacks the OLG put in charge aren't treating patients, they're slicing and dicing their brains. People go in but never come out, Briar."

Maybe her mother needed to be admitted into the hospital. It seemed she'd suffered a stroke. "Mom, you're talking crazy. It's a treatment center, not a black hole. People get better and they leave. Haven't you watched the warm and fuzzy commercials?"

Her mother shook her head. "Staged. Every last one of them. Frankly, I don't care if you believe me or not, because you're never going there. Ever. Your father died and left me with nothing. Not even a life insurance payment because his death was a suicide. His reputation and influence are all that remain, and I will use them as weapons to fight the OLG. I'll not lose you, too."

Dr. Bingham tapped on the door while opening it, and then shut and locked it behind him.

"Did you lose Dr. Play-Pretend?" Briar's mother tossed her gaze skyward.

"We need to speak privately." He dragged his previous chair closer to her mother's and sat down. "Mrs. Lee, I have a solution that could prevent Briar's admittance to the ARC. But first, I need the word of you and your daughter that the information I am about to divulge will remain strictly confidential."

"Agreed." Mrs. Lee nodded along with Briar.

He took turns studying their eyes for a moment. "A colleague of mine, Dr. Frank Rosen, is the chief of program development for Operation Level Ground. Dr. Rosen has a special interest in Stone Labs, a Nevada laboratory that is developing an abstergent to eradicate the use of SAP. To be complete, the research needs only to be tested on a human subject."

His speech quickened. He paused and cleared his throat as if to keep his enthusiasm in check. "A few moments ago, I spoke with Dr. Rosen and told him the details of Briar's situation," he said in a lowered voice. "I mentioned her father was the reputable Windsor Lee, and asked if that could work to her advantage. He became very excited at the prospect of Briar becoming Stone Labs' subject."

"Hold it. Are you suggesting I send my daughter into exile over a thousand miles away to become a human guinea pig? That's your solution? No thank you, Doctor."

"Stone's Abstergent is organic, Mrs. Lee. Comprised from the nectar of an indigenous cactus plant. Unlike SAP, it doesn't travel through the bloodstream. The serum is injected directly into each Agathus, meaning exposure to the heart and other vital organs is nonexistent. Instead of merely numbing the Agathi in the manner SAP does, this new serum dissolves the areas away completely. It will be as if Briar's Agathi never existed."

"This is the first I've heard of it. I'm sure my husband would've mentioned such a thing. He never was good about keeping secrets from me."

As if her Agathi never existed? Excitement welled inside Briar. There was a good chance, an *extremely* good chance, that she would be able to interact with real live people—other than her own mother and the clinic faculty?

"Your husband realized the importance of keeping the research under wraps" The doctor said. "The development of this new product will not only eliminate the demand for SAP, it will eliminate the need for the Alternative Research Center. The ARC will lose millions of dollars in government funding, thousands of jobs, and ultimately collapse. For that reason, Dr. Rosen will not disclose his department's involvement in the project until after the research is complete."

"No." Her mother exhibited a series of rapid blinks and headshakes, as if to prevent the doctor's proposal from settling in her brain. "Absolutely not. I don't know anything about this so-called lab. Place could be worse than the ARC. You can forget all about that idea."

"I want to go." Briar's voice overtook her mother's and reverberated from the walls. The words leapt from her tongue—her voice hadn't even shaken.

Briar's mother stopped twitching and stared. "Nonsense. This isn't up to you. Now wipe that grin off your face, you appear disturbed."

Briar turned to Dr. Bingham. "How long will I be there?"

"Upon your mother's consent, your virtual chart will be sent to Dr. Rosen, who will forward it to Stone Labs. Your scans and blood sample information will be analyzed. If there are no hindrances, you will receive the injection and be under observation for a week or so. You could possibly be home before your eighteenth birthday."

"Get that, Mom? Home by my birthday—three weeks from now."

"I heard. Assuming everything goes right. But what if something goes wrong?"

"Mrs. Lee, I assure you, there's nothing to worry about. The OLG will fly in one of the country's top neurosurgeons to perform the procedure—Dr. Randall Fuller from Baltimore, Maryland. The abstergent's immediate dissolving of Briar's Agathi will eliminate the risk of recollection. Her God-zones will no longer exist—she can't recollect what isn't there. The entire process is foolproof."

"Doctor, I've been around much too long to buy into the 'nothing can possibly go wrong,' spiel. Something can *always* go wrong. What will happen to my daughter if things don't turn out as anticipated?"

Dr. Bingham sighed. "The OLG can't afford to rouse suspicion concerning the project. If by some slim chance Briar's brain doesn't react as expected, she will be transported to the ARC by OLG officials. Otherwise, she will be deemed a defector for failing to appear."

Mom shoved back from the table and stood, yanking her purse strap over her shoulder. "Come on, Briar."

"Mrs. Lee, please understand. I'm opposed to the ARC as much as you. By allowing your daughter this opportunity, you will directly contribute to closing its doors forever."

"Mom. Listen. I want to do this. Let me get it over with so I can be back home for my birthday. We will actually be able to go out and celebrate over dinner—at a restaurant. I've waited forever to do that. But I still want your homemade vanilla cake with chocolate frosting."

The ice in her mother's blue eyes melted as she held Briar's gaze. "I can't bear the thought of losing you."

"Let me do this, Mom. I'm a big girl. Trust me to make this decision." Briar stood and wrapped her arms around her. "Besides, it's not like we have options."

"You just get yourself back here by your birthday."

Briar nodded against her mother's stiff hairdo. "I promise."

Dr. Bingham deactivated the cube and stood. "I have a few forms for you both to fill out, and Briar will be on her way."

"On her way?" Mrs. Lee asked sharply, breaking Briar's embrace. "As in today?"

He raised an eyebrow. "As in immediately. The sooner the lab can begin the study, the better. Time is crucial. The abstergent has a very short shelf life."

"But how will she get there?"

"Private jet. As soon as I call Dr. Rosen, he will remotely reconfigure Briar's ankle bracelet to allow her to travel. She will be assigned two escorts who have recently received SAP boosters."

"So that I can't contaminate them with my gospel-soaked Agathi." Briar rolled her eyes.

"Pretty much." Dr. Bingham half-grinned. "You will have minimal exchange with the escorts, and will not be allowed to read or browse the Internet. You will be required to turn over your cell. In fact, let me have it now." He held out his hand as Briar's mother once again deep-sea dived the depths of her purse. "Thank you," he said, flattening Briar's cuffphone and sliding it into the pocket of his lab coat.

"She won't be allowed to contact me?" Briar's mother asked, her limp tissue leaving white bits of paper on her eyelashes.

"Three weeks or less, Mom. We can do this."

But could she really? Something her grandmother would have called conviction gnawed her insides.

"For what shall it profit a man, if he shall gain the whole world, and lose his own soul?"

The verse was found in chapter eight of Mark. Granna Grace taught it to her over a plate of fresh chocolate chip cookies. She could still see the Bible's worn leather cover and hear the rustle of the pages.

Is that what she was doing? Forfeiting her soul? God had given her a rare gift, and she was dissolving it in acid. But could God blame her? It wasn't as if she had a choice in the matter.

When her Agathi were gone, she would be allowed to work with children face-to-face. Counsel them about grief and loss. Hug them if they needed it. Wipe their tears when they cried. Didn't God also gift her with that desire? Wasn't that also His will for her life?

How can you counsel others if you have no soul?

"I'll be right back with those forms." Dr. Bingham walked to the door.

Briar's stomach rumbled loudly.

He turned around. "And a package of miniature doughnuts from the vending machine."

3

Lukas Stone again peered through the vertical blinds and sighed. He stepped back and shook his head. "I bet you're getting a kick out of this, Roxy. A twenty-four-year-old medical laboratory scientist acting like a kid on Holiday morning. Staring out the window every five minutes as if searching for Santa's sleigh."

The dog gazed up at him and wagged her massive tail.

He knelt, took her big face in his hands, and scrubbed her jowls. "So, I'm a little excited, OK? This is a big deal to me. I finally get to test my abstergent on a real live person and in the process, help someone. Help a lot of someones in the long run."

Roxy's tail thumped rhythmically against the polished tile.

"But you don't care about that, do you girl? Everything is right with the world, so long as you get your ears scratched." He gave her head a brisk rubdown, patted her sides a few times, and stood. Roxy gave an immense shake, as if she'd just had a bath.

Lukas cringed as a sprinkling of golden hairs floated to the tile. He hoped the test subject wasn't allergic to dogs. He'd have Derby sweep the waiting area right away. He turned his hand over and glanced at his palms. Probably a good idea to wash his hands, too.

He crossed the small waiting area, stopping at the doorway behind the reception desk. "This is as far as you go, girl."

Roxy's tail slowed, her brown eyes pleading.

"I'll be right back." He opened the door and stepped down the chilly hallway to the staff restroom, rolling his shirt sleeves as he walked.

He wondered for the dozenth time if he could be dreaming. For months, he'd heard nothing from the OLG, and was beginning to think they'd lost interest in the project. Now suddenly, without warning, *bam!* Not only did Dr. Rosen call, he was supplying a test subject who would step through the laboratory door at any moment.

He glanced in the small mirror as he scrubbed his hands. Appalled by the ridiculous grin that overtook his features, he worked his facial muscles to get rid of it. The silly thing crept back to his lips as he held his hands beneath the dryer. It was no use, he couldn't contain his exhilaration.

In his defense, having the opportunity to perfect what nature hadn't was kind of a huge deal. To dissolve away the tiny area of the brain within the temporal lobe that kept the human race from being level, would not only impact society, it would change history. Soon the God-zone of every newborn baby in the United States would be dissolved at birth. His research would be a fundamental part of that future. The thought filled Lukas with pride. The day was quickly arriving when his father would take his research seriously.

The Agathus was as useful as wisdom teeth or the appendix. Centuries ago there may have been a need for the pesky thing, though he couldn't imagine why.

Perhaps the hope of a higher deity kept prehistoric man from throwing himself under the massive foot of a brachiosaur.

In modern society, the Agathus wasn't merely useless, it was dangerous. It gave a sense of piety to those susceptible, and tormented the minds of those who ignored it. It caused sensations of guilt and shame, making it nearly impossible for individuals to find peace of mind. Pre-Commandment Christians referred to these unfounded bouts of the conscience as "sin." Thank goodness society came to its senses and realized with regard to lifestyle there was no such thing as right or wrong, only varying perceptions.

Leveling freed society of the detriment of the Agathi—except for a fraction of the population resistant to SAP. The ARC wasn't really a solution, it was a holding tank. He wasn't exactly certain what transpired there, but judging from the commercials it was some type of glorified health spa. Soon there would be need for neither SAP nor ARC.

Regarding the human testing of his abstergent, everything was lined up and ready to go—except for one small hitch. His grin faded as he stepped from the restroom and tugged down his sleeves. The antidote wasn't complete. In his excitement of receiving an unlevelled test subject—and his fear of never receiving another one—he may have failed to mention the oversight to Dr. Rosen. The formulation was almost absolute, but not quite.

As Lukas reentered the reception area, Roxy barked twice—her usual way of informing him of an approaching car.

His breath caught in his throat. The test subject. He cursed the obstinate grin that split his face as he rushed through the waiting area to the front door.

~*~

Briar strapped her bag over her shoulder and exited the shiny black vehicle. She gazed at the mountains, still unable to fathom their beauty, even though she'd stared out the window the entire drive from the small airport. Who would dream there could be such majesty in desolation?

"Can you keep up? I need a cold drink and a nap." Reid Laughlin, Briar's escort, glared at her from the veranda of a rock veneered building. High on the multi-hued wall behind her, an elegantly engraved sign declared the structure to be Stone Labs. "All this time I thought I was a clinical laboratory technologist, not a spur of the moment chauffeur," she muttered, raising her oversized sunglasses from her face to the top of her blonde head.

Briar stepped up the walkway, stopping to admire a spikey plant that resembled a small tree. "Wow. I've never laid eyes on anything like this in Oklahoma. Is it a cactus?"

Reid shrugged and examined a fingernail. "Read the plaque. To yourself. And make it quick."

Briar silently skimmed the information: *Grusonia pulchella—aka—sand cholla. Rare. Protected species of cactus. Medicinal qualities. Specimen obtained by Stone Labs with special permission from the Nevada Department of Conservation.*

Below the description was a small image of the plant in bloom, covered in stunning reddish-pink flowers.

Reid cleared her throat.

Briar snapped her gaze from the cactus and hurried up the veranda steps. "I'm sorry. It's just so fascinating. The plaque says it has medicinal qualities. Do you know what kind?"

"Guess you'll find out when the stuff gets squirted into your brain."

Briar froze on the top step.

"Lukas—I guess I should start referring to him as *Dr. Stone* since you're here, even though it sounds ridiculous." She rolled her eyes and started over. "Dr. Stone used the nectar to make his abstergent. You'll have plenty of time to ask him all about it—if we ever make it through the door." Reid gave the doorknob a brisk turn, annoyance huffing from her overblown sigh.

Briar followed, still thinking about the cactus. How could such a delicate plant be so powerful? Could it really make her normal?

"I'm back, finally," Reid said to the unexpectedly young and good looking man standing on the other side of the door. "This is your test subject."

Reid gestured to Briar who gave a little wave and knelt to scratch the brown-eyed creature staring up at her, wagging its enormous tail.

"Here's her GPS receiver and dock." Reid pressed a black, zippered case into the man's hands. "I'm off to shower away this day." Reid raked both hands up the back of her scalp, giving her long, highlighted hair a toss. "Have fun, you two." She turned and crossed the small waiting area, hips swaying as if she knew someone was watching.

Briar returned her gaze to the dog that was practically smiling. One hind leg knocked the floor in rhythm with Briar's scratching.

Lukas bent at the waist and extended his hand. "You must be Briar. Welcome to Stone Labs. I'm Dr. Lukas Stone—please leave off the Dr. and call me Lukas." He gave Briar a firm handshake. "You've met Reid, my assistant—why do I feel the sudden need to apologize?" He raised his eyebrows and whistled out a breath. "And, of course, this is Roxy. Therapy animal slash guard dog." He patted the dog on the head. "She's a good judge of character, by the way."

"Glad she likes me." Briar stood and readjusted the bag's strap on her shoulder. "I'm surprised to see a dog in a laboratory. Guess I assumed there were rules about that."

"There used to be. Ten or so years ago, Roxy wouldn't have been allowed on the property. The Animals as Emotional Aides Act changed that. Now certified animals are allowed in hospitals, labs, and other healthcare facilities as long as they have all of their vaccinations and are kept from sterile rooms and equipment."

"Cool." Briar smiled. She glanced around the small waiting area, wondering if anyone ever really waited there. And if so, what would they wait for? Serums, potions, and special tonics, concocted in test tubes and beakers, cooked on Bunsen burners? The lab was out in the middle of nowhere. The vibe was very sci-fi flick-ish. She couldn't wait to tell Mouse about it.

Although...Lukas Stone looked unlike any mad scientist she'd ever seen in the movies.

"Ready for the tour?" Lukas asked, giving Roxy a final pat before stashing the black GPS case beneath his arm and dusting his hands together.

"Sure."

Briar followed Lukas to the reception counter,

impressed by the way Roxy halted and sat before reaching the doorway.

"She's aware of her boundaries." Lukas tipped his chin toward the dog.

"You've trained her well."

Briar stepped through the doorway behind Lukas. The hallway was freezing. She rubbed her hands over her exposed arms as the scent of bleach and disinfectant watered her eyes. "Now this is what I expected a laboratory to feel, and smell like. Cold and chemical-laden."

"The living quarters where you will be staying are behind the laboratory area. You'll be able to control the climate in your apartment. And Derby insisted on buying a whole array of air fresheners. He said women like their surroundings to smell good." He shook his head. "Reid, Derby, and I each have a small efficiency apartment similar to yours. Think of it as a hotel room, without glitchy technology and noisy neighbors."

"I've never been in a hotel room."

"I think you'll find it comfortable. I'll have Derby bring your luggage in from the car after the tour." He stopped in front of a door with his name on it.

"I don't have any luggage. Only this." She shrugged her shoulder, causing her single bag to rise and fall.

"Your purse is all you brought with you?"

"I didn't really have a choice. I was at the clinic in Greenfield, Oklahoma for my usual scan. The next minute I was on a private jet, headed for Sickle Ridge, Nevada. Dr. Bingham said the lab would provide whatever necessities I needed—clothes, shampoo, whatever."

Lukas nodded, a frown pinching his brow. "I'm

sure we can manage. We have plenty of scrubs on hand, which is all the wardrobe you'll need. As far as toiletries go, you can make a list of items for Derby to pick up for you—unless you'd rather go shopping with Reid."

"No, thanks," Briar replied, maybe a little too quickly. "I don't need much. I'm sure Derby can manage. I can't wait to meet this Derby-guy, by the way. Sounds as if he does a lot around here."

"Derby Jenkins. You'll meet him soon. He's a real jack of all trades. Takes care of the lab's custodial and maintenance duties, works as our security guard, runs our electronic surveillance equipment, takes care of Roxy and, on his down time, pulls extra duty as my personal hot air balloon pilot."

"You have a hot air balloon? No way—"

"Step in to my office, and I'll show you." Lukas fished a key ring from his pocket and jiggled it. "No keycards, fingerprint access pads, or cornea identifiers at Stone Labs. Only metal keys. My father insisted. He likes the feel of tumblers turning. Reminds him of opening the door to his first laboratory." He unlocked the door, pulled it open, and held it for her.

"First things first, let's get your monitoring equipment squared away." He unzipped the small black case Reid gave him, slid out the GPS, and keyed in a series of numbers. He then placed the charging dock on the counter, plugged it in, and slid the GPS into place. "I feel as though I'm dealing in antiques, here. How old is your ankle monitor?"

"I've worn it for ten years—" she stepped away from him, distracted by the many official looking certificates and awards mounted on the stark-white walls. Her homeschool-earned high school diploma and online cos-play contest ribbons sure wouldn't measure up against this guy's accomplishments.

"Hey, is this it?" she asked, pointing to a framed photograph of a red hot air balloon hanging amid the documents.

"Yes, that's her. Picture was taken last October, right here in Sickle Ridge at the Hot Air Balloon Festival."

"The plant painted on the outside—is that the cactus from out front? I recognize the flowers from the photo on the plaque. Sand cholla, I think the nameplate said."

"Yes. Grusonia pulchella, if you want to get scientific about it. I adopted that particular cactus to be a kind of logo for Stone Labs."

"Because your abstergent is made from its nectar."

"Someone's been doing their homework."

"Actually, Reid told me. I think it pleased her to inform me that you would be 'squirting the stuff into my brain.'"

Lukas set his jaw and shook his head. "I'll have a talk with her."

"No, don't say anything. It's OK, really. She explained how tired she was. I'm sure all the driving made her irritable. I shouldn't have said anything." Briar stepped to the wall, touching her toes to the baseboard to get a closer look at the balloon. "I think I can see you in there."

Lukas chuckled. "Your eyes are playing tricks on you. You wouldn't catch me flying that thing."

She turned from the picture and stared. "You're joking, right?"

"No. I'm serious."

Briar couldn't stop the corners of her lips from

twitching. "You own a hot air balloon. But you've never been up in it." It wasn't a question. It was a statement designed to make him realize how crazy that sounded.

"I don't have a pilot's license. A lot of people don't realize a person has to have a pilot's license to fly a hot air balloon. Not only that, there are different types of licensing—personal and commercial. Balloon piloting requires a lot of time, dedication, and resources. Derby can tell you all about it, and I'm sure he will. He loves flying. Once he starts talking about it, you can't get him to stop."

Briar turned back to the picture and let out the laugh she'd been holding. "That makes more sense. I thought you said you'd never been up in your own balloon. You meant you've never *piloted* it." She pressed a hand to her chest, stopping the next wave of laughter. "I was really beginning to wonder about you. I mean, why would someone who's afraid of heights own a hot air balloon, right?" As she looked into his eyes, the grin froze to her face and melted away.

He wasn't laughing.

"If you must know, I have the balloon for PR purposes. The logo gets a large amount of publicity in the air. And lots of important people attend balloon festivals. It's proved to be a wise investment. In addition, I aided in advancing the technology that got that particular balloon prototype off the ground."

Briar nodded. "But you've never been up in it."

Lukas's nostrils flared as he inhaled deeply. "Let's get you settled in your apartment. I'm sure you could use a good night's rest."

"Actually, I'm not tired anymore." She started to mention that the laughter perked her right up, but thought better of it.

Lukas's footsteps were quick and brisk compared to the relaxed gait he'd used earlier. Was he angry? Maybe she shouldn't have teased him about the balloon. He must be sensitive about his acrophobia. She'd have to be more careful.

Without a word, they walked down a broad corridor lined with four widely spaced doors. He fished the large ring from his pocket and examined the keys. "This one is yours. Number three." He stopped at one of the doorways and twisted a silver key from the ring. "Don't lose it."

She nodded, took the key, and unlocked the door.

Lukas reached around her and switched on the light.

"It's very clean." *And very white,* she observed, squinting as she dragged her gaze over the bright white walls, gleaming porcelain tiles, white enamel furniture, and bleach-white bedsheets.

"I'll pass your compliment on to Derby."

He stepped to a recessed area that housed a mini-fridge, microwave, and small sink. A little table with two chairs stood nearby. "Kitchenette," he said, gesturing to the appliances. "You'll find provisions inside the refrigerator and pantry. Nutrient-rich food to optimize brain function."

Briar opened the fridge. "Mmm. Nothing like a big old helping of microwaved fish to make the brain—and taste buds—happy. Makes the neighbors happy too, if the ventilation system isn't functioning up to par."

Still no smile. She was beginning to think Lukas Stone had, literally, turned to stone.

"If you don't prefer fish, there's a variety of other

proteins available."

She shut the refrigerator door. "Fish is fine, I was only joking." *Lighten up, guy. So you're afraid of heights. I get it. Now move on, already.*

"The lab should be quiet over the next few weeks. Calls will be fielded by Stone Labs' remote answering service. With the exception of Reid and Derby, I have relocated all other employees elsewhere until the project is complete. By 'project,' I'm referring to your preparation, reception, and tested response to the abstergent. The less people aware of what's going on, the better."

Briar crossed the room to a half-opened door and switched on the light. More white glared from the sink, tub, tile, and toilet. Good thing she didn't suffer from migraines.

"As I mentioned before," Lukas was saying, "Derby runs our surveillance equipment and reviews all of our internal and external camera data."

Briar snapped to attention and flicked her gaze to each corner of the room.

"Don't worry. There's no surveillance in here. Cameras are only mounted in the technical areas of the lab. A few more are outside the building, directed at the doors and windows. Rest assured, no one is interested in watching you apply your lip gloss."

She was pretty sure that was a jab—though not a very good one, since she didn't even wear lip-gloss.

"We clean up after ourselves. Wash your own dishes, change your own linens, be sure your dirty clothing makes it into the hamper."

Briar walked to the closet and peered in, taking the opportunity to roll her eyes. She knew how to take care of herself.

"Derby will be taking out the trash, doing the laundry, and sweeping up. During the day, you will be undergoing tests in the lab with Reid or myself. In the evenings, you may relax in your room. At 10:00 PM it's lights out and doors locked."

"So…I noticed no gazing devices or flexpanes."

"No outside stimulation during the study. I can have some books brought to you, if you'd like."

"Comics, if you've got them."

His face was a blank.

Briar sighed. "Never mind. I'll be fine."

Lukas wouldn't know a trade paperback from a graphic novel, anyway. Besides, she needed to work on some new scripts for the kiddos.

"That about covers everything. Do you have any questions?"

"Nope. Think I've got it."

"Excellent. I'll have Derby bring some fresh scrubs to your room later this evening. Do you want to scratch out a quick list of essentials? There's a pad and pen in the nightstand."

She leaned over the nightstand and opened the drawer. "What, no Bible?"

The joke was inappropriate, given the reason she was there in the first place. Just the same, she found it pretty hilarious. By the expression on Lukas's face, he'd never heard the legends about how back in the old days, a Bible could be found in every hotel room in America.

"Kidding." She removed the pad and pen, made a small list, and handed it to Lukas.

"Shampoo, soap, toothpaste, toothbrush, antiperspirant—any brand," he read. "That's it?"

"That should do it." She sat on the bed and patted

her bag. "I have a comb in here—right next to my lip gloss."

4

Lip gloss sarcasm. Very funny. She probably thought he deserved it. On his way out, Lukas turned the knob on Briar's door and then paused.

What he didn't deserve, was another juvenile to put up with. He was already putting up with Gatlin, his brother's kid. He loved his six-year-old nephew like crazy, but the kid's silliness and incessant teasing sometimes drove him out of his mind. Briar stirred up that same annoyance.

At first, he'd had high hopes for her—the way she'd petted Roxy and memorized the name of the cactus really impressed him. But then she'd humiliated him by making fun of his fear of heights. Acrophobia was a legitimate disorder. How would she like it if he'd teased her for having functioning Agathi? Made fun of her God-zones? He'd be willing to bet that wouldn't make her break into laughter.

He clenched his teeth and drew a breath through his nose. He was behaving like a child, and he knew it. His oversensitivity regarding his phobia was beyond ridiculous. He was a grown man—a *scientist,* no less.

Besides, Briar Lee hadn't come here to be his friend, she'd come to be his test subject. They'd gotten off on the wrong foot, and it was all his fault. If he'd remained professional in the first place, instead of yakking away like a college roommate, his feelings wouldn't have gotten hurt.

No choice but to man-up and apologize. It was his

responsibility. Afterward, they could start fresh, forego the chitchat and solely be professional. He opened his mouth to speak just as the door pushed open, knocking him backwards.

"Roxy! Come back!" Gatlin hollered as the yellow Labrador retriever bounded into Briar's apartment at full speed. Lukas's nephew right behind her, grasped for her tail.

Briar, all smiles, scrubbed the dog behind the ears as the animal jumped onto the bed beside her. Roxy panted through her own smile as she surveyed the room and snugged closer to Briar, giving the girl's cheek a swipe with a wet beach towel of a tongue.

Giggling, Gatlin hopped on the bed and wiggled in between Briar and Roxy.

"Gatlin, take Roxy outside immediately. You are perfectly aware she is not allowed in this area."

"I know. That's why I was chasing her." The little boy jumped from the bed and tugged Roxy by the collar. The big dog didn't budge.

"I'm sorry about this, Briar. It won't happen again."

"Roxy's a therapy dog," Gatlin explained, still yanking her collar. "Uncle Lukas says she'll be safe around you, even though she doesn't have SAP. You can't brainwash her with Jesus talk because she can't absorb it."

"Gatlin!" The skin on Lukas's cheekbones and ears sizzled as he narrowed his gaze at his nephew.

The little boy stiffened and widened his eyes. "What? That's what you said earlier, before she got here. I told you I was afraid she'd turn Roxy into a Christian, and you said dogs don't have God-zones in their brains. Remember?"

Lukas pulled Gatlin's hand from the dog's collar. "Roxy, down!" He snapped his fingers and pointed to the floor.

Roxy drooped her ears and snatched a last kiss from Briar's cheek before jumping from the bed.

"Uncle Lukas, remember you said that?"

Lukas growled inwardly. The kid wasn't giving him a break.

"It's OK, really." Briar smiled at Lukas. "I don't mind explaining." She turned to Gatlin. "Roxy and I are a lot alike. She doesn't have SAP in her brain, and neither do I. I'm one of the few people in the United States who is immune to SAP. 'Immune' means it doesn't work on me. That's why I'm here, at your uncle's lab. So he can give me something that works."

Gatlin nodded. "Abstergent."

Briar's mouth dropped open, and she widened her blue eyes. "That's right. I can tell you're extra-smart."

The little boy offered her a closed mouthed grin, a twinkle of pride lighting his eyes.

Lukas's anger melted away as he watched her interact with his nephew. For a brat, she sure could handle kids and dogs.

A loud knock on the doorframe drew his attention.

Reid caught his eye through the opening and stepped slowly into the room. Folding her arms on her chest, she stared at Gatlin and Roxy.

"Gatlin, please take Roxy to one of her designated areas. As a matter of fact, I bet she'd love to go outside and run off some energy."

Lukas inwardly cringed at the mock-sweetness of Reid's voice.

"Come on, girl." Reid cooed, reaching for Roxy. The big dog sidestepped her, adding a small bark when Reid made a second attempt to snatch her collar.

Reid glared at the dog while addressing Briar. "You wouldn't believe how much time and money was wasted on this mutt. Doggie vitamins and specialized trainers—*please*. And to think Geoffrey, the head dog-guru of the free world, said she held some kind of 'heightened perception' when it came to people. That she could gauge a person's character with 'uncanny precision'. *Right*. All I see is an oversized fur bag with an attitude problem."

Roxy snarled, a low growl rumbling in her throat.

A grin crept to Briar's face as she reached down and patted the dog's head. Lukas wondered if her thought was the same as his—that Roxy was an excellent judge of character.

~*~

Briar ground her teeth, blocking a scream of pain. Just her luck, the stupid fleshcard wouldn't cooperate. Again, and again Reid loaded the little square into what looked like a sophisticated staple gun and jammed it against the thin, now tender, skin on the back of Briar's left hand.

She squeezed her eyes shut, bracing for the next assault. "Ouch!" she yelped, the exclamation bursting right through the barricade of her sealed lips. That one nearly brought her out of her chair.

Reid slammed the gun to the countertop and yanked off her gloves. Her ragged breathing and stiff movements alleged that the trouble was all Briar's fault.

"Complications?" Lukas stepped into the exam room and closed the door behind him.

Reid stamped hard on the trashcan's lever, banging the lid open. "The fleshcard's not taking." She flung the rolled gloves into the can and kicked the side, causing the lid to slam.

"The reason it's not taking?" Lukas slid on a pair of blue gloves and examined Briar's throbbing hand, frowning at the redness.

"There's something wrong with the gun. It's jammed." She tossed an angry gaze to Briar. "The fleshcard is stuck inside."

Lukas removed his gloves and picked up the silver gun. "It's wedged tight," he said, peering inside the mechanism. "The card was loaded crooked. I can tell by the angle."

A bitter little smirk twisted Reid's lips. "I know how to load a fleshcard. It slid into the chamber without resistance. Your theory's wrong."

He squinted into the gun and turned it over in his palm. "Regardless, the thing's fried. So is her fleshcard." He shrugged and returned it to the counter. "I'll order her a new one." He turned to Briar. "The card is equipped with tracking technology. You'll have to keep wearing your ankle monitor until the new one arrives."

"Why? I'm under constant surveillance." She pointed high on the wall, to the camera in the corner.

"Protocol." Lukas moved to a small desk with wheels, snatched the flexpane from the surface, and administered a succession of quick, expert taps across the keyboard.

Disappointment settled in Briar's shoulders. The thought of being free of her cumbersome device had excited her. She lowered her gaze to her ankle monitor. Heavy, uncomfortable—a modern day shackle. Only it wasn't really modern day; everyone said it was ancient. The fact that she'd been so close to being rid of the thing now doubled its weight. She hoped the fleshcard arrived soon.

Or did she? Something tapped on her insides, as if to get her heart's attention.

What if God was protecting her by jamming the gun?

She pictured the Agathi inside her brain, her tiny God-zones, at this very moment, glowing a brilliant red—brightening and changing hue every time she thought about God. Proof she belonged to Him.

Would the fleshcard pick up on the reaction? Of course, it would. Her Agathi activated some sort of chemical, she assumed. All of her brain data would be recorded and assessed.

"All taken care of. The new gun will be here in a week. The fleshcard should arrive shortly after. In the meantime, Reid and I will continue to take your vitals and run your labs the old-fashioned way." He returned the pane to the desk.

"Yay. I envision more ice-cold stethoscopes, vein piercing needles, and flimsy urine cups in my future."

"For the time being, I'm afraid so. The advanced fleshcard will keep track of your vital signs and bloodwork. As soon as it arrives, I'll upload your medical history and other information from your chart and proceed with the implant. After that, with the exception of an occasional hypodermic needle, you shouldn't be subjected to these primitive devices of medical torture." He plucked a stethoscope from an implement holder above the counter. "Will you move to the exam table, please?"

Briar rose from her chair and hopped to the edge

of the exam table, crinkling the tissue-paper overlay.

Lukas donned the stethoscope. "This might be a bit chilly."

Briar braced herself, yet jumped anyway when the cold metal touched her skin. "Sorry." She giggled.

Lukas chuckled. "I warned you."

Reid slammed a cabinet door and turned to face them. "If you'll excuse me, I have work to do. I'll leave the two of you alone to laugh yourselves silly." She left the room, shutting the door too loudly behind her.

5

Briar slept deeply, dreaming of her grandmother. The sound of a rattling doorknob startled her awake. She strained blurry eyes. Someone was opening her door. Had she forgotten to lock up last night? She racked her sleep-fogged brain, but couldn't remember. The hinge squeaked loudly. Seemed the hinges would be quieter in such a sophisticated laboratory.

An eye peeked through the crack. Lukas's nephew. Briar hid her smile beneath the blanket and pretended to sleep. She tried to keep her eyelids from trembling as she watched the boy tiptoe into the room then disappear to the floor.

Listening to the thump of little hands and knees, she pressed her lips together to restrain a giggle. It was all she could do to keep from rolling closer to the edge to find out what on earth the kid was doing.

Suddenly, Gatlin's face was close to hers, his gold-green eyes wide with curiosity. His strawberry scented breath puffed in and out from the exertion of his mission. He reached out, slowly extending his pointer finger until it lightly touched her pillow, his eyes never leaving her face.

Briar snatched Gatlin's wrist and roared like a lion, giving his arm a gentle shake.

The little boy jerked and shrieked, trying to twist his arm from her grip. She sat up and held tight, tickling under his arm as she raised it high in the air.

Laughing and squealing, Gatlin twirled and flailed until something clunked to the floor. "Wait!"

Briar loosened her grip.

Gatlin fell to his knees and scuttled under the bed. He crawled out and stood in front of her. "I want to show you my rock." He placed an object in her hand.

"It's plain brown, but if you wiggle it, it turns into gold." His wide eyes urged her to try it.

Briar rolled the jagged chunk over in her palm. Tiny gold flecks caught the light and glittered throughout the stone. "Wow," she breathed, shifting her gaze to Gatlin. Her heart warmed at the sight of his proud grin. Was anything on earth as rewarding as a child's smile? She held the rock between her thumb and finger for a closer look.

"My mom liked those kinds of rocks." His gaze fell from his prized possession to the cold tile floor.

"She did?"

Gatlin mentioning his mother in past tense caused Briar's chest to tighten.

"Well, I can certainly understand why. This is a beautiful rock."

"My mom's dead, now. But Lira said she's not really dead, that nothing ever really dies. She said Mom's part of the amissfear. That she turned into air and I breathed her in, like this." Gatlin closed his eyes and widened his nostrils, sucking a deep breath into his nose. He peeked at Briar through one squinted eye. "And back out like this." His words were strained as he attempted to hold his breath and speak at the same time. Squeezing both eyes shut, he exaggerated an exhale through puckered lips.

"Who is Lira?"

"My nanny. Dad said she's full of it. He said dead means dead. He said the earth's amissfear is nothing but a mixture of gasses, and that people can't be breathed into your lungs. He said that would probably cause cancer."

"And what do you think?"

Gatlin's sneaker slipped from the sheet as he tried to climb onto the bed. Briar clutched him gently beneath the arms and lifted him to the mattress. He wiggled in close to her. "I think maybe they're both right. Maybe the part of her that's in the amissfear isn't skin and hair and teeth and stuff. Maybe it's the part you can't see. Is there a part of people you can't see?"

The soul.

Deep inside Briar, something hummed—a vibrational energy resonating in her bones.

Quickening, Granna Grace called it. *"That's the Holy Spirit nudging your insides, Briar. When you feel the quickening, God's telling you to pay attention."*

She gazed down at Gatlin, his eyes filled with questions and pain.

She glanced at the door. They were alone. Just the two of them. No cameras to record their conversation. No fleshcard to document the activity of her Agathi. She licked her lips. "You know, Gatlin. This isn't all there is—"

The door swung open with an earsplitting creak. Miraculously, the flimsy doorstop jutting from the baseboard kept the knob from impaling the wall.

In the doorway stood a tall, broad shouldered man with eyes the color and sharpness of knife blades.

The child stiffened. "Dad," he whispered.

"Gatlin, come." The man pinned the little boy in his gray glare as he took deliberate steps toward the bed.

Gatlin jumped from the mattress and scrambled to his father's side.

"I am Caster Stone, Lukas's brother." He extended a hand. "You must be Miss Lee."

Briar mirrored the gesture, fighting the chill brought on by his cold, smooth fingers. "You can call me Briar, if you don't mind. Nice to meet you."

"I see you've already met my son." His grip tightened. She got the uneasy feeling he was practicing restraint. "I apologize for Gatlin's disrespect of your privacy." Like a hunting dog reluctantly obeying a command, he released her fingers, and took a step back. "It won't happen again."

"Don't apologize, please. He wasn't bothering me at all. In fact, I really enjoyed his company. We talked about rocks. It was a fun visit, wasn't it, Gatlin?"

Gatlin stared at the floor in silence.

Caster looked into Briar's eyes and smiled, his straight teeth glistening like little ice cubes—only colder. "Miss Lee—how can I put this delicately?" He cut his gaze to the ceiling and frowned, then swooped his attention back to her. "Well, I'm afraid I can't. I've never taken a course in sensitivity training. So, I'll simply tell you how it is."

Briar wanted to wiggle away from those dagger-eyes skewering her in place.

"In your present condition, my son will not benefit from a relationship with you."

His words hurt far worse than the insults she'd received from online haters. She'd almost gotten used to those. Discrimination—ugly, hurtful, and humiliating, was perfectly allowable in politically correct society—providing the target possessed functioning God-zones. But an up-close-and-personal punch to the gut was different from a virtual slap in the face. Caster's words didn't leave behind a sting.

They left a bruise.

"Because I'm unlevel?"

"Understand, it's for your own good. Imagine what would happen if I were to walk in on one of your 'fun visits' with my son to find you unwittingly filling his head with poison? What if—through no fault of your own—the runoff from your diseased Agathi flowed through your mouth to his ear, and seeped into his still-developing brain?"

Briar's mouth turned dry as the surrounding hills. "Hasn't Gatlin received his SAP injections?"

Caster's icy smile disappeared as he moved closer. The man was a mountain, and she was a severely underdressed molehill.

"What is in my son's brain is not your concern. Ensure you don't make any contributions. Otherwise, I will be paying my own unexpected visit."

Briar swallowed, hating the click in her parched throat. She noticed he'd left out the word "fun."

Caster led Gatlin to the door, his cold grin returning. "I'm sorry it was necessary to take up so much of your time, Miss Lee. We'll be going now." His strong fingers curled around the doorknob.

She clutched the sheet to her breastbone, half-expecting wintry steam to escape the man's lips.

"Wait!" Gatlin dodged beneath his father's arm and darted to the bed, his sneakers squeaking as he slid to a stop. He grabbed Briar's hand, pressing his prized rock into her palm. "Keep it." He ran back to his dad's side.

Caster frowned down at the boy and shut the door.

Briar fell back on the bed, releasing the breath she didn't realize she'd been holding. Gatlin's rock was warm in her hand. She raised the stone, twirling it above her, watching the light bounce over the golden glitter. A tear slid down her cheek with another close behind.

She missed her little friend already.

~*~

"Are we hungry?" Lukas asked, determined not to laugh at the angry growls echoing from Briar's stomach.

"We? I can't speak for you, but I'm starving."

Lukas hid a smile as he positioned the small foam cushion beneath her knees. "Ready for your headgear?" he asked, holding up the contraption.

"Oh, no. Not a helmet." She rocked her head back and forth on the table.

"The sooner you comply, the sooner we can get this over with."

"There you go with that 'we' stuff again. Fine. Lay it on me."

Lukas positioned the white dome over her face as she squeezed her eyes tight and stuck out her tongue. He shook his head. What was it about this girl? She annoyed and enchanted him all at the same time. She made him jumpy when he wanted to relax and—most irritating of all—smile when he didn't feel like smiling.

Her stomach gurgled again. "Are you listening to this? I think my stomach is devouring itself. Too bad this isn't a full-body scan, we could watch."

That did it. Lukas dropped his hands to his sides and laughed. "I give up," he said, letting his chin fall to his chest as he continued to chuckle. "You caused me to lose my composure. Are you satisfied?" He peered down at her through the apparatus covering her face.

"Extremely." She brought a hand to her stomach. "Still hungry, though."

Lukas laughed harder.

"I don't know—or care—what's so funny, but I don't have time for this." Reid's angry voice blared through the headphones sitting beside Briar on the table. Thank goodness he hadn't put them on her yet. At that volume level, Reid would've blown both of Briar's eardrums.

"Sorry," Briar whispered. "Didn't mean to get you in trouble."

Lukas shook his head. "It's my lab, remember? Besides, she's only blowing off steam. She'll be fine."

"She had a tough morning?"

"The worst. First, the sun had the nerve to come up. After that, I think a few birds were even caught singing."

Lips tight and shoulders shaking, they looked through the headpiece at each other in silent laughter.

"I can hear you whispering!" Reid roared, flying from the technician's booth.

"Calm down. I'm lightening things up for Briar. Things are too dull around here, I don't want her dying of boredom." He snapped his gaze to Briar. "Figuratively, of course."

"Of course." She nodded, bumping her face on the helmet. "Ouch. I'm OK."

Reid swished to the side of Briar's table. "I hate to break this to you, but having a brain malfunction doesn't make you royalty."

"Darn. I thought this was my coronation, and that this cage over my face was a crown."

"You think you're so witty," Reid spoke through

clenched teeth. "Well, let me tell you what *I* think—I think you're a spoiled brat who's screwed up in the head. Deep down you're miserable, and want everybody else miserable, too. I think you enjoy having functional Agathi. You believe those stupid, glowing God-zones make you somehow special. Queen of Stone Labs. Well, they don't. They make you pathetic."

Heat flashed behind Lukas's eyes. "Reid, back off."

"Back off?" Reid stepped closer to Lukas. "Oh, how sweet! The big, bold, scientist is coming to the aid of his weak little test subject. Or maybe you're testing out more than just your abstergent on her? Perhaps the two of you have some extracurricular experimentation going on."

"Leave." The word left his lips in a quiet explosion. Never had fury overtaken him like this. Not even when as a child, Caster tripped him, causing him to land face-first in the dirt, embarrassing him in front of his friends. The anger he'd experienced then was a summer breeze compared to this.

Reid crossed her arms and settled into one hip. "You're joking."

"Leave. Now."

Her lips twisted into a bitter smirk. "You'd better watch yourself, Lukas. She might be contagious. I suggest running a few tests on your brain to make certain your SAP level is still where it should be. To be sure the serum is still doing its job." She leaned over Briar and smiled. "Enjoy your brain scan, test subject." Nose in the air, Reid stepped briskly across the tile and slammed the door.

Heat rose to Lukas's ears. "I'm at a loss for words. Reid's behavior is inexcusable—and an embarrassing representation of Stone Labs. I don't understand what's gotten into her. I mean, she's not normally all sweetness and light, but she's not usually a full-on wicked witch, either."

"She's jealous. She has feelings for you and having another female around makes her feel threatened."

Lukas shook his head. "Reid, jealous over me? No way. We've worked together for nearly a year. She's never shown any signs of being interested."

Briar chuckled. "Trust me. I'm a psychology major—although I wouldn't have to be to notice. Anyone could see that she's jealous. It may as well be tattooed on her forehead. If you don't believe that, maybe you're romantically challenged as well as elevationally challenged."

"Is that another crack about my acrophobia?" Unbelievable. The girl was relentless. She'd actually gone there again. Lukas couldn't decide whether to laugh or be insulted. "I told you, the fear of heights shouldn't be taken lightly," he said, knocking on her headpiece, causing her to blink.

"I realize that—psychology major, remember? But for some reason, I can't resist."

Lukas could relate. He shook his thoughts back to reality. He'd better start resisting, immediately, or he wouldn't accomplish a thing in the way of research—the whole reason Briar was here in the first place.

He picked up the headphones. "Seems I should've put these on you before positioning the headpiece."

She shrugged. "Do I really need them? The sounds the machine makes won't bother me. I've undergone dozens of scans. I'm used to noise—in fact, I prefer it."

He nodded. "OK. We're ready to do this. I'll step into the technician's booth and fire up the machine. Lie completely still, and it will be over in a few moments. I'll be monitoring you on the screens and watching through the glass." He stepped from her side, taking the headphones with him.

"Wait. Lukas? Do you think, after my scan, we could have lunch together?"

"You usually eat in your room."

"Yes. But yesterday your burned popcorn fumes choked me out, and I literally almost died. I think I'd like some fresh air today. Maybe eat outside on the bench, beside the little cactus?"

Lukas didn't have to be a psychology major to ascertain the reason behind his increased heart rate. "Sure. Sounds fine." He stepped to the technician's booth and started the machine.

6

"So, what did my scan reveal?" Briar forked a cherry tomato from her salad. "Am I a robot, an alien, or something else?" She smiled as she chewed.

"Afraid not," Lukas said, poking around in his own salad. "You're a regular girl with Agathi that doesn't know when to quit." *Regular girl,* he mused. The description was highly inaccurate. Briar Lee was anything but regular. But, he couldn't very well tell her that. Besides, in general, girls probably didn't like being told they weren't regular. For that matter, young women probably didn't like being called girls, either. Briar was by no means a child.

"Did you find out why my Agathi are still functional, no matter how much SAP they pour into my veins? No one has ever been able to come up with a reason. I have my own theory, but it's not scientifically sound."

"Honestly," Lukas answered, "I don't understand how they continue to function. According to scientific research, your Agathi should not be thriving. Enough SAP has pumped through your brain to disable a hundred Agathus."

"Or the Agathi of one gigantic elephant—if elephants had Agathi." She plucked a black olive from the bowl with her fingers and popped it into her mouth. "Can you tell me more about the God-zone? Dr. Parker never told me much about it. Everything I know I've learned from the Internet."

"Well if you learned it from the Internet, it must be true, right?"

Briar's smile reached the corners of her dark blue eyes. He'd caused that smile. His insides warmed with the knowledge.

"Not to dispute the Internet, but can you tell me about it, anyway?"

"With your father's background as a chief leveling researcher, I assumed you'd be well informed." Halfway through the sentence, Lukas felt like a jerk. Only months ago, her father committed suicide. The last thing he wanted to do was upset her. He wondered if he should apologize.

"Dad rarely mentioned his work. Maybe the irony of having an un-levelable kid made it hard to talk to me about it." She shrugged.

She didn't seem upset. Relieved, Lukas rose with his nearly empty salad container and held out his hand for her container. "Finished?"

She swiped out the last bit of dressing, licked her finger, and handed him the paper bowl. "I've learned a little bit about SAP, but not much. I know that it's an acronym for Serum to Accelerate Progressivism. I also know that inoculation by SAP injection became mandatory in the United States ten years ago, and that it doesn't work on me and a couple thousand other people in the U.S."

Lukas returned the few steps from the recycle bin. He reclaimed his spot on the bench next to Briar, an inch or two closer than before. "What else do you want to learn?"

"Tell me about the Agathus itself. How it works. Why it's so dangerous. I've been held prisoner by this tiny little whatever-it-is in my brain for my entire life. I want to find out more about it. From someone I trust."

"I've never thought of myself as much of a teacher, but I'll give it a shot." He leaned against the backrest and squinted at the cloudless sky. "Thought and emotions of Christian nature are housed within a specific area of the brain referred to as the Agathus, singular, or Agathi, plural—think of cactus and cacti. Agathus is derived from the Greek word for thorn, named for the minuteness and curvature of the segment. Located on each side of the brain, in the medial temporal lobes, the Agathus, in true thorn characteristic, is imbedded between the hippocampus and the subtantia nigra." He turned to her. "Am I being too technical?"

"No, not at all." Briar's gaze snapped with curiosity. "So far, I follow."

"The job of the hippocampus, with help from the frontal cortex, is to analyze sensory input and decide what's important enough to remember. Information deemed worthy ends up in the long-term memory, which is stored in different parts of the brain. The exact reason the Agathus stores information exclusive to the Christian religion has yet to be determined. Despite millions of dollars exhausted on countless studies, the cause remains a mystery."

"Maybe God designed it that way."

Lukas chuckled and then noted the somberness of her eyes. She was serious. The laughter died in his throat. He lowered his gaze, embarrassed for her. It was the Agathi talking, he reminded himself. She couldn't help it. "Should I continue?"

"Please. Keep going."

This time he'd appeal to her logical mind. It was difficult to argue with history. Shifting on the bench, he angled toward her. "Around twenty-five years ago, the government determined there was no longer a need for the Christian religion. Once upon a time, long before society became self-sufficient, belief in a supernatural savior may have supplied a kind of hope—a false sense of security essential to the survival of our culture. But not any longer. The Christian faith, it was decided, was doing society more harm than good."

Briar frowned. "You'll probably write this down in your notes, and I'll get in a lot of trouble for saying it, but what right does the government have to remove the belief system of an entire group of people? Or even from one person, for that matter? Isn't that terrorism?"

"Actually, it was quite the opposite. According to broadminded society, Christians were the ones doing the terrorizing. Claiming anyone who didn't worship Jesus Christ would end up in hell, insisting abortion was murder, refusing to validate homosexuality and transgender lifestyles after being ordered to do so—these so-called believers made it impossible to maintain freewill society."

"So, one day the government up and started shooting SAP into people's brains to destroy their convictions? The solution was to turn the Christian population into a bunch of empty-eyed zombies?"

Lukas blinked, confused. "No, that's ridiculous. Efforts were made to rectify the situation civilly. Sanctions were put into place to prevent church leaders from referring to specific behaviors as sin. Some churches complied under the threat of legal ramification, but many remained rigid. Their defiance not only slowed progressivism, it nearly tore the country apart. As a last resort, a group of government-funded scientists were called upon to develop a serum to erase information stored in the Agathi."

"Tore the country apart, how? Did Christians force people to convert to their beliefs? Hold their heads under baptismal waters?" Briar was less relaxed now. She perched on the edge of the bench, spine straight and shoulders back. "Or were they deemed terrorists simply because of what they believed?"

Lukas shifted on the seat. What was she twisting this into—a societal war on Christians? "It was more than that. Their beliefs were accusatory. The Bible, the very book their religion was organized around, encouraged discrimination by classifying specific actions as sin. Homosexuals, for example, were lumped in with liars, murderers, and slave traders."

"First Timothy, chapter one." Briar said, barely above a whisper.

Lukas lifted a shoulder. "I wouldn't know. I've never seen a Bible. Father and Mother never owned one that I'm aware of. Even before Bibles were banned." The admission made him feel deficient. To scientifically prove or disprove a theory, correlative aspects must be studied and compared. Without Biblical knowledge, even a theory as flawed as the Christian religion couldn't be disproved. In the subject of faith, Briar was his superior.

"My grandmother was a Christian. She taught me some verses." Her eyes shimmered, and for a moment Lukas thought she would cry. Instead, she raised her eyebrows and clasped her hands together. "For the love of SAP, don't tell your brother that," she mock-pleaded. "He despises me enough already."

Lukas's heart cracked its knuckles. "What did Caster say to you?" He didn't even realize they'd met, let alone shared a conversation.

She stared past him. "It's not important." She craned her neck, trying to see around him. "Hey, is that a path over by the side of the building? Can we take a walk?"

Lukas turned to follow her gaze. "Sure. But don't be disappointed. The path doesn't lead anywhere interesting."

"I'll be the judge of that." She hopped from the bench and made her way across the yard, careful to stay on the row of decorative stepping stones.

Lukas followed behind, somehow moved by her respect for the sparse, patchy turf. From what he'd gleaned about Oklahoma, there was no shortage of green grass. In the sandy soil of Sickle Ridge, however, a lawn didn't spontaneously grow, it was cultivated. Nurtured by hard work, dedication, and near-constant watering. Without being told, Briar seemed to understand that.

"Are you coming?" she asked, standing on the last stone, hands on her hips.

"I'm not as young as you are."

"Older by six whole years. *Puh*lease. Twenty-four is by no means old. That reminds me—how does someone become a doctor at such a young age?"

He picked up his pace. "Accelerated education—and no social life. I graduated high school at sixteen and earned a Ph.D. in biology by twenty-three."

He caught up with her and they stepped together onto the narrow gravel path. He wanted to press her about what Caster had said. Obviously, his brother had upset her, and he wanted get to the bottom of it. But he couldn't risk her shutting down on him. The last thing he wanted was an atmosphere of distrust. He and Briar were colleagues. More like partners, really. She was his key to a scientific breakthrough. He was her key to freedom. They needed each other.

"Your grandmother raised you?" Embarrassed that such a short trek left him winded, Lukas struggled to keep his voice steady.

She turned to look at him. "You really should get out of the lab and get some exercise. Weed the flowerbed, take Roxy for a walk. Do *something*. I'd give anything to be able to go outside and work up a sweat while breathing fresh air. Instead, I'm stuck inside every day, working out to techno pop with some muscle-head on a flat screen."

Apparently, she'd not only noticed the wheezing, but felt compelled to comment on it. That settled it; subtlety was not one of Briar Lee's attributes. Discretion simply wasn't in her nature. For their partnership to work, he might as well thicken his skin and accept it.

"Granna Grace, that's what I called my grandmother. You could say she raised me. She moved in when I was a baby and lived with us until she died, when I was ten. Even though Mom and Dad were around, I spent most of my time with her. I preferred it that way, and so did she. We were BFFs, best friends forever. I'll never have a friend like that again. I'm thankful I experienced ten wonderful years with her."

"She was your namesake. Briar Grace—your full name is on your chart."

She nodded. "Yep. Though I'm not very graceful. But she was." She stopped short and knelt on the path. "A lizard. Come here, little fella." She held her fingers to the ground, coaxing the slender creature onto her hand. "What kind is he?" she asked, rising slowly, lightly stroking the mottled gray-and-brown tail.

Lukas leaned closer. "Side-blotched lizard. Very common in this area. They only grow to about six inches long. This guy is probably full grown."

The lizard climbed higher on her wrist, and she cupped her palm gently around him. "That's far enough, Blotch. Don't want you down my shirt or in my hair. Go back to your family. Tell them about your exciting day on the path, how you ended up in the hand of a giant." She stooped and opened her fingers, smiling as the creature slipped into the larger rocks beside the path.

Lukas chuckled and shook his head. "I'm picturing Reid right now. Screaming, running for shelter willy-nilly because a lizard got too close to her foot."

"Fear's ugly." Briar shrugged and began walking again.

"You don't experience fear?"

"I didn't say that. I said it's ugly. Makes you do ridiculous things—like run willy-nilly. I'm not even sure what that means, but it sounds really unattractive."

Lukas laughed. "I'm having a hard time picturing you being afraid."

"Here, let me give you an eye full." Briar stopped walking and turned to him. "I'm afraid right now. Standing on this path, breathing in clean, crisp air, surrounded by scenery more beautiful than I could ever dream or imagine, conversing with the smartest person I've ever met—I'm terrified."

Lukas's scalp slipped back. "Of what?"

She lowered her eyes and shook her head. "You wouldn't understand."

"Maybe not, but I'd still like to know."

She took a deep breath, dropping her shoulders as she exhaled. "I'm afraid of unplugging from God. I mean, it's not like I can help it—my God-zones are being destroyed by order of The Commandment, not by my own free will. But will God understand that? I'm not sure He will. And I can't stand the thought of not knowing where I will spend eternity. I've always believed I would go to heaven when I died, that I'd be with Granna Grace again. But after the abstergent..." She massaged her collarbone. "Not knowing will be like living in hell already, minus the brimstone and flames."

Lukas tried to trade places with her, tried to relate to her fear. But it was impossible. Instead, he felt sorry for her, and a powerful resentment toward her grandmother's ignorance. The superstitious old woman had really done a number on Briar's psyche. Thankfully, his abstergent would be able to alleviate her torment. The sooner, the better. To witness a young woman of Briar's intelligence and fortitude trapped by the irrational fear of a make-believe god infuriated him.

"I'm sorry." It was all he could manage to say. If he spoke ill of her grandmother, she'd never talk to him again, let alone forgive him.

"You have nothing to be sorry for." She half smiled. "Since you asked the question, and now you've got me on a roll, would you like to know what I'm more afraid of? Even more than losing my connection with God?"

"Tell me."

"I'm afraid that deep inside, I'm secretly glad." She swallowed. "I'm scared I'm relieved, because things will be so much easier. I'm so tired of being isolated, lonely, shunned by society. Never being allowed to attend public school, or even to go shopping. Forbidden to dry the tears of the children I so desperately love and want to help." She wiped at her own tears. "I'm only seventeen. It kills me to think of spending the rest of my life this way."

"Relief, gladness, the anticipation of change—those thoughts should bring you comfort, not fear. Things *will* be easier once your Agathi are eliminated. Think of them as a ruptured appendix or compacted wisdom teeth. Painful. Excessive. Unnecessary. But easily removed by a pair of skilled hands." He opened his hands like a book and held them palms up in front of her. "These hands."

Briar sniffed and cleared her throat. "Are you being for real right now? Because I seriously can't tell. I mean, how melodramatic can you get?"

His face warmed as he dropped his hands to his sides. Joking. She was only joking. He stretched a smile over his clenched teeth.

She gave a surprised laugh. "Glad to see you finally found your sense of humor!"

She threw her arms around him and squeezed, causing Lukas to sputter a surprised laugh of his own.

~*~

"Hello? Anybody here? Delivery."

"Coming." Lukas stepped quickly down the hallway toward the front office. "I'm sorry. We're running on a skeleton crew." He signed the electronic clipboard held out by the delivery man. "Thank you."

"You, too. Have a nice day." He handed Lukas the large padded envelope imprinted with the government seal and then walked out the front door.

Lukas pressed the envelope face down to his hip, and hurried through the empty waiting room and down the hallway. He ducked into his office, locked the door and sat at his desk. Sliding a pair of scissors from the top drawer, he carefully slit the top of the packet and slipped his hand inside. Heart tunneling toward his toes, he tweezed the postage-stamp-sized object between two fingers and slowly drew it from the opening. Briar's fleshcard. It stared coldly from inside the clear plastic case.

What was he supposed to do now?

He frowned at the tiny chip, less than a quarter the size of its casing. He didn't like the idea of tracing Briar's every move. The thought was absurd, and he was well aware of it. Monitoring and testing was the sole purpose of Briar's residence at Stone Labs.

What was the big deal? It was a fleshcard. He held the small, transparent case under his desk lamp and rotated his wrist, scrutinizing the chip. He'd seen hundreds of them before, exactly like it.

No. Not exactly like it. This one belonged to Briar.

Once the card was under her skin, she would no longer be her own person. He would know the levels of her biological chemicals. He would know the precise area of her brain that was processing information, not only when she was undergoing a brain scan, but all the time. As she conversed, ate her meals, brushed her teeth, and went about her daily routine, her brain would be an open book. Even while she slept.

He would discover her chemical responses to stimuli. The chip would track her every move, record her every word. Tell him if she was lying. It would give him a read out, essentially, of what she truly thought of him.

He would be alerted when her Agathi were active. He would know exactly when she thought about her god. The times when she remembered special moments spent with her grandmother, heads together over an open Bible. He would be aware when she prayed.

Installing the fleshcard would obliterate what sliver of freedom Briar had left. He might not have God-zones, or a *soul,* for lack of a better term. But he did have a conscience.

Lukas pulled his key ring from his pocket and selected a small silver key. He unlocked the third drawer on his desk, tucked the chip inside, and locked it back.

Shipment companies weren't what they used to be. No telling when—or if—Briar's fleshcard would arrive.

7

The quick knock on Briar's door bounced off her ribs. She dropped her book to the bed, forgetting to mark the page. "Come—" she croaked out, cleared her throat, and tried again. "Come in," she said, praying it wasn't Caster.

"Hello, Miss. Hope I'm not bothering you too much." A man with sandy blond hair sticking out from under a red ball cap stepped through the doorway. In both arms, he held a stack of neatly folded clothing. "Name's Derby Jenkins." He stuck out the fingers of his right hand. "I'm the guy who's been bringing by your laundry and grooming supplies when you're out. Sorry we haven't already met. First time I've caught you here."

Briar smiled. "I'm in the lab a lot. Let me help you with that so we can properly introduce ourselves. I'd feel terrible if you dropped all that perfectly folded laundry."

"Fresh from the wash."

Briar took the stack from him, setting it carefully on the bed. The clothes were soft and smelled heavenly—like spring rain, fresh cut grass, and sunshine. Sunshine? How was that even possible?

"What kind of detergent did you use? My mom would love it. She's all about great smelling laundry." A wave of nostalgia overtook her as she thought about her mom. She hadn't realized how much she already missed her.

"Spring…something. Found it on sale at The

Dollar Save. Thought it smelled nice."

"It smells great." She held out her hand. "I'm Briar Lee. Nice to meet you, Derby."

"Pleasure." He pumped her hand and grinned. "I was hoping to make your acquaintance sooner, but this place keeps me hopping." He leaned in closer, as if someone might hear. "Tell you the truth, I'm enjoying my work more now with most of the staff gone. I can do things my own way, without anyone complaining." He let go of her hand and readjusted his cap. "Want me to take out your trash, Miss?"

"It's Briar, remember?" She glanced at her trashcan. "Nothing in this one." She stepped to the bathroom. "Let's see…A string of used dental floss and a soap wrapper in this one." She stood in the doorway. "Safe to say my trash doesn't need emptied today. But I appreciate the offer."

"No problem. It's part of my job." He glanced at his cuffphone and tapped the screen. "Sweeping's next on the agenda. I'll be back to take care of the floor and clean your bathroom later, when you're in the lab. Lukas—I mean Dr. Stone—said you were scheduled for some appointments this morning."

"There's no need for you to pick up after me. I'll sweep up and clean my bathroom this afternoon." She returned to his side.

"That's my job, remember? You trying to get me fired?" He nudged her shoulder.

"Never." She lifted a scrub-shirt from the top of the stack, careful to keep it folded, and held it to her nose. "I'll let you clean my bathroom twice, as long as you keep the fresh laundry coming."

He chuckled. "So how are you liking it here?"

She shrugged. "It's OK. Maybe a little lonely. I

mean, I was isolated before, but I had my phone and flexpane. Because of my condition, my conversations were monitored, but at least I could talk to my kids." The look on Derby's face caused her to rethink her words. "Not my own kids." She laughed. "I meant the kids I talk to online. I love interacting with children. I'm majoring in child psychology." She wondered what Mouse was up to lately.

"I thought you seemed a little young to have ankle biters." Derby stepped to the door. "I'll catch you later. Still a lot to get done this morning. Real nice to meet you, Miss Briar." He tipped his hat and left, closing the door behind him.

Briar scooped up the stack of scrubs, burying her face in the fabric as she carried them to the dresser. She got a good vibe from Derby Jenkins. Fun loving, nice, polite. Visiting with him was like kidding around with a good-natured uncle. She hoped to see more of him.

~*~

"The color looks good on you. Brings out your eyes."

Briar glanced down at her turquoise scrubs and hopped onto the exam table. "Thanks. They smell really good, too."

Lukas nodded. "Derby's a regular laundry connoisseur. I can use the same detergent and softener, but try as I might, can't get the clothes as clean or smelling as fresh."

"They say everyone has a talent. Did you pick out the colors?"

His cheeks pinked slightly. "Most of them. Reid chose a couple of sets—the brown ones and the mustard yellow. I picked out the rest. We ordered them from a medical supply store. We concluded they'd be an acceptable option to accommodate your daily procedures."

"Gee, and I thought you guys were thinking of my comfort. Didn't realize scrubs could be so technical." She tugged up her waistband. "Be sure to tell Reid the brown ones are my favorite, followed by the mustard yellow. I'm saving both pair for a special occasion."

Lukas glanced up from the flexpane where he was recording her vitals. He locked gazes with her for a second and grinned. "I'll do that."

She smiled back, glad he was finally able to tell when she was joking.

"Or you could tell her yourself. I won't be in the lab this evening. Reid will be conducting your after-dinner testing. It will just be the two of you."

"Can't wait." To her annoyance, Lukas chuckled. So now he was going to laugh at her every sarcastic remark? She didn't find the thought of being alone with Reid very funny. "So, where are you going tonight, if you don't mind my asking?"

He set the pane back down on the wheeled desk. "My father is flying in from Maryland, which is somewhat of a rarity. My brother and I are taking him to dinner."

Caster. She almost shivered.

"I'm hoping spending time with Father will be good for Caster. Lighten him up a bit, emotionally."

She shouldn't say it, but she was going to. "What is the deal with him, anyway? He seems so cold and bitter. Of course, that's strictly a first impression."

He removed her blood pressure cuff. "He has his reasons. Life hasn't been good to him."

"His little boy sure is cute."

Lukas's countenance brightened like the sun moving from behind a cloud. "Gatlin is a great kid." He slid a tongue depressor from the glass container on the countertop. "Open wide."

She opened her mouth and stuck out her tongue.

"You mean that's all it takes to keep you quiet?" He flattened her tongue with the wooden stick and shined his penlight into her mouth.

"Very funny," she mumbled around the depressor.

"Shhh!" His light brown eyes sparkled with mischief.

This guy was having way too much fun at her expense.

~*~

"Does this table meet your approval, Dr. Stone?" The blonde hostess glided her manicured fingers above the table as if she were about to make it disappear.

"Is it the best in the house?" Lukas's father asked, standing up even straighter, dwarfing the young woman despite her high heels and towering up-do.

She smiled. "Yes, it is."

"Then it meets my approval."

She seated them, promising the swift arrival of a server. The older man's gaze followed intently as she walked away. Whether she also met his approval or didn't measure up to his standards, Lukas couldn't tell.

"Caster, I was hoping to spend time with my only grandson this evening."

"Gatlin's with the nanny. Lira's teaching him how to make cookies or candy. Something that rots the teeth."

"Boys don't belong in the kitchen. He should be

here with us, talking business. Learning the ropes. Time passes faster than you realize. Soon he'll be part of Stone Labs."

"He's six, Father." Caster cut his gaze around the dimly lit room. "Where's the waitress? I require wine immediately." He frowned and snapped his fingers, beckoning the blonde hostess, now seating other guests.

She hurried to the table.

"Is there a reason our server has been detained? Perhaps the words on the menu are too hard to pronounce, or some catastrophe has occurred?"

"My apologies, sir. I'll find someone right away."

"When you find this 'someone,' be sure to tell them I tip according to service."

She hustled away, looking somehow smaller.

"Was that necessary?" Lukas asked, his ears warming.

Caster smirked. "She's a *hostess* who's gone searching for a *waiter*. She can handle it. It's not like I sent her on a scavenger hunt in a cannibalistic jungle."

Lukas pondered on the analogy. In a way, Caster was a cannibal. An eater of human self-esteem and dignity. An emotional cannibal. "Your rudeness is embarrassing."

"Enough." Lukas's father looked at Caster and back to him. "I didn't fly from the other side of the country to listen to the two of you bicker."

"You're right. I'm sorry, Father." Caster lowered his eyes, offering a smug wink to Lukas when their father glanced away.

"Good evening, gentlemen. I am so sorry to have kept you waiting. My name is Marco, and I will be your server this evening." The waiter distributed three menus with black covers. "May I show you the wine list?"

"That won't be necessary," Caster said, rattling off the name of a doubtlessly expensive wine Lukas had never heard of. "That will be all for now. And leave the bottle." Caster glanced at Lukas. "Please."

"Yes, sir. I will bring your bottle of wine and a nice basket of warm bread, right away."

"Thank you."

The waiter turned to go.

"Say, Marco?" Caster said, calling him back. "I've been informed that my mannerisms could be interpreted as insulting or rude. Would you say you agree?"

"No sir, not at all. You seem very polite."

Caster shrugged. "See there, Lukas. Marco, here, thinks I'm polite."

Lukas glared at his brother as the server left the table.

The eldest Dr. Stone cleared his throat. "If you two are finished, I'd like to discuss the reason I'm here." He fixed his sharp blue eyes on Lukas. "How's the research coming? I trust things are working out well with the human test subject?"

Here it came—the thumbscrew pressure Heston Stone was famous for. Lukas opened his menu. "It's a day-by-day process. Thus far, I'd say it's going well." He slid his gaze down the list of entrees. "I believe I'll have the eggplant parmesan. No, scratch that—there's mushroom in the sauce."

"The procedure was a success? No adverse reactions to the abstergent?"

"Do you suppose they offer an alternate sauce?" Lukas asked, avoiding his father's questions. His mouth, a moment ago watered by the aroma of garlic bread and fresh oregano, went dry as the Mojave Desert.

"Lukas." His father reached across the table and slid the menu from his hand. "I don't need all of the details. I realize there is extensive follow-up monitoring to be done. All I'm asking, is did the subject tolerate the abstergent? Did it effectively dissolve the Agathi?"

Lukas breathed a sigh of relief as Marco returned, making a show of presenting Caster with the wine bottle and distributing the stemware with flair. Another server accompanied him, holding a basket of bread. "Gentlemen, are you ready to order?" Marco asked, taking the bread from the younger server and shooing him from the table. Marco took their orders and retrieved the menus.

"More water, please," Lukas said, before draining his glass.

"Back to Father's question," Caster said. "How is what's her name—Briar, isn't it? How is Briar adjusting to the aftereffects of your abstergent?"

Lukas stiffened his neck. "You are quite aware I haven't given it to her yet."

"Haven't administered the abstergent?" Lukas's father set down his water glass, hard, sloshing liquid onto the white tablecloth. "You can't be serious."

"She's been at the lab for less than a week. I refuse to rush the process."

"There is no *process*," Caster hissed the word like a desert sidewinder. "The abstergent's been ready for weeks. Shoot it into her brain."

"I'm not the one doing the shooting. That's Dr. Fuller's job. And there are a few more tests to perform before she's ready for treatment."

"What type of tests, little brother?"

Lukas narrowed his gaze at Caster. "This has nothing to do with you. I refuse to say another word until you either leave this table or shut your arrogant mouth."

"Quiet, Caster. I want to hear what Lukas has to say."

Caster aimed his white-hot gaze at the wine, nearly bursting the bottle.

"The abstergent is not the problem, Father. It's the lack of antidote that's causing the delay. I'm not comfortable experimenting on a human subject until the antidote is fully developed. It's good medicine—and proper scientific procedure—to have a viable antidote."

"Nonsense. You're wasting time. There's no need for an antidote. You've run test after test with favorable results—make that *perfect* results—every single time. Nothing can possibly go wrong."

"This is the first test I've administered on a person, Father. A *human being*. In the infinitesimal chance that something does go wrong, an antidote would have to be administered in less than five minutes—almost instantly. The abstergent begins to dissolve brain tissue very quickly." For the first-time Lukas could remember, he looked his father squarely in the eyes. "I will absolutely not administer my abstergent to Briar Lee without the safeguard of a fully developed antidote. Period."

Caster licked his lips, undoubtedly anticipating their father's response like a decadent dessert.

Heston Stone sighed. "Very well. To preserve your peace of mind, I will give you exactly one week to finish concocting this imaginary necessity of yours. After which, you will immediately instruct Dr. Fuller to inject the subject with your abstergent and report back to me. Better yet, stream the procedure to me live. I want to watch the future unfold in my son's hands."

With a loud scrape of his chair Caster rose, threw his wadded linen napkin to the table, and left the room.

Their father didn't seem to notice. "One week, firm. Rosen's department has been breathing down my neck, demanding to know when the abstergent will be ready for public consumption." He lowered his voice. "There are rumors surfacing about the ARC. People are starting to ask questions about what goes on there. If the truth leaks out, it will destroy my reputation as well as my career. Not to mention your mother's chance to become Maryland's next state representative."

Unease squirmed through Lukas's insides. What was going on inside the ARC that could ruin his parents' careers? Through the years, he'd shrugged off a few ridiculous rumors he'd assumed were distorted gossip, but had he somehow ignored something valid? Something he should have already known? Something everybody else knew? He supposed that's what happened when a person spent every waking moment either in college or in a scientific lab—or both. And did he really want to find out what went on inside the ARC?

Fear of the answer stopped him from asking the question.

"One week, Father. You have my word."

"Good." Heston Stone smiled and reached over the table to give Lukas's forearm a hard squeeze. He glanced at Caster's empty chair. "Where has your brother run off to?"

~*~

Lukas returned his father's hug, wincing at his firm pat on the back. "Send Mother my love."

"I will—providing I can pull her away from the campaign podium." His father turned to Caster, giving his eldest son an identical hug and pat, then reached under his suitcoat to retrieve his airline ticket from his breast pocket. "Lukas, I expect to hear back from you in exactly one week."

"I haven't forgotten."

He watched his father fall into the long line of early risers leading to airport security. The deadline played over in his mind. One week until his patented abstergent made scientific history, forever altering the future of the entire country. No more mandatory boosters to combat diminishing SAP levels. It was merely a matter of time before other countries followed suit. Soon, Stone's Abstergent would change the world.

On a smaller yet equally important scale, his abstergent would end the suffering of the unleveled population. Others like Briar, shunned by society because of functional Agathi—a defect beyond their control. There would be no more need for questionable holding facilities. Permanent leveling would not only cure the encumbered, but secure for them a well-deserved place in society, enabling them to learn and grow without the fear and judgment synonymous with their present condition.

Briar would be free. He'd been aware of that from the beginning. So why did the thought fill him with inexplicable dread?

"One thing I'll never understand, little brother. How those strings you've attached to Father reach all the way to Piper, Maryland. Hope he doesn't yank back one day. Wouldn't want you to get whiplash."

His brother had been through a lot. Lukas had to remember that. He couldn't imagine the devastation Caster must feel over losing his wife. As far as Lukas knew, Caster had never broken down or even shed a tear. Undoubtedly, he held it inside for Gatlin's sake. He wanted to be strong for his little boy, but that level of pent-up grief, coupled with a ravenous hunger to be the driving force behind Stone Labs caused Caster to overstep his bounds.

Lukas grinned. "Then you'd have to stand in for me at the lab and enjoy Father breathing down your neck for a change. You'd find out who really holds the strings."

Truthfully, Lukas felt guilty over the restrictions Father placed on Caster. Though his brother would never admit it, Caster would give anything to trade him places. He wanted control of Stone Labs—quite possibly even more than Lukas. He'd had his chance, a short-lived stint that ended in failure.

Afterword, Father insisted on bestowing Stone Labs upon Lukas. He'd said he was the right man for the job. The "level-headed" son, pardon the pun. Father felt Caster was led by emotion—and most of those emotions were rooted in anger. He was right.

Since childhood, Lukas had been the rational one. Calm and composed. Sensible. Briar's face—blue eyes bright with mischief, pink lips curved in a smile—flashed into his mind.

Until recently.

8

Briar stood, frozen, in the center of her room. The anguished scream from next door turned each vertebra into an individual ice cube. Was there an axe murderer on the loose?

Oh, no. Reid!

Briar ran from her room, skidding to a stop at Reid's doorway.

Roxy, collarless and soaking wet, dashed around Reid.

"Get out of my room you, stupid animal!"

The dog hunched down on her front legs, wriggling her hindquarters. She opened her huge mouth, appearing to smile as she wagged her massive tail.

"I said out!" Reid kicked at Roxy, who barked playfully and sprang, nearly knocking Reid to the floor. The dog snatched a black garment from the tile as she darted around the room.

Derby rounded the corner at the end of the hallway and sprinted toward them, empty leash in hand. "Miss Reid, I'm so sorry. I was finishing up her bath when she got away."

"Get this ridiculous beast out of here!"

Roxy shook the article of clothing hanging from her massive jaws.

"And give me that!" Reid dove for the sheer garment and missed. Yelling what sounded like a battle cry, she lunged again, this time snagging the fabric. "Let go!" To Roxy's excitement, she yanked the cloth back and forth, propelling the overgrown pup into tug of war mode.

Briar scooted back.

Derby stepped into the room and circled the opponents, knees bent and hands splayed like a lion tamer. "Roxy? Easy, girl."

Reid pulled away as Derby reached for the fabric, wadding it up in his fist, holding it tight as the dog tugged and growled teasingly.

"Now drop it!"

Just like that, Roxy released the garment. She backed up, smiling again, tail proudly wagging as if she'd handed Derby a prize rabbit.

"What on earth is going on in here?" Lukas joined Briar in the doorway. "Sounds like a hostile takeover."

"It is." Briar nodded toward the display.

Derby blushed at the skimpy black panties in his hand. "I'll take these over to the laundry room."

"Don't bother." Reid snatched the underwear from him and tossed them into the wastepaper basket beside the desk.

Roxy barked once, her damp tail picking up speed.

Derby nudged her with his foot.

"Perhaps you should keep your clothing off the floor instead of leaving it for Derby to pick up. In case you haven't noticed, there's a hamper right over there." Lukas tipped his head toward the corner of the room. "That would decrease your risk of undergarment casualties."

Roxy gave a massive shake, creating a torrential rainstorm in the middle of Reid's room.

"Get out of here! All of you!"

The dog yipped and dashed from the room.

"Sorry, Miss Reid." Derby followed, pulling the

door closed behind him.

"Don't ever come in my room again! You're all banned! That means you too, Derby! I'll do my own laundry!" Reid's furious yells echoed through the closed door.

~*~

Lukas pressed the hypodermic needle to Briar's skin, a few inches under the rubber tourniquet. He pulled away as her arm began shaking—again. This was getting ridiculous.

"Let me know when you're finished," he said, backing up for the third time.

"I'm sorry." Briar pressed her lips together, squelching her laughter. She opened her mouth wide, closed it, and massaged her jaws. "Let me relax." She took a deep breath, her cheeks puffing with the exhale. "OK. I'm ready."

"You're sure?"

"Yes. The giggles are out of my system. Draw my blood. Third time's a charm."

"This is attempt number four." He tapped the skin inside the crook of her elbow. "Squeeze the rubber ball a couple of times." The vein plumped up. "Perfect. You'll feel a little stick." He pressed the tip of the needle to the vein—and she jerked her arm. Lukas slammed the hypodermic to the sterile tray.

"I can't help it!" She shrieked through jags of laughter. "I keep thinking about Roxy taking off with Reid's panties! It was hysterical—how can you *not* be laughing, right now?"

He glared at her. "Like everything else in life, there is a time and a place for laughter. And this is neither."

Briar's lips twitched and she slapped a hand over her mouth. "I'm sorry," she mumbled through her fingers. She closed her eyes for a moment and dropped her hand. "OK." She breathed in through her nose and out through her mouth. "Time and place—I understand all that. But I really don't get why you are so serious all the time. Even when Derby was standing there, beet red, holding Reid's unmentionables, you never cracked a smile."

Lukas lowered himself onto a stool. "My upbringing, I suppose. I've worked for my father, in one form or another, since I was a boy—for as long as I can remember, really. Our home was strict. No nonsense. There was little to no time for play. Everything was a competition, and not a friendly one. Caster and I were raised by nannies and homeschooled by the best online tutors money could buy. We were very isolated as children." He lifted a shoulder. "Not much has changed."

"At least now you're doing what you love. I hope to one day do what I love, too—working with children, face-to-face. Making them laugh. Laughter is healing. You should try it sometime." She nudged his knee with the toe of her lab issued slipper. "You have to admit, the scene with Roxy and Reid was funny, right?"

"Hilarious." Lukas chuckled. "Satisfied? Can we do some bloodwork now?"

She nodded, and to his astonishment, sat perfectly still as he drew three vials of blood from her vein.

"Very good. Thank you." He placed the stopper on the last vial and discarded his gloves. "Reid will be in to finish up your session. Odds are, she's not in a good mood." He moved to the sink, lathered, and dried his hands. "I don't suggest laughing. Or you might find the blood pressure cuff around your neck."

"Would it work that way?"

He raised an eyebrow and she cringed.

"Don't answer that."

~*~

Briar breathed in through her nose and out through her mouth as she waited for Reid to enter the room. She didn't have to wait long. The door banged open and Reid blew in like an Oklahoma whirlwind.

"Let's get on with it," she snapped, slapping a clipboard to the countertop. She snatched a small device from the wall and clipped it roughly to Briar's fingertip. Lukas was right. Reid definitely was not in a good mood.

"What is this thing?" Briar asked, needing to fill the awkward, angry silence.

"Pulse oximeter. If you had a fleshcard like a normal person, I wouldn't have to waste time taking your vitals."

"Has the new fleshcard arrived yet?"

Reid glared. "I have no idea."

Briar returned her gaze to the device on her finger. "*Pulse oximeter*. Interesting. Measures the pulse?"

"Don't attempt to chitchat with me. In fact, you need to shut your mouth altogether. I need to work in silence."

Reid seized the device from Briar's finger, marched to the counter and scribbled something on the clipboard. "Bad enough I had to deal with that ridiculous beast this morning. Now I have to put up with an overcurious juvenile," she muttered under her breath, loud enough for Briar to hear.

Briar wished she hadn't heard. Desperately. The corners of her mouth twitched and shot upward, as if yanked by double fishhooks, while the battle between Roxy and Reid played out in her mind. She coughed, hoping to disguise her laughter and hide her smile at the same time.

"Something funny?"

Attempt failed.

"No, it's nothing. I'm sorry…something Lukas mentioned."

Reid banged the clipboard to the counter, cracking off one of the plastic corners. She whirled around, emerald eyes on fire.

"Don't get any ideas about Lukas. He's not interested. Believe me, I've tried. He didn't go for my advances—you're crazy to think he'd go after yours." She stepped to the exam table and leaned forward, her face close to Briar's. "It's pitiful, really. The way you tag along after him like a runt pup. Did you think I hadn't noticed? Well, let me set you straight. You're nothing but a test subject to Lukas. A means to his success. He's only being nice because he pities you, cooped up here in the lab. Trust me, once that abstergent hits your brain, the romance will be over." She stood up straight and crossed her arms. "Take my advice and give up this fairytale fantasy of being Lukas's little girlfriend before you make an even bigger fool of yourself."

Briar forgot how to speak. It didn't matter, because she'd forgotten every word in the English language as well. She remembered only how to blink and swallow.

"Maybe you should set your sights on someone more attainable. Like Derby." Reid's smirk turned into a full-blown smile filled with too many teeth. "Now there's a catch." She laughed loudly.

Turned out Reid had a sense of humor after all.

~*~

Breathing a relieved sigh, Briar turned the doorknob to her apartment. Never was she so ready to be alone. Nothing like a couple of hours with Reid Laughlin to make a person long for isolation.

"If you need anything, call Derby or Lukas. I'm taking the night off."

Briar nodded. As if she would call Reid for any reason—*ever*. Not on a bet or a dare. Not even if she awoke in the night with her head stapled on backwards. Asking for Reid's assistance was not happening.

"I heard my name." Derby appeared in the hallway, his usual lopsided grin glued in place.

"Hi, Derby. Reid was telling me to call you if I need anything later on. In the event something comes up."

"Miss Laughlin's a smart lady. Mighty good looking, too." He glanced at Reid, turned back to Briar and winked.

Without a word, Reid spun on her heel and walked away.

Derby watched her go. By the glint in his eye, he enjoyed the view.

Briar wondered what he could possibly see in Reid. She wished she could tell him what the woman had said earlier—the cutting remark she'd made about him—but she never would. It would shatter him.

As she surveyed Reid's departure, Caster turned

the corner, slamming into Reid at the end of the hallway.

Briar lunged inside her apartment, heart racing. Something about Caster Stone made her uneasy. *Uneasy?* Who was she kidding? The guy terrified her. She couldn't stomach the sight of him.

"Hey, where'd you go?" Derby stuck his head into the doorway. "You missed the collision. Dr. Stone nearly knocked Miss Laughlin to the floor at the end of the hallway. She's all right, though. He caught her on the way down and steadied her upright."

"Come in and close the door. Hurry."

He stepped over the threshold, closing the door behind him. "You OK?"

Briar shook her head. "I'm sorry. Lukas's brother makes me really nervous for some reason—as if I'm doing something wrong by existing. Pretty much the same as Reid does. I think they're a match made in heaven." She mock-glared at Derby. "You're not going to turn me in for mentioning heaven, are you?"

He grinned. "No, ma'am. Not a chance."

"So, what is Caster's deal, anyway? I mean, I realize he lost his wife a while back, and that is completely terrible." Briar pulled out her desk chair and motioned for Derby to sit. "But is that really what makes him behave so…superior?" She sat on the bed.

Derby frowned and tugged at the brim of his ball cap. "Superior. Not so sure that's the right word. I'd say it's more like he's desensitized." He glanced at the closed door and lowered his voice. "It wasn't only that his wife died—sure, that's bad enough—but she'd left him six months before. Caster's always been difficult, so the fact Kate left him wasn't a surprise. But no one could believe she'd leave Gatlin."

Little Gatlin's hazel eyes flashed through Briar's mind. How could anyone, let alone his own mother, abandon that sweet little boy?

"As you can imagine, Kate's leaving so abruptly caused people to whisper. Everyone assumed she was having an affair and that she'd up and left her family to be with the other man. Was quite a scandal. Caster paced around here like a caged lion, eaten up with rage." Derby shook his head. "None of it sat right with me. I knew Kate. She was a good wife. The type of woman who would put up with anything to keep her family together. Heck, she already had, the way Caster was always runnin' around on her…" He blew out a breath. "Disgraceful."

No wonder Briar knew instinctively Caster was a jerk. He was putting off some kind of lecherous vibe. "How did she die?"

"Cancer. There'd been no love affair. Only radical radiation and intense chemotherapy. For months, she'd known she was dying. She'd checked herself into a cancer treatment hospital someplace in New York and kept it under wraps. She'd given the doctor specific orders not to tell her family. Kate thought of everything—even prepaid the funeral home director to take care of the final arrangements. When the time came, they picked up her body at the hospital and she was cremated. No muss, no fuss."

"She never got the chance to say goodbye, I love you, or maybe even, I'm sorry?" Needles of sadness pricked the corners of Briar's eyes. "No one was allowed to see her?"

"She wanted it that way. Caster saw her, briefly, right before the incineration. That's when he discovered the truth about why she'd left." Derby looked down at his folded hands. "The next morning, he brought the urn back to Sickle Ridge and we had a little memorial. Just the five of us—Caster, Gatlin, Lukas, Reid, and me. A small celebration of life with a few flowers. Afterward, I took Caster and Gatlin up in the balloon to release her ashes. Lukas stayed on the ground, of course."

"What about her family? Mother, father, siblings? None of them came?"

Derby shrugged. "Subject never came up. And I'm not the type to ask personal questions, especially at a delicate time like that. Especially not to Caster Stone."

Briar nodded, seeing his point.

Derby tapped the screen of his cuffphone, pried it from his arm, and snapped it flat. "Here's a picture of her. The only one I've got. Maybe the only one in existence, for all I know. She took down all of her social media sites when she left town. Everyone figured it was to hide her new life. Turns out it was to hide her death."

Briar took the phone from Derby, caught off guard by the woman's coal black hair and charcoal eyes. "Striking," Briar's mother would have said. Looking closer, she could see Gatlin shared his mother's pert nose and dimpled chin. "She was beautiful."

"That she was." Derby stroked a finger lovingly over the screen before snapping the phone back around his forearm. "The whole thing was such a shock. No one could believe it." He frowned as if swallowing a bad taste. "Caster has always been callous, but he's gotten worse since Kate's death. He's desensitized, like I said earlier. Unfeeling. And he's extremely protective over Gatlin."

"Yeah, I got that message loud and clear." Briar

lowered her eyes. "He doesn't want me around his son, period. He thinks I will contaminate him."

Derby concentrated on his hands, rubbing one thumb over the other. "I might have some insight on that. I gather a lot working behind the scenes—and not on purpose, either."

"You know why he's so adamant about keeping Gatlin away from me?"

"He doesn't trust SAP, and he's completely paranoid about it. That's why he's pushing Lukas so hard to hurry with the abstergent. He wants Gatlin's Agathi dissolved away."

"Gatlin's Agathi? That doesn't make sense. I'm sure his Agathi are nonfunctional. Caster would make certain Gatlin stayed current on his SAP boosters."

Derby shrugged. "As I mentioned, he doesn't trust the stuff. I didn't say Caster was logical. I said he was paranoid. He doesn't want to risk any of your Christian nonsense leaking through—no offense."

"None taken." She actually felt a little sorry for Caster. He'd taken such a blow. Trauma sometimes caused people to question everything they believed in. Although, in Caster's case, she had no idea what that could be—if anything.

And poor little Gatlin, believing what—that his mother simply ceased to exist? That she became part of the "amissfear" as his nanny believed?

She turned to Derby. "Do you believe this life is all there is?"

"I believe Kate lived, and then she died." He stood and returned the chair to the desk. "That's all there is, Miss Briar." He tipped his cap at her. "I enjoyed our chat."

"Me, too."

He closed the door behind him.

That's all there is, Miss Briar. Derby's words resounded in her head. She couldn't imagine what it would be like to live without the hope of eternal life. To believe this life was the end of existence.

But soon she would believe it—wouldn't she? The thought tinkled down her vertebrae like an ancient requiem over piano keys.

9

Briar unwound the towel from her head and tossed it into the hamper. The scent of her damp hair caused her chest to ache. Hunger pangs of an empty heart.

She was homesick. And although she missed her mother and longed to once more see her departed father, tonight it was Granna Grace she yearned for.

She sat on the bed and tugged a section of hair toward her face—the strands barely reaching her nose—and inhaled. Lilacs. The shampoo Derby bought smelled so much like her grandmother. Amazing how aroma could transport the senses. Granna Grace had been gone for ten years yet there she was, sitting on the bed next to seven-year-old Briar, combing the tangles from her hair.

She leaned over and pulled the strap of her bag, hauling it from under the nightstand to her lap. She unzipped it, pushed the blue wig aside, and rifled through the odds and ends until her fingers wrapped around the stuffed lamb keychain Granna Grace had sewn. The ring was filled with random keys, the old-fashioned metal kind no one used anymore, with the exception of Lukas's father. She didn't have a car, and had no need for a house key because she never left home. The keychain was a diversion to distract from what really mattered. To preserve what was on the inside.

And it gave her an excuse to play with a stuffed animal despite her age. She smiled and gave the lamb a gentle squeeze. As always, her pulse quickened when she felt the tiny book buried in the sheep's belly. The Holy Bible. A final gift from Granna Grace tucked into the tufts of cotton.

The book was smaller than a pack of sugarless gum and twice as thick. Granna had let her hold it before sewing it inside, explaining that God's word would be hidden away in the lamb, just as it was hidden away in Briar's heart.

She'd said there would be hard days ahead and that she was old and wouldn't be around much longer. She'd prayed for the light of God to glow eternally inside Briar so that others could see it.

Yep, others could see it, all right. "Thanks, Granna." Briar held the lamb to her chest and sighed. Her light of God was, literally, glowing. Every scan she'd ever had proved it. And now it had gotten her into deep trouble. Those blazing red God-zones were the whole reason she was here, forfeiting her soul.

So, she was going to give it all up, just like that? The virtues Granna Grace instilled in her. God's never ending love. The truth about eternal life and salvation through Jesus Christ—a truth the world needed now, more than ever. Everything Granna Grace taught her, wasted. Dissolved to nonexistence by the prick of a needle, and she would do nothing to stop it?

She drew a deep breath through her nose and exhaled through her mouth. Had the air become suddenly thicker? It was like breathing fog.

Did she really expect God to forgive her? To shrug off her decision as if she was tossing a pair of outgrown shoes into a donation box? To watch, unmoving, as she surrendered the priceless gift His Son bled and died for? Was He simply to let her slide?

Briar smoothed her hair, pretending Granna Grace was stroking it the way she used to. The scent of lilacs surrounded Briar. She closed her eyes as she imagined her grandmother wrapping her arms around her, holding Briar close to her side. "It's hard to explain, Granna. I feel like a thief is peering through my window, leering at my most prized possession. His mouth is watering, he wants it so bad. But he's not breaking in, he's waiting. Patiently waiting until I turn my back. When I do, he'll simply walk inside and take it. Take my soul."

She rested her head on her grandma's shoulder. "I don't know what to do. I'm scared, Granna," she whispered, tears slipping down her cheeks. "I'll lose you all over again."

Who knows whether you have come here for such a time as this?

Briar sat up straight and opened her eyes. The sound of her grandmother's voice, loud and clear as Oklahoma hail on a new tin roof, lingered in the room.

The verse was from Esther, chapter four. The part where Esther's uncle told her not to assume she would escape death simply because she was queen. Outside the castle her people were being destroyed in the streets. If she was silent, she and her family would die.

"Queen of Stone Labs," Reid had once called her. Of course, that was ridiculous. Briar was no queen. However, she couldn't deny she'd been granted special provisions. Because of who her father had been, she was safe. Resting comfy-cozy in her own private apartment while hundreds of other Christians were being stripped from their families and held captive at the ARC until the leveling process was complete.

Held indefinitely, according to her mother's sci-fi

version. "They're slicing and dicing their brains. People go in but never come out, Briar."

Hidden camera footage, secret documents. She'd have said anything to keep Briar away from the OLG. She was convinced the insufferable amount of work Dad accomplished for Operation Level Ground is what drove him to suicide. To Mom, the ARC really did seem like a chamber of horrors.

But it wasn't. It was a treatment facility. A place where unleveled patients received treatment based on their specific needs.

Needs? Briar frowned. Was that really the right word? Did people like her *need* to be fixed? Have their brains evaluated, medicated—in her case dissolved—for the sake of progressivism?

Briar's heart trembled. Something precious was about to be stripped from her. And not from her alone, from hundreds who shared her affliction. Who had labeled it an affliction in the first place? An affliction was a hardship—a weakness. Maybe having a working Agathi wasn't a weakness. Maybe it was a strength. A mixture of clarity and outrage rose in her soul. The time had come to stand up and fight. Blood blasted through her veins like a call to arms. It was as if God Himself were leading her in battle.

And she was terrified.

Fight who? The OLG? She must be insane. She was no fighter. She was a floater—a go-with-the-flow kind of girl. Her encounter with Reid today was the closest she'd ever come to an altercation, and that didn't even count. It had been an ambush. If she couldn't stand up to a spoiled lab technician, how could she hold her own against the most powerful government entity in the United States?

Maybe Granna was trying to tell her that soon her suffering would be over. "Such a time as this," could mean the abstergent would be a success. That Briar would soon be a part of a medical breakthrough that would change the world. Yes, that was probably it.

Her soul knew better.

The walls seemed to close in. She closed her eyes to escape, only to find Granna Grace shaking her head slowly.

"I'm sorry, Granna. But I can't fight. I'm too afraid."

She wished this was all behind her. If Lukas would only give her the abstergent, she could stop dwelling on the fact she was a miserable coward, and get on with her life. What was taking him so long?

A tap on the door rattled her thoughts. She pushed the lamb under her pillow and bolted from the edge of the bed. "Who is it?" she asked, padding across the floor.

"It's Lukas."

She tightened her bathrobe and opened the door.

"May I come in?"

~*~

Lukas pulled the chair from beneath the desk and sat down. "I wanted to check in with you before you turned in. Find out how things went in the exam room today after I left."

Briar slumped on the edge of the bed. "Epic fail." She dropped her gaze to the floor.

He didn't like the crease in her forehead, or the way her mouth dipped at the corners. "How so?"

"Let's just say I didn't take your advice. Reid

mentioned the Roxy incident from this morning, and I might have laughed a little." She flicked her gaze up and right back down.

Lukas fought a grin, the image of Roxy shaking off water in the middle of Reid's room nearly getting the best of him. "I'm sorry. She'll get over it."

Briar nodded as she stared at the floor.

"Hey. Don't let her get under your skin. I'll have a talk with her."

She shook her head. "It's not Reid. I mean, she's no ray of sunshine, but I can deal with her." A tear splashed to the tile.

"What is it?" He glanced from the tear to her bowed head. "Briar?"

She sighed. "I'm stressed, I guess. I know, it sounds stupid. What do I have to be stressed about, right? I have this really nice apartment, clean clothing, nutritious food, I'm surrounded by good people—for the most part. Still, I feel anxious."

Lukas pulled a tissue from the box on the desk and handed it to her. "Of course, you're anxious. That's perfectly understandable. You're over a thousand miles from home in a strange place, surrounded by people you hardly know. That's enough to stress anyone out."

Briar twisted the tissue between her fingers, her hands trembling as she wound the paper tighter and tighter. Her jittering leg kept a quick rhythm against the side of the bed. The poor girl was a nervous wreck.

"Why don't you turn in for the night? Get some rest."

"I don't think I'll be able to sleep." Her fingers worked over the tissue, shredding it to bits.

"Would a hot bath help?"

"I already took a shower."

Lukas inhaled, catching a whiff of her clean scent. She smelled like flowers.

"Would you like a sedative?"

"No, thanks. I don't like taking medication." She glanced down at what was left of the tissue. Little more than a pile of dust in her palm.

Lukas reached for the wastepaper basket and slid it in front of her. "The sedatives I'm offering are very mild. You won't even realize you've taken them. Tomorrow morning you'll wake up refreshed and energized, with a lot less anxiety."

"No, thank you." She dusted her hands together over the trashcan. "Lukas—can't you just do it? Give me the abstergent and be done with it? I can't stand living this way anymore. Unable to interact with the kids that I love, or to fulfill my passion to help them. Living as a shut in, having no contact with the rest of the world. And the guilt—I can't cope with the guilt. There's a tug of war going on inside me, and I'm ready to throw down the rope. Can you do it tomorrow, Lukas? Please? I'm prepared for the next step."

Tears flowed down her face, dripping to her light-blue bathrobe, turning the fabric a darker shade that matched her eyes. He pulled another tissue from the box and handed it to her, aware it would soon be minced to powder. "What about some tea?"

She blew her nose and nodded weakly. "Tea sounds fine."

"Good." He rose from the chair and slid it under the desk. "I'll be back in a few minutes."

She nodded again and offered the saddest excuse for a smile he'd ever witnessed.

Lukas closed the door behind him and hurried

down the hallway to the kitchen.

Reid stood at the double sink, dousing a glass of ice cubes with water.

"Excuse me," he said, opening a cupboard door beside her leg and retrieving the teakettle.

"Tea at this hour? The caffeine will keep you awake." She swirled the ice in her glass and took a long drink.

"It's not for me. It's for Briar." He set the kettle on the stovetop and turned the dial.

"Ah." Reid clinked the glass to the countertop and wiped her mouth with the back of her hand. "She was pretty high strung today during her exam. The only vital I logged was her pulse, and I practically had to fight her for that."

"Glad you brought that up. We need to talk." He opened a high cupboard and reached for his favorite red mug. He tore a paper towel from the roll, polishing the cup as he leaned against the counter.

"Bringing out the good china." Reid smirked. "Styrofoam might upset her fragile sensibilities."

Lukas tightened his grip on the ceramic handle, pointing the mug toward her. "That's exactly what I want to talk about."

She cocked an eyebrow.

"You always have something snide to say about her. It's bad enough she's been shipped a thousand-plus miles from home to be a test subject in a scientific lab that's operated by total strangers. But that's not quite torturous enough. You have to make her life as miserable as possible." He set the mug solidly on the counter and extinguished the heat under the kettle. "A specific type of depression exists with Briar's condition. When she thinks of what the future holds, the Agathus generates feelings of hopelessness and loss. It's like a built-in emotional defense mechanism. The sensations are very strong, and comparable to grief."

Reid opened one of the matching canisters on the countertop and retrieved a teabag. "Are you saying she is in—mourning?"

"Essentially, yes."

Reid placed the bag into the mug. "Poor girl." Her voice softened as Lukas poured the bubbling water. "I had no idea."

Was she being sarcastic? Wasn't she always? He gave her a quick glance before setting the kettle in the sink. Head down, gaze on the floor. If so, she was hiding it well.

"Your cutting remarks and general rudeness toward Briar aren't helping matters. Your behavior certainly isn't advancing the clinical process. Oppositely, the hostile environment you've created is hindering progress."

That should do it. If she came unhinged, it would be now. No way could she fake a calm demeanor following that speech. Not the Reid he knew.

"I—I don't know what to say." Reid dragged her sad gaze to his. "This is hard for me to admit, but I've been a little jealous of Briar. Before she came along, I received much more attention around here. More attention from you." She swallowed, her eyes never leaving Lukas's. "Now I fade into the woodwork."

He glanced over her perfectly styled blonde hair, made-up eyes, bright pink scrubs and matching lipstick. No woodwork in the world could camouflage that.

"Today in the exam room—well, to tell you the

truth, I was embarrassed. Briar was distracted. She kept snickering, so I asked what was funny. She said she was thinking about something you'd said earlier, but I knew that wasn't the truth. She was thinking about the incident with Roxy. Stupid dog. Do you think I enjoyed watching Derby pry my underwear from that beast's mouth?" Reid inhaled through flared nostrils. "It was humiliating. When Briar laughed about it, I guess I lost my temper." She widened her eyes and stood up straight. "Should I go and apologize? Would that make her feel better?" She took a step toward the door.

Lukas touched her shoulder. "Not tonight. It's a nice gesture, but she's pretty distraught. I'll take her the tea and hope it calms her nerves. A good night's sleep would do her a world of good."

"Maybe you should suggest a sedative. Something to take the edge off, so she can rest."

He shook his head. "I offered. She isn't comfortable with the idea of taking anything that makes her sleep."

"What about an anti-anxiety compound? Not enough to knock her out. A light dose to loosen her up so that she can fall asleep."

Lukas frowned and bobbed the teabag inside the red mug.

"Look, I hate that I've contributed to Briar's misery. I'll do my best to make things right, starting tomorrow. Would you please give the poor girl something to help her rest? I can't stand the idea of her lying awake all night because of my inexcusable behavior. That thought will keep me from sleeping. Then you'll have two insomniacs on your hands."

He held the dripping bag above the cup for a

moment and walked it to the trashcan. "She really needs the rest. We have an early testing session."

Reid nodded. "I'll bring her breakfast in bed first thing in the morning. Fruit, toast, and coffee with a heartfelt apology on the side." She placed a hand on her chest.

"A mild sedative," Lukas said, picking up the mug.

"A few sprinkles in her tea. She'll never know the difference." Reid touched his elbow. "It's for her own good."

"I'll go and prepare the compound." Lukas fished the key to the pharmaceutical closet from his pocket as he left the kitchen.

10

"Rise and shine, Sleeping Beauty." Reid's voice, dripping with artificial sweetener, roused Briar from a dead sleep. She clattered something onto the nightstand and tapped Briar on the cheek. "Briar—that really was the name of the princess in the story, wasn't it? Sleeping Beauty's name was Briar Rose. I don't know why I didn't think of that before." More clattering. "You share the same name as a princess whose only responsibility was to look pretty and get plenty of rest. Fitting." She tapped Briar's other cheek, harder than the first.

"What time is it?" Briar asked, lifting her head from the pillow and letting it fall back down. Her skull was made of solid lead. "I feel like I've only been sleeping a few minutes."

"It's almost noon. I tried waking you earlier, but you were dead to the world. Now sit up and eat your breakfast. Fruit, toast, juice, and coffee. I threw away the first tray and made fresh."

"Noon?" Briar shot straight up into a sitting position and wrapped a hand around her forehead. "*Ugh.* My head." The room spun. She closed her eyes to get her bearings.

"Hangover?" Reid chuckled. "I'm not surprised, with the amount of sedative you ingested. I told Lukas you were a lightweight, but he insisted you could handle it."

"Sedative? What are you talking about?"

"Last night. Lukas slipped a sedative into your tea.

Nothing harmful, just something to curb your anxiety and help you sleep."

"I don't believe you. I told Lukas I didn't want any drugs. I made myself clear."

Reid was lying, she had to be. Lukas respected her. He would never…

"It was for your own good. He was blathering on about your being in mourning because a portion of your brain will soon die, and how isolated you are here at the lab." She lifted the tray and sighed. "What I'd give for a little isolation."

Sharp tears pricked the corners of Briar's eyes. He'd told Reid about her emotional state. Her private fears. She'd never been so betrayed—not even when her father killed himself. Dad hadn't been thinking clearly. His final decision was made in a pressurized cloud of depression. Last night Lukas was expressive and alert. He'd known exactly what he was doing.

Reid tried to set the breakfast tray over Briar's lap. Briar brought both knees up and blocked the tray, ignoring Reid's growled explicative.

"I'm not hungry."

"Lukas wants you to eat before starting your testing session. You're already hours behind." She forced the tray over Briar's knees.

Briar straightened her legs with a jerk, rattling the dishes.

"Knock it off. You nearly spilled your juice."

"Take it away. I said I'm not hungry." Briar clamped her mouth shut. She wouldn't say another word. She couldn't. If she tried, the sobs would take over. She'd explode before she'd let Reid see her cry.

"I had nothing to do with it. Slipping you that sedative was all Lukas's idea." She marched to the small wastepaper basket and dumped the tray, dishes and all. A piece of toast landed butter-side-down on the tile. "Starve, for all I care." The tray banged against the doorframe as she left, slamming the door behind her.

Briar stared at the soggy toast on the floor until her vision blurred. She dragged the pillow to her lap, buried her face, and sobbed.

~*~

Briar guessed the silence would have been awkward, had she not been so angry. The testing session seemed to drag on forever, and she'd managed to stay silent the entire time. Now she was paying for it. She opened her mouth wide and massaged the areas under her ears. Her jaws ached from gritting her teeth and her stomach gurgled, filled with the bitter words she'd continually swallowed.

"You seem tense." Lukas glanced up, his fingers still tapping away at the flexpane in front of him.

Briar slammed her mouth shut, refusing to wince at the pain.

"Sleep OK last night?"

He did *not* ask her that question. Angry words charged from the holding tank of her stomach and raced up her throat. Let them come.

"Like a rock. Same as any other woman who's had a roofie slipped into her drink at a party, I suppose."

The tapping stopped. Lukas blinked at her over the opalescent screen.

She crossed her arms over her chest.

"I-I'm glad you rested well."

He lowered his shocked gaze to the flexpane and

hammered the surface at what sounded like triple-speed.

"Unbelievable." She dropped her head back and stared at the ceiling.

He didn't respond. Chances were he hadn't even heard her over the maddening tap of his fingers. She seriously doubted he was really typing words. Probably pounding random letters to fill the silence. Disheveled hair, perspiration on his brow—Lukas looked like some piano prodigy from an old-time movie banging out a symphony. Minus the music.

Her blood simmered. Avoidance was not an option.

"Lukas!" She hopped from the edge of the exam table, sticking a solid landing directly in front of him. It took all she had to resist snap-kicking the pane into his glistening forehead. Instead, she bent the screen downward. "Look at me."

He dragged his gaze up to hers, his brown eyes softer than usual.

"Reid said you put a sedative in my tea last night."

"Reid? Since when do you listen to—"

"True or false?"

Lukas closed his eyes and drew a long breath. His slight Adam's apple bobbed twice. "True," he whispered, opening his eyes.

Briar turned away, tears already spilling as she stepped toward the door.

"You were so upset. You needed to rest. And the sedative was extremely mild—barely there at all."

She swiped the back of her hand across each cheek and turned to glare at him. "I slept until noon, Lukas. *Noon*. And you're telling me the drugs you slipped into my tea were mild as mother's milk? Give me a break."

"Drugs? Wait. No, Briar, it was nothing like that. You needed to rest. It was only a mild sedative. I would never—"

"I told you no sedatives. No medication. I made myself clear."

Lukas nodded slowly, dropping his gaze. "You're right. I'm sorry."

His apology should've made her feel better. It didn't.

"Actually, I'm glad this happened. I was starting to think of you as a friend. Now I realize what a gigantic mistake that would've been. From this point on, no more sharing interests, talking about emotions, or swapping childhood stories. Our relationship is strictly professional—although you've made it obvious you are, by no means, a professional."

His gaze snapped to hers. "Please, be reasonable. I meant you no harm. I was trying to help." His focus turned to the baseboards. "As you've probably figured out by now, I don't have many friends. And I would really love—" He winced. "*Like* to be your friend."

His voice was low and rough with emotion. She nearly caved. Instead, she swallowed and straightened her spine. "If you crave friendship, I'm sure your accomplice—oops, I meant to say, lab technician—will be happy to oblige. The two of you are so much alike, I'm surprised you aren't finishing each other's sentences by now." She turned away, making it all the way to the door this time. Without looking back, she closed it behind her.

~*~

Lukas sat on the little wheeled stool, flexpane on

his knees, staring at the closed door.

Why was the place so cold? The exam room felt like a meat locker—or how he imagined one would feel when there were such things. He blew out a breath, half expecting a white plume of smoke to escape. He ran a hand across his slick forehead and grimaced. Clammy. That explained it. He was in shock.

And with good reason. Briar accused him of slipping a—what had she called it? A *rudy*? A *roofie*? Lukas rubbed his temple. He was the doctor, for goodness sake. He should know drug-slang better than a girl who'd been under house arrest for most of her life. A *rookie*?

"Does the name really matter?" Lukas demanded from the empty room. He stood and slapped the pane to the counter. "Whatever the street name, it's a date rape drug, OK? Some type of amnesia-invoking muscle relaxant from the benzodiazepine family, I presume." He rolled his eyes. "And she strongly suggested—make that obstinately insisted—that I slipped it into her tea!"

He paced the white tile, inhaling and exhaling out of flared nostrils. A traitor. That's what she'd made him feel like. A schemer. An opportunist. "Some kind of pervert," he muttered.

She'd been so anxious last night. So, distraught. He'd only been trying to help her get a little rest. How could she think he would intentionally harm her?

You betrayed her trust, Dr. Tactless.

It was such a small amount—he never dreamed there'd be adverse effects.

Lukas stopped pacing. He pressed his forehead to the wall and gave the drywall a few soft bangs. How could he be so careless? So, stupid? Not only had he betrayed Briar's trust on a personal level—an atrocity in its own right—he had threatened, quite possibly destroyed, the integrity of the doctor-patient relationship. Inexcusable.

He wanted to blame Reid. With everything he had, he wished the whole thing had been her fault. Anybody's fault but his. But that wasn't the truth. To say Reid was responsible for what he'd done to Briar was to say he was incapable of making his own decisions—that he was without the ability to say no. For Lukas to believe that about himself, or to have anyone else believe it, would be worse than death. He was a scientist. A doctor. He lived to improve the lives of others. It was his passion. A doctor unable to make his own decisions wasn't a doctor—or a man—at all.

Lukas walked to the door. He had to make things right. But how? By talking to her?

He pictured Briar as she'd looked the night before; hands shaking, chest hitching, tear-filled gaze and trembling lips tugging toward the floor. Overwhelmed with stress and anxiety, she'd begged him to give her the abstergent and put her out of her misery. He hated himself for adding to her pain.

Maybe she was right. He should give her the abstergent and be done with it. If he was honest with himself, he'd admit the antidote was as perfect as it ever would be. He was killing time, putting off the inevitable. Because...why? He wasn't exactly sure, but it felt a lot like dread. It wasn't that he was afraid of his own serum. His formula was failsafe, and his research sound. All he knew was that something inside of him shrank at the thought of inserting that needle into Briar's brain.

What had he gotten himself into? Behaving like

some junior high kid, nervous because he'd been assigned a pretty lab partner. Pathetic. He didn't have time for emotions, or hormones, or whatever ridiculousness this was. He must take care of things. Concentrate on what he was supposed to be doing in the first place—his job. Briar was unlevel. Unresponsive to SAP. To be injected with the abstergent was the reason she was there.

"The only reason." He exited the exam room, leaving his foolishness behind.

11

"Who is it?" Briar glared at the closed door. If Lukas knew what was good for him, he wouldn't be the one knocking.

"It's Derby, Miss Briar."

She turned to the nightstand, setting down the ink pen she'd been using to scratch the skin under her ankle monitor. Stupid shackle itched like crazy sometimes. "Come on in." She pulled herself upright and slid her legs over the edge of the bed.

Derby poked his head inside. "Didn't wake you, did I?"

"No, not at all. I was just sitting here, thinking."

"Thinking's hard work. I try not to do much of it." Derby's grin put her at ease, and she smiled back. His easygoing nature was good medicine.

"I brought you a visitor. Hope you don't mind." Derby opened the door a bit wider.

Her smile fell. Lukas—that snake. Using Derby to gain access to her. Probably to offer some lame apology that she would immediately throw back in his face. She narrowed her eyes at the doorframe, waiting for Lukas to show his long face so she could order him away. To her surprise, in darted Roxy, banging the door against the wall with her spring-loaded tail as she galloped through the opening.

"Roxy!" Briar held her arms open to the big yellow dog that bounded to the bed and stood on two legs, painting her face with wet kisses. "It's so good to see you, girl." Briar scratched Roxy's back and rubbed the top of her massive head. She buried her nose in the dog's warm fur. "She smells fantastic."

"Thanks. Gave her a bath this morning. Thought I'd wait until she was good and dry before letting her anywhere near the lab this time. Didn't want to make the same mistake twice."

"Yeah, I get that." Briar held her palms under Roxy's jowls and planted a kiss between the dog's big brown eyes. "You're a sweet baby." Roxy licked Briar on the chin and then lowered her front legs to the floor. She walked in a circle, finding just the right slice of tile to curl up on.

"Time for her afternoon nap," Derby said. "Guess we should be going."

"No, don't go. I'm enjoying the company. Let me pull you up a chair so we can visit." She slid from the mattress and shuffled to the desk, turning the chair to face the bed. "You won't get in trouble for hanging out in my room, will you?"

"Nah. I've had all my shots," he said with a wink. He sat down and leaned back, pulling an ankle to his knee.

She shrugged. "That's not saying much—so have I."

Derby frowned for a moment, and then grinned. "SAP joke. I get it."

Briar joined in his laughter as she tugged the covers from the bed, piling them on and around Roxy, who let out a content sigh. "It'll be nice to have someone to talk to for a while. Someone civil, that is." She shot a bitter glance to the doorway as she sat on the bed.

"Hope I don't disappoint you. I'm not very interesting."

"Are you kidding? What's more interesting than being a hot air balloon pilot?"

Derby nodded. "You got me there. Ballooning never loses its excitement."

"Can you describe it to me? With the exception of the plane ride here, I've never been off the ground."

He frowned and tugged the bill of his hat down and back up a couple of times. "Trying to think of how to explain it. Guess the closest I could come, would be to say it's like being in love. Floating on air. Not thinking about eating, sleeping, or any of the other things you think about when your feet are stuck to the earth. Yep. Being in love. That's what ballooning is like."

"I wouldn't know." But she almost did. Lukas flashed through her mind. Pre-betrayal Lukas. Before the sedative incident. Briar shifted her gaze from Derby's. "But I suspect it's a great feeling."

"The best. Let me describe it another way. A way you can relate to."

Briar returned her gaze to Derby.

"I remember you telling me you enjoy interacting with kids."

Briar nodded. "I love kids. I'm going to be a child psychologist."

"There's your example. Imagine the way you feel when you make a child giggle—or outright laugh. Maybe a little one who doesn't have much to smile about. Think about that instant peace that coats your insides. The sensation of your heart, so filled with love it'll float to the clouds and take you with it. That unshakable notion that in that moment, everything is right and beautiful and perfect. *That* is what ballooning is like."

"*Wow.*" Briar breathed the word out in a sigh. For the first time, she could imagine floating miles above the earth. *Really* imagine it. How cool it would be, if hot air ballooning could be used in children's therapy. Maybe she could make it happen someday. Now that the abstergent was close to being a reality, the possibility seemed attainable. Once her Agathi were dissolved, she could not only make a child laugh via flexpane, she could tickle their ribs. Hug them. Wipe away their tears.

"Most incredible feeling in the world." Derby uncrossed his leg, thumping his boot to the floor. "I'm still trying to get Reid to go up in the balloon with me, but she'll have no part of it."

Reid. The name sent Briar crashing to reality. Reid was the last person she wanted to think about right now—with the exception of Lukas. On second thought, maybe Reid did need to go up in a hot air balloon. Way, way up. To view the world from new heights instead of slithering around the lab making Briar miserable. And she could take Lukas up there with her.

"Where did you learn to fly?" She asked, anxious to get her mind off the diabolical duo.

"It's not really flying. It's floating. Got my license eight years ago at a facility in New Mexico. Place called Dreamers. They have pilot training all year round there. The course takes about three and a half weeks and costs five grand, not counting the propane. They even provide the balloon, but it costs less to use your own—so that's what I did. Granted, the balloon I had back then wasn't as flashy as Dr. Stone's—didn't have a fancy logo on the side or anything. But it was mine. Saved and scraped for months to get that faded old balloon, then saved and scraped some more to pay for licensing." He shook his head. "I'd have to say it was worth every penny. I'll never forget the first time I took her up on my own."

"How do they fly—float?"

"It's actually pretty simple. The design's stayed basically the same for the past hundred years except for a few minor modifications—Lukas could give you the technical spiel on those. There's a propane burner inside the balloon that heats the air. Hot air is lighter than cool air, so the balloon rises. The altitude is adjusted by opening or closing the propane valve. A balloon can't really be steered, it floats with the wind. But when you adjust the altitude, you can find currents of air to guide it. That means no two balloon flights are ever the same. You never know exactly where you're going." He grinned. "If that's not a metaphor for life, I don't know what is."

Briar tilted her head. "How high do they go?"

"I usually keep her at a couple thousand feet, but she'll go higher. Highest I've taken her is double that—a little over four thousand. But I'd rather take it easy on my fuel—and my nerves." He gave Briar another wink. "I'd be glad to take you for a ride sometime."

She lifted her foot and bounced it in the air, jiggling her shackle. "Thanks, but I doubt that will happen. At least, not for a while."

"Shame." He shook his head at the ankle monitor. "The annual hot air balloon festival is coming up this weekend. Balloons will be here from all over the country. So many colors, your eyes can barely take them all in. Every year thousands of people pour in to Sickle Ridge to participate. Maybe I can talk the doctor into letting you venture outside for a bit to watch the sky."

"That would be amazing."

"I'll see what I can do." Derby stood and gave a soft whistle.

Roxy let out a huge, squeaky yawn, stretched, and rose to her feet.

"Come on, Rox. Time to get back to work. Tell Miss Briar goodbye."

Briar scooted from the bed and knelt beside the dog, scratching her behind the ears. "See you later, girl. Thanks for stopping by."

"Nice visiting with you. I'll wash the bedding." Derby tipped his cap, scooped up Briar's covers, and followed Roxy from the room.

~*~

Lukas wadded up another page of nonsensical drivel from his spiral notebook, took aim at the wastepaper basket, and missed. Again. What was he doing, anyway? Composing a handwritten apology to Briar would accomplish exactly what? That he was a jerk? She'd already established that—obviously. That he regretted his decision to put a dash of barely-there sedative into her tea? If she'd been listening, she already knew that, too.

He forced a sigh through the tight line of his lips and stood. He stretched his back, readying to pick up the dozen or so paper balls scattered around the trashcan, and the streamer-like wisps of confetti that fell from the edges of the paper.

Briar would never trust him again. He'd never be able to make things right. Not ever. The knowledge sank into his chest like cactus thorns.

"Knock-knock," Derby called, opening the door.

"Here for your trash, boss." He stepped into Lukas's office, his eyes widening at the mess on the floor.

"Sorry, Derby, I was about to clean that up." He stooped, picking up several bits of spiral edges from the light tile.

"I got it. No trouble at all." Derby stepped into the hallway, returning with the broom from his cleaning cart. "Ever thought of putting carpet in here? An office should be comfortable to work in. White tile isn't exactly cozy. Plus, paper scraps would be easier to spot on carpet."

"I'll keep that in mind," Lukas said, barely listening.

"I took Roxy to visit Miss Briar a while ago. Earlier in the day I'd seen her in the hallway on the way to her room, and she looked so sad. I thought the dog might cheer her up, and boy, was I right!"

Lukas frowned. A visit from Roxy cheered her up. Of course. Why hadn't he thought of that? He cleared his throat. "Did she say anything? About why she was sad?"

"No. But like I said, she wasn't sad for long. Roxy perked her right up, and she started chattering like a chipmunk. She asked me to tell her all about hot air balloons. She went on and on about it. Seems she has a real interest in how they work. She mentioned wanting to take a ride in one, but being unable to because of that monitor she wears on her ankle."

Derby dumped the last of the paper scraps from the dustpan to the wastepaper basket. He crossed the room and straightened Lukas's hot air balloon photograph on the wall, making a bigger show of it than necessary—moving the frame this way and that, backing up to gaze at it before moving it again.

Lukas was about to tell him to stop touching the picture, it was fine exactly the way it was, when a realization hit him. Briar had shown an interest in his hot air balloon the first day she'd arrived at the lab. She'd even teased him about owning a balloon that he'd never been up in. Several times since, she'd taken good natured jabs by asking if he'd "watched his balloon float around lately." He hadn't taken her curiosity seriously before, but he was definitely taking it seriously now. Very seriously. He'd just found a way to make up for his unforgivable misstep with the sedative.

Lukas joined Derby in front of the picture. "Derby, the balloon festival is coming up, correct?"

"Yes sir. October third. This coming Saturday."

Five days away. Lukas scrutinized the photograph. "Do you think it would be a good idea if I—"

"Oh, yes. Without a doubt. Miss Briar would absolutely love to go to the festival with you. You should ask her right away." Derby slapped Lukas on the back twice, grabbed his broom and hurried from the doorway. "Goodnight, boss," he called over his shoulder as he shut the door behind him.

Lukas blinked at the closed door. "Thanks for letting me run my idea past you," he said to the empty space, wondering what had just happened.

~*~

Lukas stood outside Briar's door, his knuckles an inch from the surface. He glanced at the ceiling, then down at his necktie, deciding to straighten it one more time. He didn't really like the tie. It was too…navy blue. Maybe he'd go to his apartment and change it. Swap it for the forest green silk.

The knob rattled and the door opened. "Did you need something?" Briar glared, hand on her hip, the other still gripping the doorknob.

Her dark blue eyes snapped like lightning, vaporizing his thoughts. He had needed something—hadn't he?

"Uh-hum?" She cleared her throat.

"I-I was walking by. I'm sorry if my footfalls disturbed you."

She snatched her hand from the knob and stepped from the doorway. "Are you sure about that? Because I've been watching you through the peephole for five minutes."

Lukas's cheeks warmed as he relived the past five minutes in his head…holding his fist up to knock. Letting his hand drop so he could kneel to adjust his shoes. Preparing to knock again. Retracting his hand to run a palm over his hair. Raising his knuckles to the door. Pausing to inspect his shirt buttons, the ceiling, his tie…how ridiculous he must have appeared.

She crossed her arms. "Well?"

Lukas struggled to get ahold of himself. Here he stood—what was left of him, anyway—with Briar right in front of him. That had been his goal, right? The reason he'd been standing outside her door like a pizza delivery guy who'd forgotten the goods. He could do this. Not the way he'd rehearsed it, but he could still pull through. There was no guarantee she'd say yes, but he could at least pose the question. A laboratory scientist had to be able to ask a simple question. Essentially, that's what science was—a bunch of answered questions combined with a bunch of unanswered questions.

"Listen, if you can't say anything, I'm shutting the door. I need to get back to my—" She turned to glance over her shoulder. "Boredom." She took a step back and pushed the door toward him.

"Wait!" Lukas stepped forward, planting his foot on the threshold, stopping the door.

Briar dragged her gaze from his leather loafer to his face.

"The Sickle Ridge Hot Air Balloon Festival starts on Saturday. It's a huge event. The entire community will turn out for it."

"OK?" She raised her eyebrows.

"You should come with me."

Her eyes calmed—or did they?

"I *should* come with you? As your test subject? So, everyone in the community can gawk, stare, and point? No, thanks." She squeezed the door against his shoe. "Please remove your shoe from my doorway."

The lightning was back, looking more like bolts of ice. He'd mistaken cold for calm.

"My test subject? No, of course not. That's ridiculous."

"The two words I detest above all others are *should* and *shouldn't*. You're talking to a person who, with the exception of doctor visits, hasn't been more than a hundred and fifty feet from home since age seven. No one has the right to put shackles on what little freedom I have left. Call me rebellious, but I will travel outside that radius every time. And since you're so convinced I *should* attend the balloon festival, I've determined that I absolutely, positively *should not*."

He'd blown it. Again. He'd spoken presumptuously. Made it sound as if she didn't have a choice. He'd repeated the same mistake, the one that had torn out their budding relationship by the roots. He'd made the choice for her. Just as he had the night he'd slipped the sedative into her tea.

Normally, he was a fast learner. Not so in matters of the heart. Emotions weren't cut and dried. They were uncomfortably warm, and oftentimes indirect. In those matters, he was the slowest pupil in the class. But this wasn't a classroom. It was a field test. And this time Lukas would pass. Or die trying.

He drew in the synthetically-freshened air flowing from Briar's room as if it was steeped with courage. He squared his shoulders and once more straightened his tie—this time with purpose. He removed his foot from the door, looked straight into Briar's deep blue eyes, and watched the lightning fade. "I realize the choice is completely up to you. But it would be my pleasure if you would consider accompanying me to the Sickle Ridge Hot Air Balloon Festival. I would be honored to share the experience with you. Not as an associate of Stone Labs, but as my friend."

Her eyes, still locked on his, appeared hazy and a bit unfocused. She snapped her gaze away and turned her head, taking a sudden interest in the door hinge.

"Why?" Her voice cracked on the word. Her hand flew to her neck and she cleared her throat. "For what reason would you like to take me?"

For what reason? What kind of question was that? Lukas puzzled over the answer. She was testing him. He was sure of it. Everything inside told him he shouldn't answer. If he did, she would know the truth. He would be exposed. Vulnerable. There'd be no going back. He should listen to his inner voice. He shouldn't answer. *Should. Shouldn't.* Lukas never realized how much he hated those words.

"Because I want to start fresh. I didn't realize how much I truly enjoyed your company until you stopped speaking to me." Granted, there was a point in time, early on, when Lukas thought she'd never shut up, but it was best not to say so. Seemed he'd learned a few things after all. "I miss you, Briar. There is no other person in the world I'd rather be with. And for that reason, I would love, more than anything, to take you to the balloon festival on Saturday."

Briar blinked a few times and closed her mouth. She raised her pant leg and pointed her toe, letting him see her ankle monitor. "What about this?"

"It won't be a problem. I'll request a code from the OLG, allowing you to leave the lab for a predetermined length of time. I'll carry the GPS in my pocket."

"Meaning I can't be more than a hundred feet from your side."

For the first time in days, Lukas smiled. "You got it."

Her eyes sparkled and then dimmed. "I don't have anything to wear."

He thought for a half-second of suggesting she borrow something from Reid—strictly as a joke—but immediately decided it wasn't funny.

"And don't you dare suggest I borrow something from Reid." She narrowed her eyes at him.

"What? Why would you think such a thing? I would never—" He pulled his wallet from his back pocket and handed her a silver SphereSwipe card.

"What's this?" She eyed it suspiciously.

"This is your clothing allowance, courtesy of the OLG. The same funds that bought those fancy scrubs you love so much, and those attractive rubber flip-flops you are so fond of. And there's plenty of money left over, trust me." He tucked his wallet back into his pocket. "You should—" He caught himself and started again. "I hope you will consider choosing something casual for the outdoor festival, and something a little more formal for the ball that follows. Please opt for overnight shipping to be sure everything arrives on time. Shoes, jewelry, hair ornaments—pick out whatever you'd like. The accessories are covered as well."

Briar wrinkled her nose. "What's a hair ornament?"

He hoped she was teasing, because he really had no idea. It had sounded legitimate at the time.

"Don't look so scared. I'm joking. Fancy hair combs and barrettes. I get it."

She laughed. A bright, joyous sound he could listen to all day. *For the rest of his life.*

The abstergent would have to wait. He wanted her Agathi intact when she experienced the balloon festival. He anticipated the aftereffects of the abstergent to include grogginess, lethargy, and moderate depression. Of course, all effects would be temporary. But he couldn't be certain how long they would last. Those types of afflictions wouldn't mix well with the festivities. The experience could completely overwhelm her senses—and not in a good way.

But Father had allowed him only one week to administer the abstergent to Briar, and that time was almost up. If he waited any longer, what would Caster say? Would he run and tattle to Father, as when they were children? Get Lukas into trouble? A gnawing in the pit of his stomach accompanied the thought of his father's disapproval.

Briar's laughter tapered off slowly, leaving sparkles in her eyes and a pink glow on her cheeks. Her smile remained, sweet and genuine, the most beautiful he'd ever seen.

Who cared what his brother thought—or even his father? The only person who mattered was standing before him right now. And making her smile was worth the risk.

12

Briar gazed into the bathroom mirror, turning this way and that. She grabbed the hand mirror from the top drawer of the vanity and turned, holding it up to check her look from behind. The deep-blue silk enhanced her form in all the right places. Feeling Cinderella-ish in the delicate silver heels, she twirled like a little girl, smiling as the skirt fanned about her knees. She absolutely loved this dress. If not for the clunky ankle monitor, the outfit would be ball-perfect.

She carefully slid the formal over her head, returned it to the clothes hanger, and slipped it into the plastic garment bag. She placed the fancy shoes at the bottom before zipping it closed and hanging it on the shower curtain rod.

Time to change into casual wear. And this time, it was for real. Briar's tummy swirled like an Oklahoma twister. She'd tried the new clothes a dozen times, but this time she would actually be leaving the lab. She pulled the lavender sweater from the hook on the bathroom door and tugged it over her head. Running her fingers around the sweetheart neckline, she shrugged at her reflection. Could use a little bit more up top, but not bad.

"Not bad at all," she mused, sliding on her new jeans and zipping them. After wearing scrubs day in and day out, it felt good to dress in clothes that actually hugged her body. Clothes that fit. The ankle monitor hindered her from wearing boots, so she'd settled for a pair of canvas shoes—purplish, to match the sweater.

A knock on the door upped tummy-tornado's status to F-5 on the Fujita scale. "Yes?" she called, shrugging on a light jacket.

"It's Lukas. Are you ready?"

Briar massaged her midsection. "One more minute, please." She glanced in the mirror, fluffed a few flattened hairs, and then folded the garment bag over her arm. "Coming."

~*~

Briar closed her eyes and inhaled. The air smelled wonderful. Crisp and clear with a hint of something sweet on the breeze. Cotton candy, perhaps. Or funnel cake. Some type of delicious festival food. She shaded her eyes and looked at the sky, already dotted with brightly colored balloons. A beautiful contrast to the muted browns and grays of the stony Nevada hills.

"I'm sorry. We've got quite a walk ahead of us. I assumed the parking lot would be crowded, but didn't realize there'd be no spaces closer than a half mile from the gate." Lukas used his cuffphone to arm the car's alarm and then stuffed a hand into the pocket of his fancy pants. Not the type of pants she'd call casual. But that was OK—fancy looked good on him. She'd discovered that five days ago, when he'd come to her door dressed in a suit to invite her to the balloon festival.

"Don't apologize. I'm looking forward to the entire outdoor festival experience. Blisters on my pinky toes, sand in my shoes, shin splints—I want the works!"

"You got it." He held out a small package. "Gum?"

"Thanks." She slid a piece of cinnamon gum from the pack.

He grinned and extended an elbow. "Shall we?"

Briar took his arm, her gaze wandering over the crowd as they joined the pilgrimage from the parking lot to the event site.

Children giggled and squealed, some chasing one another through the throng of people. Shoulder-to-shoulder, people from all walks of life chatted excitedly about the festival, some recounting what they'd experienced at other balloon exhibits, others talking about what they hoped to see today. Old men studied the clear blue sky and commented on the wind being just right. Husbands talked about propane tanks and burners, while their wives carried on about all the beautiful balloon colors and designs. A girl who might've been Briar's age complimented her hair.

Briar thanked her and said she liked the girl's boots.

So, this is what it was like to be part of something. To laugh and talk with people outside her own family. To be normal. To be free. Is this how life would be after abstergent? Because she could definitely get used to it.

"The gate. Finally." Falling into line at the nearest ticket booth, Lukas slid his wallet from his back pocket and thumbed through the contents.

Briar stood on tiptoe and bobbed her head to see through the crowd. Her breath stilled at the plethora of color awaiting them through the gates. She glanced up at Lukas to find him looking at her, an amused expression on his face. "You haven't seen anything, yet." He grinned and turned his attention to the ticket taker who handed him two neon orange wristbands along with his SphereSwipe card and receipt.

"Deluxe package includes entry to the event, fifty dollars' worth of food and drink items from select vendors, and two ten-dollar souvenirs from the gift shop." The woman reached into a box on the countertop. "And these." She placed two pairs of yellow plastic binoculars in front of Briar. "Enjoy the festival."

"Thank you, ma'am." Lukas stretched one of the rubber bracelets onto his wrist and motioned for Briar to hold out her hand. "Perfect fit," he said, snapping her band in place.

She held up her wrist admiring the band as if it were a gemstone in the sunlight. "Why, it's just lovely," she drawled, giving her eyelashes several exaggerated bats.

"Glad you like it," Lukas said. "This way, please."

She scooped up the binoculars and followed Lukas through the turnstile.

"Wow," she breathed, coming immediately to a standstill in the short grass. "I've never seen so many colors in one place." She handed Lukas a pair of binoculars and brought the other pair to her eyes. "Some of the balloons are shaped like cartoon characters! Hey! I see Bucky Blitz!" She pointed to the bucktoothed animal with black-framed glasses and bright blue hair floating high to the west. "Mouse would pass out from excitement."

"Mouse?" Lukas sounded confused.

She lowered her binoculars. "A kid I talk to online. He's a huge fan of Bucky. I cos-play for him sometimes. I still have the blue wig in my purse from the last time we chatted." Her heart panged when she thought of her little friend. She wondered if Mouse missed her as much as she missed him. She sure hoped not. She couldn't stand the thought of his small heart aching the way hers did.

"Cause play?"

Briar chuckled and settled the binoculars back over her eyes. The guy was clueless. "Cos-play. C-O-S. It means to dress up in costume. Cartoons, comic book characters, sci-fi—whatever piques your interest."

"Dressing up in costumes." Lukas spoke slowly, as if having trouble processing. "For fun."

"Yes." She turned to look at him through the binoculars. "Didn't you ever play dress up as a kid? It's the same concept. Only there's no age limit. There are huge communities of us online. You should check it out sometime. Might be just the thing to loosen you up."

He frowned, the lines in his forehead looking like the ridges of a sand dune through the magnified lenses. "I need loosening up?"

She laughed louder than she meant to. "A little."

The sheer size of the balloons amazed Briar as they walked farther into the venue. They seemed so much smaller floating above the earth than sitting on the ground. Lukas said something she couldn't hear. The sound of running motors drowned out his words.

"What?" she asked, cupping her ear. The noise level was much higher near the center of the stadium. She felt that she'd entered the world's largest blow dryer.

"The envelope," he said, louder. "That's what the canvas part of the balloon is called. The pocket that holds the air." He pointed to one of the huge industrial size fans inflating a balloon with air. The balloon lay on its side, basket and all. "The fans are blowing in cool air. After it's partially filled, the burners will blow in the heat to make it rise."

Slowly, the inflated balloon rose from its side, and the basket sat upright on the grass.

Briar tiptoed to put her mouth close to Lukas's ear. "Seems you know more about balloons than you let on."

He shrugged. "Only the scientific stuff. The practical stuff I leave to Derby."

The pilot climbed into the basket and gave the burner another blast. Catching Lukas's eye, he cupped his mouth and shouted. "Would the two of you like a ride?"

"He's afraid of heights," Briar shouted back, getting a kick out of the astonished expression on Lukas's face.

He jabbed her ribs lightly. "No, thank you." He waved to the pilot.

"What about a ride for the lady?"

Briar clasped her hands to her chest. "Lukas, can I?" Her insides tickled at the thought.

He shook his head. "Your ankle monitor won't allow that much distance from the GPS." He touched his jacket pocket that held the receiver.

Her shoulders dropped. "What if I take the GPS receiver with me? To keep it from being separated from the ankle monitor." Asking made her feel like an audacious child—but she really, *really* wanted to go up in that balloon.

"I had to obtain permission from Rosen to bring you here. He gave me a coordinate code to key into the receiver. If either the ankle monitor or receiver travels outside the vicinity, it will send an alert. Two thousand feet in the air is definitely out of the vicinity." He glanced around. "Besides, it's too risky. This is a huge festival. People come from all over. OLG personnel could be here as well as ARC representatives. If I hand you the receiver, someone could notice. They'd debunk the project if I broke protocol."

She glanced around at the children eating cotton candy, staring skyward while the older folks sat in lawn chairs. "I don't see any men wearing dark suits and sunglasses, whispering into their lapels."

Geez, was it really that big of a deal? It wasn't as though she was a hot commodity of some kind. No one even knew who she was.

"I'm sorry. But I have to say no."

The refusal stung her pride. She felt like a little girl denied ice cream because it would spoil her appetite.

She turned to him, intending to bite out a snide remark. Something in his eyes stopped her. Disappointment. He'd wanted to say yes. Lukas wanted her to take the balloon ride as much as she had—maybe even more.

"No, thank you," she called to the balloon pilot. "Maybe next year." She offered him a big smile and a wave.

Lukas's features relaxed. His shoulders lifted. "Would you like some cotton candy?" She could hear the relief in his voice.

"I'd love some."

13

Briar's stomach gave a flip as she stepped toward the lavish ballroom of the Sickle Ridge Event Hall. In the ladies' hospitality suite, she'd changed into her formalwear and touched up her hair and makeup. Her reflection passed inspection, but there was something about the word "ball" that weakened her resolve—and her knees. It brought to mind princesses, princes, and spoiled debutantes who enjoyed staring down their noses.

She glanced down at the ankle monitor which seemed to have tripled in size and doubled in weight. Why hadn't she chosen a floor length gown? Her reckless decision to show a little leg came back to haunt her in a big way. The shackle would raise all sorts of questions. It was selfish of her, not to think of how Lukas would feel. With the big black eyesore jutting out, he wouldn't want to be seen with her. She couldn't go inside. She'd be humiliated.

The tightness in her chest eased as Lukas stepped toward her. She wouldn't have to go in alone.

"You look stunning."

She'd never noticed the amber glow in his dark eyes, and wondered if it had something to do with the sable tuxedo he wore. A deeper look told her it had nothing to do with the suit, and everything to do with her. Her cheeks warmed, and she tore her gaze away. "You don't look too shabby, either."

"Thank you. How do you like the tie?"

She ran her fingers down the blue silk. "It's

identical to my dress. But how? You didn't see it before now."

He shrugged. "I have my ways."

She narrowed her eyes. "Derby."

He chuckled. "A man of many talents."

Lukas took her arm and led her toward the entrance of the ballroom. Beneath an array of expensive-looking shoes, the marble floor gleamed.

"Speaking of Derby," she said, "I was hoping to see him and your balloon at the festival today."

"He told me he was waiting until evening to take it up. Apparently, Reid needed him to run her on some errands today before the ball—teeth bleaching treatment, spray-tan session, limousine rental, a mani-pedi, and something called a French twist—you know, garden variety girl-stuff. Derby was more than happy to oblige. Reid isn't a fan of the balloon festival, but she's not one to miss a gathering of high society."

Great. Reid was slithering around the ballroom. Briar tossed her gaze around the room, trying to spot the woman. She didn't want to be caught off guard if Reid decided to strike.

No, she wouldn't to do that. She wouldn't let Reid spoil her night. So, what if she was there? Briar was the one no more than one hundred feet from Lukas's side.

"Would you care to dance?" Lukas asked, motioning to the dance floor.

"I don't really dance. Would you settle for swaying back and forth in one place?"

He chuckled and set his hands on her waist. "Indeed."

She placed her hands on his shoulders, hoping her cheeks weren't as red as they felt. She'd never danced with a man before. The only dancing she'd done was alone, to her favorite pop band, behind her locked bedroom door. She gazed up at him, forcing herself not to turn self-conscious and look away. As nerve wracking as it was, she had to admit it was nice. Very nice.

"So," she said, and cleared her throat. "I've been wanting to ask; what exactly do you do at the lab when you're not prodding me? Is there anything else you know how to do?"

"Believe it or not, I know a lot of things." He grinned. "But my primary field of study, as you may have guessed, is in the area of leveling."

"Same as my dad." She nodded.

"The work your father accomplished was monumental. I could only dream of making those kinds of strides. Without Windsor Lee's extensive research, the leveling program would not exist."

"So, I've heard. My dad was some kind of research rock star." Briar fluttered her eyelashes.

"That, he was," Lukas agreed. "My father is kind of a rock star too I suppose—but not a rock *icon* like your dad, at least not yet. He created Stone Labs from scratch, and has extensive knowledge of the leveling field. I've studied with him since I was a child. He taught me everything he knows."

"Which is?"

He shook his head and grinned. "You want me to tell you everything? If I did that, you'd have to dance with me forever."

"I wouldn't mind."

His eyes darkened a shade. "I wouldn't either."

"So, tell me, then. What do you cook up?"

"Let's see…I can make a mean batch of Serum to Accelerate Progressivism, otherwise known as SAP, as well as SAP booster. And as you know, I created a compound affectionately referred to as Stone's Abstergent to dissolve the Agathi from the brain."

"Yes, I'm well aware of that one."

"But for me, the trickiest concoctions of all are antidotes."

"What's so complicated about antidotes?"

"Lukas! There you are!" From out of nowhere, Reid's voice cut though their conversation, shattering Briar's good time.

"Reid," Lukas said curtly.

"And lookie there. It's Briar Rose!" She laughed, snorting as she raised her nearly empty wineglass in a mock-toast. "Lukas, did you realize Sleeping Beauty's real name was Briar Rose? Isn't that fitting? Because Briar's personality puts me right to sleep." She laughed again, and downed what was left of her wine. "Waiter! Come take this!" She held the stemware above her head.

Lukas stopped swaying, but kept a firm grip on Briar's waist. "If you don't mind, Briar and I are sharing a dance at the moment."

Reid stared at Lukas and did a few sways of her own. For a split-second Briar thought either Reid's wineglass or entire body would crash to the floor.

"But I do mind," she blurted, turning her attention to Briar, looking her up and down. "I mind very much. You're parading around with this lab experiment as if she's some kind of catch. Pampering her like a princess. Look at her. She's pathetic!" She turned the wineglass up, trying to suck out one last drop. "Homely Oklahoma hick. That's what she is."

"That's enough." Lukas released Briar and grabbed hold of Reid's wrist. "You've had too much to drink."

Her fingers spread, and she let the glass drop to the floor. "Oops," she said, gazing down at the shards of crystal littering the polished marble. "Look what you made me do." She pulled her arm from Lukas. "Hey!" She pointed at Briar's ankle monitor. "Sleeping Beauty is part robot!"

A busboy with a tiny broom and dustpan materialized.

Briar stepped back from the broken glass, her insides boiling. "Part robot is better than completely orange. Where'd you get your spray tan? The snow cone stand?"

Reid's nostrils flared. Her face turned from drink-mix orange to fire-engine red, matching her skimpy dress. "Don't be alarmed," she bellowed over the soft music. "She can't help it. It's her brain defect talking. She's not really supposed to be around people. That's why she has the ankle monitor—to keep her from wandering into the sane population."

Reid threw her fiery gaze around the surrounding couples who were no longer dancing. "But Lukas felt sorry for the little lab rat, so he dragged her along this evening. That's OK. Because in a few days Lukas will dissolve the part of her brain that makes her crazy, and all will be right with the world." Reid offered a fake smile so white Briar could smell the bleach.

Every ounce of air in the room disappeared. Briar didn't need to breathe anyway. She was running on fuel, not oxygen. Just like the hot air balloons outside. And Reid had provided the flame. Briar could either explode or rise above it. She chose both.

"No matter what you do to your outside, your inside is still ugly. And it shows through. There's not enough orange paint in the entire world to cover up that much ugly." Briar turned to Lukas. "I really appreciate you dragging me along to your fancy shindig. On behalf of all the lab rats of the world, thank you."

Explosion accomplished. The "rising above it" part would prove more difficult. She walked briskly as possible through the ballroom, fighting the urge to run.

"Don't go too far," Reid called, humor in her voice. "Your ankle bracelet—remember?" Her mocking laughter followed Briar out the front doors.

Briar clipped down the endless steps and rounded the building. A hot air balloon floated in the darkness, embodying a beauty and light she longed to hold inside. She'd held it once, long ago, when she was a little girl. But somehow it slipped away. Or maybe she'd blown out the flame.

What did it matter now anyway? If there was any of that light left, it would soon be extinguished. And that was fine with her.

Her eyes followed the lone balloon in the night sky. Who needed beauty and light? Those things sounded a lot like love. The Scientist and the Lab Rat. Now there was a tale for Mouse. No lovey-dovey mush or kissing, so he should like it fine.

Except it was too sad to tell.

She swiped angrily at her cheeks.

"Hey, what are you doing out here all alone?" The sound of Derby's voice made her jump.

"Oh, hey, Derby. I was taking a walk."

"By the light of the moon? In those shoes?" He shook his head at her silver high heels. "I doubt it. Something wrong?"

"OK, you caught me." She shrugged. "But I'd

rather not say, because it involves your girlfriend."

He chuckled. "Not my girlfriend—yet. Look, I know I'm a bit simple, but I do know a thing or two about women. Reid is a lot like my ex. Maybe that's why I'm so taken by her. Anyway, that's neither here nor there. My point is, she's insecure, and she's threatened by you."

A laugh burst through Briar's lips. "Oh, really? She told you that?"

"She didn't have to tell me. I can see it for myself. She's jealous—of your freedom."

"Freedom!" Briar placed a hand against the brick building for balance and extended her foot. "Shackle-girl, remember?"

"The freedom you carry *inside*. You have something most people don't. And Reid doesn't like it. Why do you think she's so gung-ho for you to get rid of it? Personally, I think people should live how they darn well please. God is real, God is a fairy tale. So, what? But it's the law."

Sighing, Briar folded her hands behind her and pressed her back against the wall. "I know."

He looked her square in the eye. "People like you make people like Reid feel as if they're missing out on something." He dragged his gaze to the moon. "In time, I'm hoping I can help fill that void that she feels inside."

"Hope you have a million years and a front loader the size of the Grand Canyon, because that chick's pretty empty."

Derby turned his cap around backwards and pretended to put up his dukes.

"I'm kidding," Briar said. She was—sort of.

~*~

"You might need to call that busboy back to sweep up your dignity." Lukas turned his back to Reid and stormed from the ballroom. He needed to find Briar.

What a jerk he'd been—again—for letting the altercation with Reid happen. He should've known the two of them would bump into each other. Or, more accurately, that Reid would steamroll over Briar the first chance she got.

Reid had feelings for him—he'd known it for a long time, but never cared to admit it. The whole thing made him incredibly uncomfortable. He'd never be able to reciprocate those feelings, and had no desire to.

But Briar was different. She had something special—a warmth he had no trouble reciprocating. Inside, she held something unique and real. Something Reid would never have.

Something he may be personally responsible for killing with his own hands.

That was ridiculous. His conscience was suggesting Briar had a soul. Years ago, it had been proven there was no such thing. He wasn't killing anything. He was making it possible for her to live.

He rounded the building then recoiled, quietly stepping backward and retreating a few feet. Normally, the sound of Briar's laughter brightened his spirits and tickled his heart. But not tonight. The sound of it rolled his stomach over.

Derby's laughter, loud and carefree, mingled with hers.

Lukas grimaced. Less than five minutes ago, she'd flown from the ballroom, upset. He'd come to console her, expecting to find her crying, curled up on the front steps or wilted under one of the large pines. Instead, she and Derby were sharing a moment alone together under the moonlight.

It was a proven fact—the soul did not exist. The heart, on the other hand, was an entirely different subject.

14

Briar peeled the blue silk dress over her head and tossed it to the floor. She kicked it to the corner, pried the silver shoes from her feet, and flung them on top. She tossed her earrings onto the nightstand and shrugged into her bathrobe.

She should have never agreed to accompany Lukas to that stupid ball. She should've known better. No, actually, Lukas should have known better. Reid daily went out of her way to make Briar's life miserable at the lab. He'd known Reid would be there, yet hadn't had the decency to warn Briar so that she could steer clear. All that talk about missing her and wanting to start fresh—*right*. He'd stood right there and let Reid sabotage her in front of all those people in their fancy clothes. What he'd wanted was a quick no-strings-attached date for the ball. And she'd fallen for the old "let's be friends" routine. Never again. She'd learned her lesson, big time.

Though she had to admit, the outdoor festival had been great. Seeing the balloons in person enhanced their beauty and intensified her desire to float high above the earth someday.

She sat on the edge of the bed massaging one foot, then the other. Just float away. Far from ankle monitors, malicious blonde lab technicians, and—best of all—Lukas Stone.

She needed to intensify her nagging. The more she bugged him about administering the abstergent, the quicker he'd cave in.

The quicker she'd be free.

A thump on her door caused the hackles on her neck to stand up. So help her, if that man was skulking outside her door again, she wouldn't be responsible for what she might do. She lunged from the bed to the door, barely touching the ground, hoping to catch him in the act.

Through the peephole she spied Roxy, big yellow tail thumping away.

"Roxy!" She swung the door open, dropped to her knees, and hugged the animal.

"Sorry, ma'am." Gatlin appeared behind Roxy. "She broke away and ran straight to your room, like she'd been whistled at or something."

"Don't be sorry, I'm happy to see her—and you." She released the dog and hugged Gatlin. "But what's with you calling me ma'am?" She sat back on her heels and looked at him.

He shrugged. "Lira said it's polite to call ladies ma'am and men sir."

She nodded. "Yes, Lira's right about that. But you and I are friends. And friends don't have to be so formal with one another. You can call me Briar."

He gazed with his greenish-gold eyes on the ceiling, as if thinking it over. "OK. If you're sure it's all right."

"Good." She patted the boy's back and stood.

"Hey, you still have my rock!" he scooted around her and into the room.

In your present condition, my son will not benefit from a relationship with you. Briar's breath caught as Caster's angry words tumbled through her mind. "I'm not sure you should come in. Your dad might be looking for you."

"Nah. He's out of town on business. Uncle Lukas picked me up after his fancy party to give Lira a break. I'm staying over."

Her shoulders relaxed. "OK, but only for a few minutes. I don't want your uncle worrying about where you've run off to." She glanced both directions down the hallway and shut the door.

Gatlin plucked the rock from the nightstand, squinting at it. "Yep. This is mine, all right."

Briar smiled. "Of course, it's yours. I keep it there because I like to look at it." She turned her gaze from the honey-brown stone. It reminded her of Lukas's eyes. That rock would go into a drawer as soon as the little boy left the room.

Gatlin put the rock back on the nightstand and shoved a hand into his pocket. "Briar, sit down with me." He sat on the floor and patted the empty space beside him. "I want to show you something."

He'd called her by name. Heart melting, she lowered to the floor and curled her legs under her.

Roxy walked a slow circle before resting at Briar's side.

Gatlin straightened the wrinkled paper in his palm. "My dad doesn't know I have this." He passed the tattered square to her.

Briar's heart slowed to a stop. The beautiful, dark haired woman with charcoal eyes smiled from the flimsy photograph. The name Kate Stone was printed beneath in calligraphy font. A picture of Gatlin's mother, clipped from her funeral pamphlet.

She slipped an arm around his slim shoulders. "Oh, Gatlin. She was beautiful."

"Where is she, Briar?" he asked, his voice a breathy squeak. "Where's my mom? Where is she?"

She tightened her grip around his small body.

"Are her eyes gone? Jack said bodies turn to dirt. I don't want her to be dirt!" His back shook with sobs.

Roxy lifted her head lazily to look at her little companion. She whimpered softly.

Briar stroked Gatlin's hair. "Who's Jack?"

"On the show Lira watches." He raised his wet face to her. "Don't tell her I listened. I was hiding behind the couch."

"I won't tell." Briar recognized the program he mentioned. A crime scene investigation series he had no business being in earshot of.

"Where is she?" He continued to stare up at her, his eyes pleading. "Is she rotten? Jack said dead people turn rotten." His breath shortened and his words hitched out. "I don't want her to be rotten!" He squeezed his eyes shut and shook his head.

Briar brushed the sleeve of her robe over the little boy's face. "Shh, it's OK." She shuddered, picturing the images that played beneath those small, trembling eyelids.

Those terrible visions were lies. Her body was under the earth, yes—but not her spirit. And her spirit wasn't part of the "amissfear," either. His mother hadn't turned into the air Gatlin breathed.

Briar knew the truth. She hugged him to her chest and kissed the top of his head. How could she refuse this sweet little boy his peace of mind? Keeping the truth from him was as bad as lying.

Worse.

Briar closed her eyes and prayed. *Really* prayed. The way Granna Grace taught her to pray. Closing out the world around her, she concentrated on the Holy Spirit, asking for His direction. Praying for the quick answer she needed. Thanking Him for the opportunity to help the sweet child hurting in her arms. Her heartbeat quickened, making her lightheaded. She breathed deeply, in through her nose, out through her mouth. She'd bet that right about now, her Agathi were glowing like crazy.

She didn't want to make Gatlin promise to keep a secret about God, but in this case, what else could she do? If Caster found out what she'd done—how she'd defied his order not to talk to Gatlin. She bit her lip, trying not to think of his angry, steel eyes.

On second thought, maybe Gatlin wouldn't need to promise. He wouldn't remember what she told him anyway, because of the leveling serum. The SAP would keep him from absorbing any information about God. Would her words be like a nursery rhyme to him? Or would they bounce off like rubber? She had no idea. All she knew was that it was important for him to hear the truth about his mother right now. He needed to be able to be comforted—if only for a moment.

"It's my turn to show you something." Briar scooped up the little boy and set him on the bed.

Roxy yawned, stood, stretched, and laid back down.

She felt under her pillow and slid the lamb keychain from underneath. "My grandmother made this little lamb for me when I was not much older than you."

Gatlin reached for the stuffed animal. "It's soft," he said, holding it to his damp cheek.

Briar smiled. "It is soft. Pretty cute, too, don't you think?"

He nodded, still holding the lamb close.

"But you know what?" She lowered her head to

whisper in his ear. "There's a surprise inside."

He jerked the animal from his cheek, jingling the keys, and squeezed it between his fingers.

"Can you feel it in there?"

He sucked in a breath, his eyes widening with excitement. "Something hard! What is it?"

"Something very special." She picked up one of her earrings from the nightstand, carefully using the metal hook at the top to break the thread. Excitement zipped through her. In a moment, she would once again hold God's Word in her hands.

Gatlin's hand shot out and back a few times.

Briar glanced at him and he licked his lips, his eyes glued to the threads popping from the lamb's seam. His anticipation made her grin. He couldn't wait to get his little fingers on whatever was inside.

Finally, the seam was open. She looked at Gatlin and wiggled her fingers inside. Slowly, she slid Granna Grace's miniature Bible from the soft cotton.

"A book!" He exclaimed.

She nodded. "Have you ever seen a book this tiny?"

"No. Never." He shook his head. "Can I hold it?"

"Yes." She placed the book into his restless fingers. "But hold it very gently. It is a very small book, but it holds the biggest thing in the whole world."

His eyes shot from the book to her face.

"Life." She tapped the black cover. "My grandma gave this book to me. It is called the Bible. It is a very special book from God."

"Who is God?" Gatlin tapped the book, just as Briar had.

"God is who made the whole world, and every person and animal inside it. He made the sky and the stars, the sun and the moon. God made everything."

"Even Roxy?"

She chuckled. "Even Roxy."

The sleeping dog twitched an ear at the sound of her name.

"Know what else? Every single thing this book says is the truth. So when it says God will make us feel better when we are sad, it is true. And it does say that, Gatlin."

He held the book close to his face and peeked inside. "Lots of letters."

"Yep. Lots and lots of letters. And those letters say that God loves you, and if you believe in Him, He will take care of you and never leave you. Know what else the Bible says? It says that we have natural bodies, and we have spiritual bodies. Our natural bodies are what we have on the outside." She ruffled his hair. "Our hair, our eyes, our noses, our feet. Our arms and legs—all that important stuff. But what we have on the inside is even more important."

He frowned. "Our guts?"

"Guts are important, too. But I'm talking about our spiritual body. We each have a spirit that lives on the inside, where no one can see. When a person dies, their natural body stops living but their spiritual body lives forever. So, the natural body turns to dust, but that's OK, because the person can't feel it. They aren't in that body anymore. They are a spiritual body."

He flipped through the pages.

"Can I hold it for a second? I'll show you in the Bible where it says that." Briar thumbed through the pages, searching for a verse Granna Grace read to her many times. 1 Corinthians, chapter 15, verse 44. If she remembered right, the last half of the verse reiterated what she'd explained to Gatlin, and was simple enough for his six-year-old mind to understand.

"Here it is." She leaned over so he could follow her finger across the tiny page. "If there is a natural body, there is also a spiritual body." She closed the book and smiled. "See, we have two bodies. A natural body." She wiggled her arms and legs. "And a spiritual body, inside." She patted her chest. "Natural bodies can't feel anymore when they die. But spiritual bodies never die."

Gatlin reached over and touched the Bible. "You're sure everything in here is true?"

"Yes. Because God says so."

He squirmed closer to Briar's side and rested his head against her shoulder. "My mom only has one body, now. The spirit one."

"That's right. The physical body was only a shell that held her spirit. Kind of like a seashell holds a crab. She doesn't need that body anymore."

He took a deep breath. His back trembled beneath Briar's fingers, and then relaxed. "Seashells can't feel anything."

"Nope. They sure can't," she answered, silently thanking God for the relief in the little boy's voice. His anguish was gone, at least for a moment. She wondered how long before the SAP rushing through his system would attack his Agathi like a swarm of hungry termites, gobbling up everything she'd taught him about God. Closing her eyes, she wrapped her arm around him.

A sudden, violent shake of the bed jolted startled cries from both of them.

"Roxy must've been feeling left out." Briar laughed and petted the huge animal now sitting practically in her lap.

Gatlin giggled and stroked her fur. "I didn't know she could jump way up here on the bed."

The dog licked his face. Stopping abruptly, she stared at the door and gave a low growl.

Briar followed the dog's gaze. The doorknob turned and in staggered Reid, still in her formalwear. Roxy stood up on the bed and fired off a series of fierce barks.

"Shut up, you stupid mongrel." Reid glared at the dog and turned her gaze to Gatlin. "It's late. What are you doing in here?"

Gatlin pulled Roxy back down to a sitting position.

Briar stroked the dog with one hand and inched the Bible beneath her thigh with the other.

Reid's green eyes cut to Briar's side. "What are you hiding?"

Briar once read a psychology article stating the best way to combat a robber or kidnapper was by using assertion. Aggression caught the offender unaware and muddled up his game plan. After the way Reid treated her at the festival, she had no problem pulling out some aggression. She straightened her spine.

"Last time I checked, this wasn't a prison, it was a laboratory. My possessions are not your business."

Reid snapped her gaze to Briar's. "Is that so?"

"That is most definitely so." Briar lifted her chin and forced her eyes to focus on Reid's irises. She could've sworn they darkened two shades. Must've been the bloodshot whites making them appear darker—or the black hatred swirling inside.

"I'm making sure you aren't exposing Gatlin to any hocus pocus. I'll be sure to warn Caster about keeping a better eye on his child."

Gatlin snatched the little lamb from the bed, holding it up. "Briar's grandma made this for her before she died."

The corner of Reid's mouth quirked in silent ridicule. "It's time to go." She shot out a hand.

The little boy pressed against Briar's side.

Reid snapped her red tipped fingers. "Now."

Gatlin turned his face from Reid and pressed in harder, practically burrowing into Briar's ribcage.

Reid's hands balled into fists. Breath blasting through her nostrils, she stepped toward Gatlin.

Roxy growled a warning then jumped from the bed and snarled.

"You just bought yourself a one-way ticket to the dog pound, mutt."

"Leave her alone!" Gatlin yelled, prompting Roxy to bark.

Reid stamped a foot in front of the dog. "Shut your fat muzzle," she hissed.

Briar's heartbeat picked up speed. Things were taking a bad turn. Roxy would protect Gatlin from mad-scientist, but who would protect Roxy?

She glanced around the room, searching for resources. The lamp on the nightstand? No. She wanted Reid out of her room, not dead. Her gaze landed on Gatlin's rock. Reid was a giant in her own eyes, plus she was still wearing six-inch stilettos. That made this a David and Goliath situation—sort of.

Briar slid her hand slowly across the bed. Maybe if she tossed the stone instead of hurling it, Reid would snap out of it.

"There you are!" Lukas stepped through the doorway, puncturing the invisible, tension-loaded balloon that filled the space. "I've been looking everywhere." He stepped up to Gatlin and ruffled his hair.

Relieved to see the person she never wanted to see again, Briar released a breath.

"And what's with you, Roxy? I could hear you barking clear on the other side of the lab." Lukas scratched the dog's head. The dog wagged her tail as if also relieved.

"Hey, it's time to get ready for bed." He held out his hand and Gatlin took it, letting Lukas help him down from the mattress. "How about some ice cream before you turn in?"

"Chocolate with sprinkles!" Gatlin broke loose and ran from the room. He returned, leaned back into the doorway, and waved to Briar. "Bye." He ran off again.

"Reid, it's time to go," Lukas said sternly, then followed after the boy.

Roxy continued to stand at Briar's bed side facing Reid.

"I do hope your little Bible study lesson with Gatlin was worth it."

Briar followed Reid's gaze to the small book peeking from beneath her leg.

Roxy growled.

"Shut up, you mangy beast."

15

"Where is my son?" Caster's voice boomed through the laboratory, driving Lukas from his office.

"With Derby. They drove into town to get cleaning supplies." Lukas glanced over his brother's furrowed brow and clenched jaw. "What's wrong?"

"Where is *she*?"

"Who? Reid?" Lukas struggled to pin down his brother's wild gaze.

"You know very well, who I'm talking about. That lab experiment you have the audacity to call a human being."

His brother was nearly foaming at the mouth.

"Caster. Calm down. What's going on?" Lukas stepped around him, blocking his access to the hallway. He sent silent brain waves to Briar, willing her not to come around the corner.

"She brainwashed Gatlin! She has a Bible, Lukas. *A Bible*. I demand to check her room immediately."

"Ridiculous. Where did you get your information?"

"Reid called, and I rushed home."

Reid. Of course. She was the fuel behind Caster's fire.

"You 'rushed home'…from Atlanta?"

Caster narrowed his eyes. "She saw her with it last night. And Gatlin was right there in the room. She thinks Briar was actually reading it to him. Reading the Bible to my son!" Caster shoved an elbow into the wall, rattling the frame of a desert scene.

"Listen, Reid is upset with Briar because of something that happened last night at the gala following the Balloon festival. Something completely unrelated. Not to mention she'd consumed an overabundance of alcohol before she called you. She was trying to get back at Briar by riling you up. Why don't you go home and sleep off the jet lag. I'll have a talk with Reid—"

Caster stepped closer, standing toe to toe with Lukas.

Lukas held his brother's angry gaze as hot breath assaulted his face. Had he eaten fire for breakfast?

"This is entirely your fault for continuing to put off what should have been done weeks ago. She's contagious. She's corrupting my son's mind—filling it full of lies. I take that personally. Now let me through." He bucked against Lukas's chest, aiming his gaze down the hallway.

Lukas rocked back on his heels then replanted his feet. "Pull yourself together, Caster. What goes on in this lab doesn't involve you. The process is in its final stages. I absolutely cannot let you interfere. You could ruin everything."

"When my son is involved, I am involved!" Caster elbowed the wall again, harder, jarring the print from the drywall. He stomped on it, grinding the broken glass underfoot.

"Father commanded you, and now I'm commanding you. Inject that diseased white mouse with your abstergent immediately, or I will."

"Get out, Caster, before I call the police."

"On what complaint? I haven't done anything—yet."

Lukas glanced down at the broken picture.

"Destruction of property."

Caster smirked. "You'd do that, wouldn't you? Jeopardize mother's political career by having me arrested. Pathetic. You care more about that Bible-smuggling nobody than your own family." He shook his head. "You won't be seeing Gatlin anymore. He deserves better." He turned from Lukas and left the way he'd come in.

Lukas closed his eyes and leaned against the wall. His muscles shook, and his lungs burned as if he'd run a marathon.

He couldn't stand the thought of not seeing his nephew. Ever since Gatlin's mother died, he'd felt a special bond with the child. At Kate's memorial service, Gatlin cried, and he'd held him. He'd held Caster, too.

His heart still ached for his brother, as it had then. His wife left him, and then died, casting him into a bottomless pit of irresolution. Caster was overflowing—spewing over—with unresolved grief and anger. Lukas had no problem being the object of his brother's rage, if it kept someone else from being targeted.

He glanced down the hallway, relieved Briar had kept her distance.

~*~

Lukas wondered if Briar had glued her mouth shut. It was the only explanation he could come up with, as to how she'd endured an hour and a half of testing without so much as a word. Even more astonishing, were her vital signs—cool, calm, and collected—despite the fact Reid was the one taking them. Last night, she'd been furious. Had she really forgiven Reid so quickly for her inexcusable behavior at the ball?

He glanced at Reid, fingertips of one hand pressed to her temple as she scribbled down data with the other. Perhaps Briar found Reid's obvious hangover to be punishment enough.

Lukas was suffering, too. Not from the aftermaths of alcohol, but from Briar's disappointment in him. Could he venture to hope she'd forgiven him as well? If so, her ability to dissolve hard feelings far surpassed the capabilities of his abstergent.

"Am I free to go?" Briar asked, revealing no emotional clues.

"Yes." He offered what he hoped was a polite smile. "Enjoy the rest of your day."

Briar left the room and shut the door.

Lukas turned his gaze from the closed door to Reid, wishing he would have asked Briar if he could borrow some of that glue. Not for himself, but for Reid. She wouldn't like what he had to say, and he had a strong notion she wouldn't be quiet about it.

"What did you say to my brother?"

Reid finished filling in the remaining blanks on Briar's chart and returned the clipboard to its slot on the wall. She stepped closer to him. "Is this about the Bible?"

Her admittance caught him off guard. He was convinced she would deny the whole thing—loudly.

"I did what I felt was right. I told Gatlin's father that Briar was reading to him out of the Bible."

"What you thought was right?" Lukas laughed. "Oh, that's rich. You make it sound as if you have a conscience. As if you have a sense of right and wrong."

"Who are you to belittle me? We are all level, remember? Well, all of us who count, anyway." She tossed an irritated glance to the door. "I answer to my own integrity. And I couldn't stand by and let her brainwash Gatlin. What if some of that garbage lodged in his brain? Do you realize how dangerous that could be for him? Yes, I have a conscience, and I could not live with that hanging over my head. I happen to love that little boy. Believe it or not, I am capable of love."

"I'm not convinced Briar was reading Gatlin the Bible, but even if she was, none of it would stick. Gatlin received a booster three days ago. The SAP in his system would take care of it."

"You can't be certain of that. Not at his age, and with this potential level of exposure to Briar's Godspeak. What if some of her mumbo-jumbo did seep through? It will be six months before Gatlin can receive another SAP booster. You know how kids are—what if he starts blurting Bible stories in public?" She rolled her eyes. "I can't believe you, Lukas. I really can't. You know better than anyone how flawed SAP is. Isn't that the whole reason you developed your precious abstergent? The hold that unlevel has on you is ridiculous."

Lukas was losing focus. What was the matter with him? Had he really allowed his nephew to be placed in harm's way? Maybe it was time to test his own Agathi—see if the SAP was still doing its job. He took a deep breath, letting it out as he sat on the edge of the exam table. It was his turn to rub his temples.

Reid moved behind him, placing a hand on each of his shoulders. "I realize I tend to come across...abruptly. But I only want what's best for the program." She slowly massaged his muscles, easing the tension from his shoulders and neck. "And what's best for you." She spoke low, close to his ear, causing a shiver to rush down his spine. Good shiver or bad, he didn't know.

But he knew one thing—his head was clouded. And he'd better get it cleared out fast, or find another test subject.

~*~

Lukas frowned at his vibrating cuffphone. He tapped the ignore key and watched his father's image disappear, postponing the inevitable for the third time that day.

He flinched at a knock on the door.

"Just a moment."

He stepped through his office with the feeling Reid would be on the other side. Uneasiness crept through him. Somehow, she'd gotten the wrong idea about their relationship—if it could be called that. He didn't look forward to setting her straight, but it must be done. He squared his shoulders, cleared his throat, and opened the door.

"Hi." Briar held up her hand in a little wave. "Can I talk to you?"

"Yes, of course. Come in." He stepped to the side, giving her room to enter. "Please, sit down."

"Thanks." She sat in the chair he indicated and leaned forward, placing her hands on her knees.

"What can I do for you, Miss Lee?"

Miss Lee? He wanted to smack himself in the forehead. He'd done it again—spoken as if she was beneath him. Why did he have to come across so arrogant? It happened whenever he was the least bit nervous or uncomfortable. *High and mighty* seemed to be his default.

He lowered into the chair next to hers. Cringing inside, he checked her expression. No visible signs of agitation. Maybe she hadn't noticed.

"I realize I stepped over the line. You won't understand this, but it's like the urge to tell the truth is trapped inside my bones, like Jeremiah."

Lukas creased his brow. "Jeremiah?"

"From the Bible." She waved a hand in front of her. "It sounds insane. But just because something sounds foolish doesn't mean it's not true. The Bible says the message of the Cross is foolishness to those who are perishing, but to those who are being saved it is the power of God." She squeezed her eyes shut for a moment. "Somewhere in First Corinthians, I think."

He nodded slowly. She was so expressive, so animated. She'd definitely changed her mind about the silent treatment. Her demeanor from this morning until now was like night and day. He wanted to ask what changed, what had suddenly gotten into her, but he needed to carefully choose his words. He didn't want to shut her down now that she was actually speaking to him. He had no idea what she was saying, but he was enjoying the show.

"Sharing my faith with Gatlin last night reminded me of how precious that faith is. I was getting used to the idea of being without it. Warming up to the thought of being like everybody else—looking forward to it, actually. But now…"

Her eyes were glistening. Should he go to his desk and offer her a tissue, or would that embarrass her?

A tear spilled down her cheek. She stood and retrieved the box from his desktop, pulling two tissues from the slot. "Now I feel that I will lose myself. My purpose. My *essence*." She blotted her eyes. "I wanted to talk to you about it this morning, but I wasn't comfortable spilling my soul all over the place in front of Reid." She blew her nose. "So…that's how I feel. I thought you might want to know—for your research. I'm sorry if I've caused problems between you and Caster. I'll really miss seeing Gatlin." Her voice was barely above a whisper.

Lukas shifted in his chair. She'd admitted to everything. She'd shared her faith with his six-year-old nephew. She had a Bible in her room. He knew what he had to do. He would stand to his feet, walk Briar to her room, and make her hand over the Bible. He would tell her she was correct to assume she would never see Gatlin again.

He drew a deep breath and stood. "Thank you for sharing. Your visit has been very—enlightening." He held out his hand and she passed him the tissue box, stuffing the used ones in the pocket of her scrubs.

She rose. "I appreciate you listening. I realize blurting my guts out like that didn't do anything—except confirm your suspicions that I'm thoroughly insane." She circled her index finger around her ear twice. "But somehow I feel better."

"I'm glad." He offered a tight smile. "And I think you're right, my documenting your emotions for posterity is an excellent idea. I'll include what you've shared with the rest of our research."

"Good." She patted her heart. "I won't remember what it feels like—this war raging inside. But others will read about it and know it existed. Documenting the conflict makes it real."

He opened the door. "Rest well."

"I'll try."

He closed the door behind her then turned, pressing his back against it. Just like that, he'd let her get away with it.

Briar wasn't insane. He was.

~*~

Briar picked up Gatlin's stone from the nightstand and caressed it. Honey-brown, like Lukas's eyes.

She wasn't exactly sure why she'd told him everything. Documentation for his research was part of the reason. But only a small part. Mainly it was because God wanted her to share her feelings with Lukas. God had talked to her all day, it seemed. His voice was a pleasant distraction, enabling her to withstand the morning testing session with ease—even with Reid at the helm.

Something big was happening to her. Sharing her faith with Gatlin made her realize she still believed strongly in the things her grandmother taught her. For the first time in a long time, she thought she could use her faith to stand up and fight.

Fight what? The abstergent being injected into her brain? Not likely.

Again, she wondered if God would forgive her for being forced to forget Him. Or would He prefer her to go down fighting—dying—if need be?

Returning the rock to the nightstand, she sat on the bed and slid Granna's lamb from under her pillow. What if instead of struggling against the injection, she complied, trusting God to supernaturally block the abstergent from her brain? Nothing was too difficult for God, right? If her soul survived, it would be what

Granna Grace called a "testimony." Her story would inspire countless other people.

Or was she merely trying to avoid conflict? Compliance would be the easy way out.

"God, I'm so confused." She slid the Bible from the torn stitching, wondering why Lukas hadn't made her hand it over.

16

Lukas magnified the image on his flexpane, leaned forward, and traced a finger over the scarlet glow. Vibrant and full of life, Briar's Agathi were truly beautiful. He clicked on the screen, creating a graphic of how the area would appear when the Agathi were dissolved. Gray. Desolate. Dead.

Animal brains were different. They weren't equipped with Agathi to begin with. The area didn't exist. As for the human brain, there was an actual space for the Agathus—that little hook that resembled a thorn. He clicked on it again, returning Briar's Agathi to radiant crimson.

Through the years, Lukas had exhaustively studied functional Agathi. Countless times, he'd viewed images nearly identical to Briar's. This, however, was the first time a shudder trailed his spine. Although Lukas didn't believe in Christ, he knew thorns were significant to the Christian religion. A symbol of Jesus Christ's suffering. The connection was almost too coincidental.

Very soon, this thriving area of human brain would be gone forever. Dissolved away.

Could he justify that, truly?

The situation would be different, were he burning off a field so that more bountiful crops could grow. What he was about to do was more like dumping acid onto the field so that nothing could ever grow there again.

Actually, it was exactly like that.

~*~

"Is it complicated to use?" Reid asked. "The videos on MediVid make it appear fairly easy."

Lukas opened his rubber-gloved hand, revealing more of the cranial drill. "It's designed for simplicity—and safety. The distraction of a complicated tool is the last thing one needs when penetrating the skull." He pointed the instrument toward her. "Unlike the older model, this one makes it impossible to drill too deeply. When the tip comes into contact with the scalp, it evaluates the skull's density. The drill automatically shuts off when it sufficiently perforates the cranium." He passed her the device. "Employing a neurosurgeon is merely a precaution. Operating the drill is so simple, Gatlin could do it." He frowned. "Not a good idea. Roxy would be in trouble."

"You'd hear no complaints from me," Reid mumbled. "I'm sure the mutt would be more agreeable following a lobotomy." She turned the instrument over and grasped the handle. "Lighter than it looks."

Lukas took the drill back, polishing the stainless-steel tool before placing it into a custom case. "I've equipped it with a sterile 16mm bit. The retractable tip will keep it contaminate-free."

"And the procedure will be performed soon?"

Lukas ignored the question. "I started Briar on a daily regimen of neuro protectants last week to prevent disruption to the blood-brain barrier when the skull is perforated."

"That didn't answer my question."

Lukas stepped away, locking the silver case into the implement vault.

"Lukas?"

He turned from the safe to find himself nearly nose to nose with Reid. He tensed, hoping she wouldn't embarrass herself by offering more unwanted advances.

She sighed and tilted her head. "So, you have some kind of hang up about administering the abstergent to Briar. I get that. But waiting is dangerous. You have to go through with the project as planned. Schedule the neurosurgeon—or grant me the authority to do so." Her green eyes skipped back and forth, gazing into one of his eyes, then the other. "Today."

Lukas's blood simmered. "I developed the abstergent, and I will see that it is administered when the time is right." He thumped his index finger against his chest. "*Me*. Not you, not my brother, and not my father."

"I'm well aware you are the creator of the all-mighty Stone's Abstergent. Just as I am aware I am nothing but a lowly laboratory technologist—your assistant. But I'm wondering if you've forgotten what—make that *who*—is at stake here. Briar's birthday is three days away. *Three days*. As precious as she is to you, I can't understand why you are dragging your feet when it comes to injecting her with abstergent. If you wait, she will end up in the ARC. And we both know what happens inside those walls. Is that what you want? For Briar to be probed? Experimented on? For her to end up some zombie with drool on her chin? Or worse?"

"Not you, too." Lukas shook his head at the ceiling. "With your level of education, I thought you'd be above believing old wives tales."

She offered a stiff shrug. "Most rumors contain a

kernel of truth."

"With the level of security surrounding the ARC, and the credentials required to get within a mile of the place, it's ludicrous to believe that Frankenstein nonsense."

"Perhaps I'm a superstitious nitwit. Briar will soon find out. You and I will never truly know." She let out a wistful sigh. "All that aside, people are getting anxious, Lukas. Are you planning to put off the procedure until the serum spoils? Hasn't it neared the end of its shelf life? Think of all the wasted funds and resources. Investors will be furious—especially your father. It won't look good for your mother either, working to become a congresswoman while her son squanders time and money."

"Enough." Lukas sliced a trembling hand through the air. He knew how Jekyll felt as he'd morphed into Hyde. "Again, I will offer the explanation not owed to you." He struggled to hold his voice steady. "According to policy and procedure, I cannot inject the subject with abstergent until the antidote is complete. Perfecting the formula has turned out to be more complicated than I anticipated."

Reid nodded. "Policy and procedure. Can't go against the handbook." She tapped her chin. "Hmm. If only we knew who penned the protocol, we could explain the situation and maybe have the rules amended. Oh, wait. I remember who wrote it. You did." She marched to the door, slamming it behind her.

Lukas chewed the inside of his cheek. Could Reid be right? And Father? Was there a nugget of truth buried inside the farfetched rumors about the ARC? Maybe he should do some online investigating.

He walked to the counter, picked up the flexpane,

and smoothed the creases from the surface. In the search bar, he typed Alternative Research Center, Fleetwood, Montana—then cleared it out before it generated results. Searching for propaganda about the ARC would make him exactly like the people he despised—tale bearers who believed everything they heard. This was the age of progressivism. People didn't experiment on other people—or even on animals. And they certainly didn't chop up brains.

The thought was absolutely barbaric. He wouldn't get caught up in superstitious nonsense. Neither would he let Reid whip him into a paranoid frenzy. Briar's birthday was still three days away. He still had time.

A slow smile lifted the corners of his mouth. But first, to put the finishing touches on a birthday surprise he'd cooked up with Derby. He cleared the pane's history and left the equipment room to search for his friend.

17

Thankful for the darkness, Briar pressed her lips together, only to have them split apart again. She couldn't recall ever having such a stubborn grin. "So, where did you say we're going?"

"I didn't." Lukas glanced her direction then returned his attention to the road. "Not the first, fifth, or tenth time you asked."

"Looks like we're in the middle of nowhere."

"I can turn the car around and take you back to the lab, if you prefer."

"No, no. That won't be necessary. I'm enjoying the ride." She flexed her toes, unable to believe how light her leg felt without the shackle. It didn't really matter where he was taking her. She was free for the time being—and loving it.

Lukas turned the steering wheel, his high beams splashing onto the empty, neglected parking lot of what appeared to be an abandoned building. "Here we are." He cut the lights.

She squinted, trying to make out a figure bustling around a large shadowy object. Suddenly, flames erupted. Her heart leapt as Lukas exited the car, the briefly opened door letting in the loud hum of a motor. What in the world was going on?

He circled the vehicle and opened her door. "Come with me," he shouted above the noise.

She took his outstretched hand. He led her in the direction of the motor, toward the bustling man and the flames. Her eyes and mouth grew wide as she recognized Derby and the realization of what she was seeing dawned on her. Derby was inflating a hot air balloon—in the dark.

"What's this about?" She was breathless. Lukas couldn't have heard her over the continuous roar.

"Happy birthday!" he shouted, sweeping an arm toward the balloon. "You're going up!"

He must be joking. "Haha, very funny. Birthday prank."

He grinned. "I'll be right back." He jogged to his car, turned on the headlights, and steered in Derby's direction. Pulling closer, he spotlighted the balloon and got out, leaving the lights on.

Briar's heart filled and turned upright, simultaneous with the balloon.

Derby turned off the giant fan motor, leaving her ears ringing. "She's ready to rise."

Lukas gazed at Briar. "Yes, I believe she is."

This couldn't be happening. She was still back at the lab asleep. She had to be. "Are you serious?" Briar yelled, forgetting Derby had cut the motor. Her voice echoed through the isolated parking lot.

"Serious as a functioning Agathus." Lukas offered her a wink.

"Funny." She tried to glare at him, but the unshakable grin was back.

Lukas scanned the sky. "Sunrise will be at seven. The weather will be cool and clear with a south wind at eight miles per hour—perfect day for ballooning. But the high will only be forty-six degrees, so you'll need to keep your jacket on."

"Wow. Somebody really did their homework."

"Actually, Derby did the homework—all the work,

actually. I just told him the date and time. Fortunately for me, the weather is supposed to cooperate."

Briar raised an eyebrow. "Perhaps there was some divine intervention."

He grinned, white teeth flashing in the glow of the headlights. "I won't argue with you on your birthday."

She gave a single nod. "Good."

"I have to get back to the lab. Derby will take it from here."

Briar frowned. "What—you mean you're not going?" She didn't have to try hard to sound disappointed, though she realized he'd prefer to spend his morning in a pit of vipers than a hot air balloon.

"Not on your life." He gave a small jump and planted his feet against the concrete. "That's as high in the air as you'll ever see me. Besides, I want to get back before Reid wakes, to cover our tracks." He gestured to Derby. "I leave you in good hands."

She stepped closer. "Thank you, Lukas, for all of this. It's a dream come true." She pulled to her tiptoes and kissed his cheek.

He turned to look at her. "Happy birthday."

Briar drew in a breath and held it. With his words, he'd wished her a happy birthday. But his eyes wished something else—something vital that pumped through her heart and rushed through her veins.

He smiled and turned away, patting Derby on the back as he walked to his car.

A longing she'd never known threatened to overtake her, tempting her to run straight past the hot air balloon and into his arms. Forget spending the morning in the clouds with Derby. She would rather spend it watching the sunrise with her head on Lukas's shoulder.

She pushed the breath from her lungs. No. That was ridiculous. He'd gone to all this trouble for her. She craned her neck, taking in the massive balloon. The ride would be incredible. A beautiful farewell to her Agathi. The glorious and final sendoff for her soul.

Would Lukas do it as soon as she returned? Would he be waiting for her at the lab, syringe in hand, neurosurgeon by his side? And there would be Reid, front and center, smirking hard enough to make her face stick that way.

"You ready, Miss Briar?"

Derby's words jarred her back to her senses. She nodded quickly and smiled. "I thought you'd never ask."

"I'm going to give you a little boost into the gondola."

"Gondola? Is that a fancy word for basket?"

Derby chuckled. "Yep."

She tiptoed next to the gondola and gripped the edge. Derby helped her inside and climbed in after. "She's going to make some noise." After stretching on a pair of gloves with leather patches on the palms and fingers, he reached overhead and pulled the trigger of a blow torch, blasting fresh fire into the balloon.

Briar's stomach leapt as the basket lifted from the earth. She'd expected a tingly feeling she'd read about, similar to a rising elevator or an ascending airplane. This was neither.

Silence enveloped the basket as Derby let off the trigger. A sensation unlike any she'd experienced, stole her away. She closed her eyes, surrendering herself to the dawn-kissed sky.

"Nice, isn't it?"

Nice? She opened her eyes. Nice is how a person

described the clerk at the grocery store, or maybe the weather. Not this. She lowered her gaze to Derby's truck, now visible in the approaching daybreak. "It's phenomenal," she whispered. Mesmerized, she watched the truck slowly shrink to the size of a child's toy. Peace settled over her, so foreign she almost didn't recognize it.

She jerked, the loud hiss of the torch startling her as Derby squeezed the trigger. Poor guy, she'd nearly forgotten he was there. Enthralled by the brilliant golds and pinks of the sunrise, she hadn't said a word in ages.

"Pretty smart of Lukas, putting the Stone Labs logo on a hot air balloon. Good publicity. I'm sure everyone stops to stare when you float by."

"No logo today. We're incognito. The envelope's a loaner, it just happens to be a similar shade of red. The Stone Labs balloon is being recoated. It's a good idea to have that done once in a while. Keeps the fabric from becoming too porous and prevents rips. The process will cost Lukas a heavy chunk of change, though."

"Guess it's worth it, if it keeps his balloon in the air."

Derby chuckled. "Yeah. Spends all that money to ensure the balloon he'll never, ever step foot in stays in tip-top shape. That Lukas is one of a kind."

"He sure is." Briar closed her eyes again, unable to believe a captive could feel so free.

~*~

Lukas unlocked the door and stepped inside. He stood still for a moment. Good. Everything was quiet inside the lab.

He glanced at his cuff. 7:30 a.m. Reid wouldn't be up for another half hour. Last night he'd told her he would be performing Briar's final tests this morning, tests that required Briar to be asleep. As a precaution, he'd assigned Reid to another area of the lab for the day. She was to work in the data room compiling a detailed report for his father—far away from where he and Briar would be working. Under no circumstances were he and Briar to be disturbed.

Reid had said she was relieved, making some adolescent comment about being glad she didn't have to look at Briar all day. He'd wanted to fire back with a few pre-pubescent insults of his own, but decided it wasn't worth the fallout. Not today.

Lukas stepped lightly down the hallway to his office and locked the door. He glanced at the hot air balloon picture on the wall, thrilled at how pleased Briar had been at daybreak. He imagined her floating through the sky, the morning sunlight in her hair. He wished he could have stayed to watch her expressions change as she went up. At this moment, Derby Jenkins was the luckiest guy in the world.

Lukas doused the tiny ember of jealousy before it could smolder. Perhaps he should have put his own fears aside and hopped into the gondola with her—after he'd taken a strong sedative, of course.

Who was he kidding? His fear of heights was severe. The thought of flying—or floating, made him sick to his stomach.

He turned from the picture. Just as well. He'd needed to return to the lab, anyway. To make sure Reid didn't become suspicious.

He unlocked his third desk drawer and slid out a small packet. Briar's fleshcard. Exactly where he'd left it—without Reid's knowledge.

He slipped the small package into his left jacket pocket. Briar's ankle monitor was in his right, and the GPS receiver was in the front pocket of his slacks. He felt like some kind of secret agent. *Stirred, not shaken…* Or maybe he had that backwards.

He frowned, not sure where to place the items. He wanted the equipment far from Reid's reach. For all he knew, her hair pins could jimmy those wimpy desk locks in a flash. He could imagine Reid as a secret agent as easily as he could fancy himself one. More easily. Oversized sunglasses and whispered cuffphone conversations were part of her daily routine. Agent Reid. Double-Oh-No-I-Broke-A-Nail.

Reid had keys to every door in the lab, except to the apartments. She only had a key to her own. However, Lukas had keys to those as well. He locked his office and stepped lightly down the hallway, a safe hiding place in mind for Briar's equipment. He'd conceal it in her room.

He turned the key in Briar's doorknob and stepped in. Her room was clean and smelled of canned air freshener. Something lemony—they all smelled the same to him. But a scent lingered underneath the fake citrus. An aroma he couldn't describe, yet knew well. A warm smell. Heavy and light at the same time. A smell that tugged at his heart. Briar's scent. The aroma of where he wanted to be.

He pulled the equipment from his pockets and grouped it together on the bed. Where to put it? He didn't want to open any of her drawers or even her closet. She might think he was snooping—and he didn't want temptation to make her assumption correct.

He glanced around, his gaze finding the floor. Under the bed seemed like the best option. He lowered to his knees and looked under. Completely bare, not even a dust bunny. He picked up the ankle monitor, frowning at the weight of it. Ten years with this thing locked around her ankle must've been torturous. And to think she was only a little girl of seven when she'd received it.

No wonder she'd looked at him that way when he'd unlocked it and slid it from her ankle this morning. She'd gazed at him as if he'd slid something precious and gold onto her finger. He'd love to compare both expressions someday. And both kisses…

He shook the thought away. She was only eighteen, as of today.

Then again, he was only twenty-four. What was six years? His father had been twelve years older than his mother when they'd wed, and as far as he knew it had never been an issue.

He palmed the other items and placed them all under the bed, scooting them near the wall, far from view. Part of him—the part he refused to accept, the part that grew stronger every day—wished he and Briar could find a place like that. A little corner where they could stay together forever, hidden from view. A secret, safe haven where he wasn't responsible for killing the God she loved so much.

He stood and walked to the door, a heaviness bending his back and stooping his shoulders. Meet Dr. Lukas Stone. Grown man who daydreams about living under a bed.

Briar Lee deserved so much better.

18

Briar's eyes couldn't open wide enough to take everything in. Lukas had no idea how priceless his gift really was—he couldn't possibly. Ten years of spiritual and bodily entrapment melted smoothly away beneath the shelter of the red balloon.

She could feel her Agathi glowing brighter than Derby's propane torch. Probably brighter than it had in her entire life. God was all around her. She silently thanked Him for allowing her this breathtaking ride over His creation. She praised Him, and she prayed. No one could keep her heart from communing with her Creator, because for a moment, she owned her Agathi—and the sky.

Derby's lips were still moving. She attuned her ears to what he was saying. He chattered on about the Stone family, as he'd done for most of the ride. She really didn't mind. She'd gleaned some interesting facts about Lukas's family and, more importantly, Lukas.

She'd already known that Lukas's father was an important man, and according to Derby, Lukas's mother was an "energetic fireball of a woman" with a head for politics.

She learned that Derby and Lukas had been friends since boyhood, Derby had worked at the lab for six years, and Lukas consistently over-payed him.

"And then there's Caster," Derby said, the smile lines around his eyes vanishing. "Behaves as if his own brother is under his feet. Jealousy is the only thing that makes a man act like that."

"Caster is jealous of Lukas?" Briar couldn't imagine the man acknowledging the rest of the population, let alone being jealous of someone.

"It eats his lunch that their father put Lukas over Stone Labs. Oh, Caster had his chance. Don't know what happened, but he must've messed up royally for Dr. Stone to jerk the rug out from under him that way. When Caster failed, Heston poured all of his knowledge and resources into Lukas. Made him director of operations, as well as chief scientist of Stone Labs."

Briar cringed. "I'm sure that sat well with Caster."

"Went over like a lead hot air balloon," Derby said. "Lukas might be younger, but he was born with the ability to run the place. He's got the knack and the know-how. Smartest man I've ever known."

"Yeah. He's pretty smart." Briar closed her eyes for a moment and inhaled the crisp air.

"Of course, Dr. Stone couldn't leave his elder son in the cold. He made him chief financial officer of Stone Labs, so he'd have a title—guess being called Doctor wasn't enough. But I'm here to tell you," Derby said, his voice becoming distant, trance-like. "Caster Stone doesn't need a title to get what he wants."

Derby's eyes took on an unfocused gaze. "He has...people." He sounded distracted, as if he were miles from the balloon basket. "People that can make things happen. Cruel people. Terrible things."

Uneasiness seeped into her pores. *Cruel people?* What was he talking about? Briar cleared her throat. She didn't like the faraway look in his eyes. The basket seemed to be shrinking.

"Wow," she said, looking below at the beiges,

grays, and occasional faded greens of the rocky desert landscape. "We really made some distance. When are we heading back?"

~*~

Lukas rolled the small container between his fingers, watching the milky liquid coat the glass. Stone's Abstergent. The stuff that would change the world—and the woman he loved—forever. He set the vial on the spotless countertop, next to the antidote. Both compounds were flawless. Every *i* dotted and *t* crossed. The serums were perfect. He wished he could pour them down the drain.

But the abstergent would save her life. Possessing a Bible was dangerous. Downright deadly. The book evoked hatred, and incited a rage in citizens that law enforcement deemed justified. She'd be better off concealing a gun—or drugs.

And the ARC wasn't an option. According to Reid, residency equaled a fate worse than death, and his father's comments echoed the same.

Abstergent was the only answer. It would release the grip religion held on her heart and mind.

He clicked off the stainless-steel lamp and stood, focusing his thoughts on Briar. How exhilarated she must be, soaring a mile above Sickle Ridge after being cooped up for so long. He recalled her kiss on his cheek again and smiled.

He picked up the vials and stepped toward the pharmaceutical closet. The rattle of the doorknob stopped him in his tracks.

"No excuses, Lukas, I know you received Briar's fleshcard. I have the invoice right here." She shook a sheet of paper.

He glanced at the printout and raised an eyebrow. "Your point?"

She shoved the page into the satchel looped over her arm. "My point, Lukas, is that you received her fleshcard and hid it away, like an obese child hoarding a candy bar. Where is it? It should be installed immediately."

"Due to the prior complications, I want to be certain the conditions are right before implantation." He no longer wanted the tracking device under her skin. In addition to reading SAP levels and vital signs, the card was designed to gauge and record Agathi reaction, as well as all other brain function. Reid—and anyone else—would, literally, be able to read Briar's physical and emotional disposition like a book.

"The new gun shouldn't give us any problems, I inspected it days ago. We're both here now. The procedure won't take five minutes."

Lukas inhaled deeply and let it out slowly. "By this point, it doesn't matter. Following the sleep study, she will receive the abstergent and be on her way within a week. Her physician's office back home can install her fleshcard." He forced the words out, hoping his eyes weren't reflecting the pain in his heart. "Speaking of—I asked you to stay out of this section of the lab until Briar's sleep study was complete." He took the remaining three steps to the vault and placed each vial next to its twin.

"The sleep study is the reason I'm here. I need the information for your father's report. Not the completed statistics, just the readings you've gotten so far. I don't even have to be in the room with her." She stepped to the counter and snatched up his flexpane. "I can glance at the data stream on your device. I only need enough to fill in a couple of blanks."

He slid the pliable screen from her grip. "I'm not streaming at the moment. I'm drawing up Briar's exit packet—follow up instructions, a questionnaire detailing her stay at the lab, confidentiality and liability forms. The usual discharge papers."

"OK, since you're making this difficult, I'll stream it from my own pane." She started toward the door.

"There's no live feed. It wasn't necessary. I'll upload the data afterward."

"How long has she been asleep?"

He glanced at the flexpane. No clock, only the Stone Labs cactus logo screensaver. He had no idea what time it was. "A while."

"Ah." Reid raised her chin. "*A while*. Sounds very clinical and precise."

"It doesn't matter. The machine records all of the data, including the time. Now if you're finished playing your little game, I have work to do. And so do you." He walked to the door and motioned for her to leave.

"Do you realize how ridiculous you look? It's no secret how you feel about her. A sleep study? What a load of garbage. We have all the information we need on Briar. Her research is complete. All that's left is to administer the abstergent. But you never will. You'll say anything to preserve that virginal brain of hers. You are supposed to destroy her Agathi, not protect them. Have you forgotten *you* are the scientist who designed the dissolving agent?"

She raked a hand through her hair and took a breath. "Tonight, you'll have another excuse—some farfetched concoction that only an idiot would believe." She stepped to where he stood in the doorway. "I'm no idiot." She slid a hand into the satchel and slipped a small item into his palm.

Briar's Bible. "Need I ask where you found this?"

"In her room, beneath her pillow. Hidden inside a hideous little stuffed animal. Much easier to locate than the ankle monitor, GPS receiver, and fleshcard stashed under her bed." She retrieved all three items from her bag and held them out to Lukas.

He took them from her hands. "Why were you snooping around in Briar's room?"

She shrugged. "Why not? She isn't here to stop me. By now she's miles away, her head stuffed in the clouds. Tickled pink to be so much closer to the God who saved her soul." She clasped her hands at her chest.

Her statement made Lukas's heart beat faster. She knew about Briar's hot air balloon ride. But how? He'd sworn Derby to secrecy. Mentally, he kicked himself. Derby was so crazy over Reid, there's nothing he wouldn't do for her—or keep from her. That explained how she'd gotten inside Briar's apartment. Derby had given her his master key.

"I've taken pictures of everything. I'm thinking of texting them to your father. To let him know how his chief scientist is operating Stone Labs. An unlevel test subject out of the laboratory without a tracking device, on the very day she turns eighteen. What if she decides to run? I don't think that will sit well with him, do you?"

Despite his burning desire to yell, he remained silent. He was sick to death of Reid, his father, and his brother breathing down his neck about administering the abstergent to Briar. Reid wanted a rise out of him.

He'd give her nothing. Not even a facial expression.

"I warned you, Lukas. Remember? I told you to quit stalling and give her the abstergent, but you did nothing." She stepped closer, tilting her head as if looking at a poor, little puppy dog. Oh, how that condescending look clawed under his skin. "You made your own bed, Lukas. But I'd be more than happy to lie in it with you." She touched his cheek.

He grabbed her wrist.

"*Mmm*. Now that's what I'm talking about." She winked, her laugh sounding like a cackle.

"Do whatever you have to, Reid. Whenever you're gone, I'll still be here."

"Are you sure about that? Maybe Daddy will see the light and put Caster in charge—as he should've in the first place."

"Doubtful. Father isn't one to repeat mistakes. He doesn't take fondly to those who undermine family, either. You'd do well to keep that in mind when you state your case. A case against Briar is a case against me."

Her eye color shifted from desert spruce to swamp algae. "Before the lab rat arrived, I thought your heart was as hermetically sealed as that fleshcard." She flicked the transparent packet in Lukas's hand. "Turns out it was as easy to unlock as that stupid ankle monitor. I just wasn't holy enough or young enough to turn the key."

She knocked into him as she walked out the door, scattering the tracking devices over the tile. He'd managed to hold onto the Bible. He dragged his thumb over the edge, ruffling the tiny pages. If only he could find a way for Briar to hold onto it as well. Not physically. *Spiritually.*

He squinted down at where he'd parted the book and read the tiny print. "For if you remain silent at this time, relief and deliverance for the Jews will arise from another place, but you and your father's family will perish. And who knows but that you have come to your royal position for such a time as this?" Esther, chapter four, verse fourteen.

"...for such a time as this." He closed the book, a determined line creasing his brow.

19

Derby hadn't answered when she'd asked where they were going. Something in his demeanor made her afraid to repeat the question. A sick feeling slid through her, settling in the pit of her stomach. She pressed a hand to her middle.

"Hungry?" Derby asked.

Her heart rose a millimeter. Maybe he would land if she agreed.

"Starving."

He fished in his jacket pocket and held a small package out to her.

Her hope took a nosedive. He'd brought snacks. Beef jerky. Fake, of course. With the exception of fish, meat had been outlawed years ago.

"I still remember what the real stuff tasted like." He pulled another stick from the pocket and ripped it open with his teeth. "And this ain't it." He took a bite.

The rich, spicy smell on his breath polluted the cool air and churned her insides. To divert her queasiness, she crushed the unopened jerky in her fist, concentrating on how the packaging bit into her palm.

Derby didn't notice. His eyes were closed, a frown elongating his features. He sighed deeply. "I like you, Miss Briar. You have a special place in my heart."

His words slammed into her chest, knocking the breath from her lungs. Was he going to try something? How could she defend herself inside this balloon? Her gaze darted around the basket. Her shoe? Maybe. If she swung it hard enough. But it was on her foot. She'd have to lean down and yank it off first. Then what? If she knocked him out or managed to throw him overboard, who would fly the balloon? Not her.

"I had to do it. I didn't want to. If it was up to me, I wouldn't have done it at all. But, you see, I *had* to."

She clamped her mouth shut, panic rising with each quick breath she sucked in. What was he talking about?

"I hate doing this to Lukas—he'll never forgive me. Caster was behind it all. He arranged everything."

Derby was crying. She swallowed what little moisture her mouth contained. Things were spiraling downward fast, and she feared the balloon would follow. She had to cheer the guy up. Redirect his thinking. Do *something*.

"Oh, I'm sure it's not all that bad." She forced herself to drop the jerky and touch his hand. "Why don't you tell me what happened? Talking about it will make you feel better."

"I don't know—I really shouldn't. I haven't told a soul."

"All the more reason to tell me." She pasted a grin to her face, remembering to crinkle her eyes for sincerity. "I'll guard your secret with my life." She pretended to lock her lips and throw the key from the gondola. Earlier he'd said he liked her. As long as he wasn't making inappropriate advances, she would play up the cutsie-wootsie stuff for all it was worth.

"Ah, I might as well let you in on it. You're never going back to Sickle Ridge anyway."

Her bladder burned with a sudden urgency she'd never experienced. The intensity rushed hot tears to her eyes. "What do you mean by that?"

"Caster told me to fly you within a quarter mile of

a tiny landing strip outside of town. Twelve-mile flight." He glanced at his cuff. "We should be seeing it here pretty quick."

"But, why?" The words croaked from her shrunken vocal chords.

"All I know is Caster wants you at the ARC really bad. Bad enough to have me manipulate Lukas to get you inside this balloon. The birthday surprise was really all Caster's idea. He told me to put a bug in Lukas's ear, and Lukas fell for it. Caster pulled the whole thing off without raising a single hair on the back of Lukas's neck." Derby shook his head. "I told you the man couldn't be trusted."

The basket, the sky, the world—everything closed in on her.

"When we land, reps from the ARC will pick you up and transport you by private jet to their facility in Montana."

He lurched forward. Briar yelped as he clutched her shoulders. "I'm sorry. But I had to do it—for Reid. I'm only a janitor—out of her league. A man has to do everything he can to keep his woman happy, or she won't stay. I learned that the hard way last time around."

Briar nodded numbly. The guy was past delusional. Could he seriously think Reid was his girlfriend?

"Caster is relocating me to New Mexico. Setting me up in some upscale town house. Balloon runs are good there. Reid will be along shortly, after she ties up a few loose ends. We'll have a good life together." He squinted up at the sky and nodded.

Of course. Caster and Reid. It made perfect sense. Reid wanted her out of the way so she could have

Lukas all to herself. Caster wanted Briar out of the way of his brother, and more adamantly, his son. They'd arranged her demise together.

"Anyway, I heard the ARC ain't so bad. Kind of a plush holding tank where people stay and get treatment." Derby cupped a hand around his eyes to shade the sun. "Like a salon or a fancy hotel. You'll be out in no time. Back to your mama in Oklahoma. You've seen the reunions."

She'd seen the reunions, all right. According to her mother, they were a warm and fuzzy cover up for what really went on within the bloodstained walls. The more Derby babbled on, the more she feared her mother was right. If Reid wanted her there—the place must be excruciating.

Derby leaned over and pointed. "Landing strip. Time to descend."

Briar's heart sank into her churning stomach. A white airplane waited below, its red tail jutting up like a knife covered in blood. Not far from the small runway, set a dark automobile with black-tinted windows.

Derby looked up and tugged one of several cords overhead. "Have to let out some of the hot air. Cool air will rush in and bring us down." He grimaced, giving the red rope another hard yank. "Vent's more stubborn than Lukas's," he grunted. "Ah, there we go. Bend your knees and brace your back against the basket. Hold onto the handle."

Briar dully followed his instructions, bending, bracing, and grabbing a rope handle fastened to the inside of the gondola. If her bladder held, it would be a miracle.

"It'll get bumpy, but hang in there. Whatever you

do, do not jump out!"

He'd read her mind.

"A sudden loss of weight would cause the balloon to take off again—with me still inside," he explained.

She considered jumping anyway. But Derby wouldn't stay in the air forever. And when he landed, he'd find her. And he'd be furious. She glanced at him, the glazed look in his eyes making her mind up for her. She wasn't a fast runner. She couldn't out sprint a crazed maniac.

Besides, she still had to contend with the plane and the ominous black car. Derby might be insane, but at least she knew him. Entering the unknown with a crazy person was less scary than facing it alone.

At first the descent was undetectable, but she could feel it now. She watched the small jet increase in size as distance closed between the plane and balloon.

"Hold on!" Derby shouted.

Briar squeezed her eyes shut as the basket crashed against the ground and toppled over. For what seemed like miles, the gondola slid on its side, scraping the earth, the wicker creaking and groaning like an old man tumbling down the stairs. Finally, the movement stopped.

Afraid to open her eyes, she lay motionless inside the basket, knees drawn up to her elbows, hands still grasping the rope-grip.

"Whoo-whee! Now that's what I call a landing." Derby's voice pulled her eyelids open. "Sorry if I rattled you, Miss Briar." He knelt and gently pried her fingers from the handle. "You'll be all right once you get on your feet." He tugged her wrists, uncurling her from her fetal position and hauling her from the basket.

She stole a glance downward, astonished her pants were still dry.

The double-slam of car doors jerked her gaze toward the approach of two tall, sunglassed men, biceps bulging under their perfectly pressed suit coats.

Her bladder screamed against the sudden cringe of her insides. She wondered how much more the poor organ could take.

"Morning, gentlemen." Derby tipped his ball cap, amazingly, still stuck to his head.

The men loomed. Silent, and without expression.

"Not too talkative, are you?" Derby peeled off his gloves and stuffed them into his back pocket.

Briar gave a startled yelp as the taller of the two giants moved toward her, wrapping his large hand around her elbow.

The other man reached into his jacket lapel and stepped up to Derby.

Briar yelped louder, prompting a rough squeeze from the hand at her elbow. Fear pounded in her ears. The man had a gun. Derby would be shot dead right in front of her.

"This is for you," the man said to Derby.

Briar shut her eyes and prayed. She trembled, waiting for the click of the trigger, the echo of the bullet.

It didn't come. She peeked through one crinkled eye. Derby was thumbing through a stack of bills. She exhaled. The man pulled an envelope of cash, not a gun. She hadn't seen paper money in years—let alone a pile like the one Derby held. Cash was untraceable. That must be the reason. But spending paper in a plastic world was bound to raise suspicion.

"That'll do fine. Thanks, gentlemen." Derby folded

the thick stack and shoved it into the front pocket of his jeans, poking it down a few times for good measure. "Take care of Miss Briar. She's a good girl. And a good friend of mine."

Briar ground her teeth. Friend? Was he kidding? Friends didn't turn friends over to the enemy. She narrowed her eyes.

He looked at the ground. "'Least she used to be."

"We're done." The man standing in front of him said, turning away. "Make yourself disappear."

Derby looked up. "Hey, wait a minute." The man turned back around and Derby tipped back his head, meeting his gaze. "I need a car—"

The man's lip twitched as though he might laugh.

Derby glanced at his surroundings. "—or at least a ride back to my truck."

"Sorry, fella. Not in Maxwell Brown's instructions." The man opened the door of the black car and slid inside.

The jet's engines roared to life, rattling every bone in her body.

"Time to make our exit." Steered by the elbow, Briar walked shakily to the aircraft and climbed the steps. Ushered into one of eight leather seats she sat down and stared out the circular window. The black car pulled away, Derby's gaze trailing after it.

"Seatbelt," elbow-man stated.

With unfeeling fingers, Briar clasped the buckle. The plane seemed to stand on tiptoe, sending her heart into her esophagus.

"Breathe," his strong voice commanded. "It's a two-and-a-half-hour flight. You may as well relax."

She sucked in a breath and glued her eyes to the windowpane. Derby waved limply beside his deflated balloon until he disappeared.

~*~

Briar crossed and uncrossed her legs. Though surprisingly plush, the small plane was obviously not equipped with bathroom facilities.

"Uncomfortable?" elbow-man asked.

She bit the inside of her cheek and shook her head no. She couldn't tell the guy she needed to tinkle or, more realistically, downpour.

"We're almost there."

A mixture of relief and dread twisted through her body—relief because she'd surely find bathroom facilities, dread because she'd find them at the ARC.

"By the way, happy birthday."

"Thanks," she said through clenched teeth. She crossed her legs again. One more minute and she'd be seeing through yellow eyeballs.

"You know, you're very fortunate."

Fortunate? Had the world gone mad, or just her?

"At midnight, the OLG would have shown up at the lab to collect you. They don't take Commandment breaches lightly. For Caster Stone to serve you up on a platter saved you some very serious repercussions."

"I'm not in breach of The Commandment. I was scheduled to receive Stone's Abstergent today, following the balloon ride."

"Caster mentioned a Bible and an abandoned ankle monitor as well. As I said, you're lucky that guy's on your side. If he'd gone straight to the OLG with the information, instead of the ARC's Director, Maxwell Brown, you'd be arrested for treason. And the OLG sees to it that Commandment breakers get extra special treatment at the ARC—if you get my drift."

A hot tear slid down Briar's cheek. She was furious. And she was drowning. She pressed her hands to her aching abdomen. Things were so much better when elbow-man kept his big mouth shut.

~*~

A zillion times smoother than the hot air balloon landing, touchdown was, nonetheless, torturous. Every jiggle and bump zapped through Briar's middle, nauseating her. All the deep breathing in the world couldn't dull the blanket of pins and needles that was her skin.

The landing strip was close to the ARC, Briar could tell from a mile away. The fortress of a building boasted its name in gigantic letters at least six feet tall, alongside the profile of a roaring lion. The place was a prison, complete with armed guards. The windows on the top three floors even had bars. Thick and tall, the building looked nothing like the health spa/massage therapy/fancy hotel image represented on the countless ARC commercials she'd watched over the years.

Her mother's worried features flooded Briar's mind. She'd been scared to death Briar would end up at the ARC. And here she was. Suddenly she wanted her mother more than anything else in the world. She'd even take the ankle monitor back—clamp it on herself, and throw away the key.

If she could only go home.

"Let's go." Elbow-man was at it again, tugging her from her chair by the crook of her arm. "The shuttle will take us to the front doors."

He led her down the airplane steps, across the

tarmac, and to the waiting vehicle. On a shiny black bus that seated at least twenty, they were the only passengers.

Elbow-man walked her to the doors and showed his credentials to the guard. He pressed his finger to a device mounted to the front of the building and ordered Briar to do the same. The doors unlocked with a mechanical click.

"This is as far as I go, kid. You'll have to make new friends, now." He turned and walked away.

A smock-clad...nurse? Orderly?—She had no idea how to address the woman—appeared and opened the door. Briar didn't wait for her to speak. "I really, *really* have to go to the bathroom." The words rushed out all at once.

"Follow me."

Briar stepped so closely behind she clipped the back of the woman's sensible shoes more than once.

Like a spa or a fancy hotel, Derby had said. He'd been wrong. Sure, the place had some fancy furnishings and nice things, but there was a sadness she could almost touch. An oppression. A wave of despair washed over her, thick and heavy in the pine disinfectant.

Death. *Clean* death.

She was being ridiculous. The place was scary because it was new to her. She'd never been there before. The least she could do was to judge her surroundings sanely, not through the distorted eyes of fear—and bladder urgency.

Besides, as soon as the personnel talked to Lukas, this would all get squared away.

What would Lukas say, when he found out what Caster had done? What would he do?

She glanced as they marched passed a virtual clock on the wall. Lukas was probably at the drop off point right now, leaning against Derby's truck, waiting for her return. How long would he wait?

Or...what if he abandoned her on purpose? Her heart stopped beating at the thought. She feared she'd faint or fall down, dead. Would the lady in the black smock with the long-stride even notice? She'd sped up, and now had at least a six-foot lead.

This was all Lukas's fault. Why hadn't he given her the abstergent? She'd practically begged him to do it—and begging was nightmarishly hard for her. But he hadn't done it. He'd always had an excuse not to.

Maybe he wanted her here as much as Reid and Caster did.

Briar plowed full-force into the nurse. She hadn't seen the woman stop walking.

"Restroom." She held the back of her hand to what appeared to be an iridescent blanket of light, dissolving it before Briar's eyes.

Briar ran through the opening and into the first stall. "Thank you," she whispered. She'd thank the woman later, right now she was thanking God.

20

Lukas walked into the lab, worry grinding against his brain like sandpaper. Where was Derby? He'd waited beside his truck in the parking lot for nearly an hour, but he'd never shown. He wasn't answering his cuff, either. Had something gone wrong? He shook his head, clearing from his mind the hundred and one images of how a hot air balloon could crash, deflate, and explode.

He'd come back to the lab to talk to Reid. She'd known about Briar's hot air balloon ride—what else did she know? Maybe Derby had additional plans that Lukas wasn't aware of, and shared those plans with Reid. The balloon ride was supposed to be a relatively brief flight—no more than an hour, total. The only landing was to be back at the parking lot where they'd started. They'd been gone way too long.

Down the hallway, Lukas spotted Reid unlocking her apartment door. "Reid." He quickened his stride. "Where's Briar?"

She raised an eyebrow. "I am not your lab rat's keeper." She snatched her key from the lock and stepped inside the doorway.

"Tell me." Lukas followed, standing on the threshold. "Now."

"I like it when you're forceful." A smirk twisted her red lips. "Please. Come all the way in." She took a step back and gazed at him from under mascara-laden lashes. "Let's…talk."

"If you value your job, you'll do all the talking

while I stand right here."

She dragged her gaze to the ceiling and back. "What's the matter? I'm not desperate enough?"

"Quite the opposite."

Her smirk hardened to a straight line. "What makes you think I know where she is?"

Lukas balled his hands into fists then crossed his arms so he wouldn't be tempted to use them. "I'm through playing games. Tell me what you know, or pack your bags."

"Your brother told me you'd stoop to this—threatening my job because of that *unlevel*. I'd hoped he was wrong. Well, I've got news for you, Lukas. This was all his idea, not mine. He's probably informed your father by now, as well."

Hot lead filled Lukas's stomach. "What are you talking about?"

"He couldn't very well let you wait forever, could he? She's eighteen years old, Lukas. If you were planning to administer the abstergent, you would've done it by now. I tried to warn you, but you refused to listen. Instead, you dragged your feet, putting all of us in danger, including your precious lab rat."

Lukas licked his lips. No. Caster couldn't have sent Briar to the ARC. This conversation was a ploy. A bluff Reid and his brother conjured up to make sure he was still onboard with the project. A last-ditch effort to ensure he would go through with Briar's injection. "The procedure is scheduled to take place this afternoon. Dr. Randall Fuller will be arriving from Baltimore in less than three hours to perform the injection."

"No, he isn't. Caster cancelled his flight. You would have never gone through with it anyway. You would have dreamed up some last-minute excuse not to do it."

Rage replaced the blood in Lukas's veins, and fury pulsed through his arteries. A growing mass of hatred thumped inside his ribcage.

"Your brother cares too much about Stone Labs to allow it to be undermined by ARC officials. What you've been working on is no secret to them—no matter what Rosen or anybody else says. They have their all-knowing eye on this place. And it's not as if they're cheering for the success of your abstergent—the serum that will put them out of business. They're waiting for you to mess up—which you've done by allowing Briar to remain unlevel. By harboring her, you've turned all of us into accessories. Caster did what had to be done. What you didn't have the guts to do yourself."

"You're fired." Lukas turned away, making long strides down the hallway. Refusing to give her the satisfaction of seeing him run, he waited until he rounded the corner before sprinting the rest of the way to the exit.

Roxy barked twice, catching up with him as he reached the door. "Sorry girl, no time to play. I'm going to get Briar." He gave the dog a quick pat on the head.

She panted, her big tongue lolling from what appeared to be a huge smile.

~*~

Lukas screeched to a halt and threw open the car door. "Where is she?" he yelled as he strode up the cobblestone walkway leading to the over-extravagant front veranda. His brother's fancier-than-thou lifestyle made Lukas want to puke. In what messed-up universe did a rotten to the core, heartless excuse for a man get to surround himself with such splendor? Caster Stone was the biggest joke on the planet. Worst of all, the joke wasn't one bit funny.

Lukas ignored the bell and beat both fists against the mahogany door. "Where is she?" He repeated, his yell echoing through the flower-filled terrace. The unsuitable beauty of the plants amplified his wrath, and the temptation to rip up a miniature rose bush by the roots nearly overtook him. It wasn't the thorns that stopped him—he would've welcomed the pain. It was the thought of frightening his nephew. He loved Gatlin, and wouldn't hurt him for anything in the world.

The thought of the little boy calmed Lukas's temper, slightly. No need to behave like a monster—he'd leave that to Caster. For all he knew, Gatlin could be on a chair staring through the peephole.

Lukas planted his shoe on the threshold as the door opened a crack.

"Oh, hello, Lukas." Lira, the housekeeper-slash-nanny stood with her hand on her chest. "You gave me a scare."

"I need to see Caster." He knew he should apologize, but didn't want to go too soft just yet. He'd make nice after he saw his brother.

She threw a quick glance over her shoulder.

He followed her gaze. "I'm coming in."

Lira stepped to the side, clearing his way to the foyer. "He's in his study. I'll take Gatlin outside to the play area, to give you some privacy."

"Thank you." He walked through the entryway.

"I'm sorry I startled you."

Lukas stepped quickly through the great room and down the hallway.

Caster opened the study door before Lukas was able to knock.

"Ah, come in. I've been expecting you." Caster motioned his brother into the room.

"What have you done? Where is Briar?"

"You really don't know? I thought surely Reid had squealed by now."

"She said you had Briar taken to the ARC. I wanted to hear it from you before I decide a course of action."

"Course of action?" Caster laughed. "It's too late for that, brother. Your course of action should have been to administer the abstergent to Briar before her eighteenth birthday."

Lukas stepped toward Caster until the toes of their shoes collided. "As you well know, the neurosurgeon was scheduled to administer the abstergent this afternoon."

"I've freed up his schedule."

Lukas drew back his fist. A born nurturer, never in his life had he wanted to hear the sound of bones breaking—until now.

Father would strip him of the lab. In an instant, everything he'd worked for would be gone. Did he really want to afford Caster that joy?

His forearm trembled. "You're not worth it," he growled, dropping his arm.

"You didn't follow protocol. The OLG was applying pressure. Father gave you a timeframe, and you exceeded it. I wasn't about to let the lab go down for your emotionally saturated mistake." Caster took a step back. "In addition, I couldn't risk her being around Gatlin. She had a *Bible,* remember? What if Gatlin's SAP levels have depleted? What if some of that venom soaked in?"

"Don't be ridiculous. Gatlin's fleshcard would alert you of a decreased SAP level. You're paranoid."

Caster's gray eyes flashed silver. "I'll be sure to pass that along to Father."

"By all means, tell Father. But you'll have to beat me to it. The next conversation I have will be with him. How are you planning to explain the cancellation of Dr. Fuller's flight from Baltimore? His plane ticket to Sickle Ridge is evidence that I was going through with the procedure. I'm convinced Dr. Fuller wasn't thrilled about the cancellation, either. He's a talented neurosurgeon and a busy man. He and Father are good friends. There's a strong possibility he's already called him to complain."

"Don't try to intimidate me, Lukas. You're no good at it. When I explain how close you've grown to the test subject, Father will understand why I was forced to do what I did. He will demand you find another test subject—perhaps ask for my help in the matter."

Lukas curled his hands in front of his brother's face. "If you knew how badly I want to wrap my hands around your neck right now, you'd shut your mouth. I'll have you arrested for this. You are an accessory to kidnapping. Briar is a human being. You had no legal reason to retain her against her will."

"Actually, I did. Briar turned eighteen without being injected with abstergent, and without checking into the ARC. You let your heart get in the way of your head's work. All that time needlessly wasted on an unnecessary antidote—admit it, you were stalling."

"Creating an antidote is as important as creating a treatment. Every respectable scientist knows that." He squared his shoulders. "But I guess that's why I work inside the lab and you don't."

"Briar is exactly where she should be."

"She's not staying."

Caster drew a breath in through his nose, the air expanding his chest. "You're too worked up over this. We both know the ARC is just a government-mandated vacation resort. Briar will be fine. Excellent, actually. Her resistance will be diagnosed, and she will receive proper treatment—intense, custom designed therapy."

"Enough. I'll deal with you later—so will the authorities."

"Please let me finish." Caster looked into Lukas's eyes.

Something in his gaze made Lukas wonder if his brother was mentally sound.

"While Briar is receiving treatment at the ARC, you can finalize the abstergent. You already have the ideal test subject. Right here in this house."

"Lira? You're not making sense, you know the subject must be unlevel." Lukas stepped around his brother, making a point to bump shoulders. "I don't have time for your nonsense."

"Not Lira. Gatlin."

Lukas stopped at the doorframe, frozen in place. He couldn't have heard his brother correctly. "What did you say?"

"Think about it. Your serum will expire in a matter of hours. If Gatlin becomes the subject, you can administer it right away. You've already done all of the preliminary testing on Briar. You know how the brain will react. Merely cut the dosage down to a corresponding level."

Slowly, Lukas turned to face his brother, terrified of the lack of sanity he might perceive in his eyes. "You are insane. Gatlin is a child. His brain has a great deal of developing to do. I still can't authenticate with one hundred percent certainty how the abstergent will affect a human—that was the point of having Briar."

"You know enough. Believe it or not, Lukas, I have the utmost confidence in your abilities." His eyes, more silver than gray, held Lukas's gaze without blinking. "Please. Inject Gatlin with the abstergent." He placed a hand on Lukas's wrist.

"You've lost your mind." He shook free of Caster's grasp. "Keep your phone on. Expect a call from Rosen."

Lukas walked briskly through the house, muttering to himself. What had he done? He'd had the antidote ready for weeks. Why hadn't he given Briar the abstergent? Because he'd been afraid, that's why.

He disarmed his car and slid behind the wheel. Briar had…something. Something others didn't. He'd waited because, deep down, he didn't want to be responsible for destroying that special something. Part of him wondered, if there really was a God, what would He think of Stone's Abstergent? And what would He think of Lukas—the creator of a serum that dissolved all spiritual content from the brain? Most assuredly, the thoughts wouldn't be positive. For some reason, the scenario bothered Lukas.

What—did he believe in God now? Was that even possible, since his Agathi were numb? That was the affect Briar had on him. She made him want to believe.

Either that, or Reid was right, and his fleshcard was on the fritz. Maybe his SAP level was low, and he didn't realize it. Maybe he truly did need his own Agathi checked out. Regardless, he would get Briar back. He couldn't help but think that would please God—if there was one.

But how would he do it? Waltz into the ARC and take her? That was a laugh. No one got within two hundred yards of the place without proper clearance. There was no way.

But there *had* to be a way. There were laws against kidnapping. Technically, Briar didn't have to enter the ARC until midnight, therefore she was kidnapped. Even if the place was as plush as a high-end day spa, what Caster had done was still kidnapping. Besides, Briar wasn't the day spa type. That was more Reid's thing. Briar belonged…Briar belonged…with him.

He pressed the gas pedal to the floor and reversed from Caster's driveway.

He had to find Derby.

21

"Ouch!" Briar snatched her left hand from the male nurse.

"Uh-uh," the man said, laying the fleshcard gun on a silver tray. "You're not finished yet." He again grasped her hand, placing it into the slot of a plastic machine. "Time to get your tattoo."

Briar cringed, but felt nothing. A few seconds later, he slid her hand from the opening. The bronze profile of a roaring lion emblazoned the back of her hand directly over the fleshcard she'd received. She stared at it, unease worming through her stomach. It reminded her of the mark Granna used to speak of from the book of Revelation.

He squinted, inspecting the tattoo, and nodded. "Perfect. Cleo will show you to your room now." He gestured to a woman with braided hair and dark eyes who stood by Briar's chair.

"Come with me, sugar."

Briar stood and followed Cleo. She couldn't keep her eyes from the tattoo, staring at it even as she walked down the hallway.

"You're liable to march right into a wall staring at that thing. Besides, it's always a good idea to pay attention to where you're going, so that you can find your way around later. The ARC is a big place. Seems even bigger when you're lost. Happened to me all the time when I first started working here."

Briar dropped her hand to her side for a few seconds before lifting it again to gaze at the tattoo.

"Here you are. Room six seventeen." Cleo nodded toward a slice of rainbow that must've been the door. "Raise your tattoo to dissolve the drape." She lifted her hand, instructing Briar to turn the back of her hand toward the iridescent shimmer in the doorway.

A gentle surge warmed Briar's hand as she followed Cleo's directions. The rainbow curtain disappeared, revealing an opening to the room. She turned her hand and gasped, surprised to see the bronze lion glowing.

"Don't be afraid," Cleo soothed. "It's harmless. Just the fleshcard lighting up under your skin. Lets you know it's working. It also makes a handy flashlight when it's dark."

Briar tried to smile, but managed only a weak tug from one corner of her mouth.

"Come inside and meet your roommate."

Roommate? Briar froze in place. The possibility of sharing a room hadn't occurred to her. Then again, until a few hours ago, being at the ARC hadn't occurred to her—nor had being on an airplane or in a hot air balloon. Things that never before occurred to her had somehow taken over her life.

The woman nudged Briar into the amethyst-hued room—the same exact shade as her new clothing.

"Briar, meet Ms. Harper Ross." Cleo placed a hand on Briar's shoulder, turning her to face an elderly woman in a plastic chair. "Ms. Ross, this is Briar Lee."

"Come closer, Briar. Let me make your acquaintance." The elderly woman stretched out a slightly trembling hand.

Briar gave the woman's hand a gentle squeeze, loving the feel of her weathered fingers. It was like touching Granna Grace again. "Nice to meet you, Ms.

Ross."

"Call me Harper."

She smiled, and Briar's heart swelled. Either nostalgia had gotten the best of her, or Harper's resemblance to Briar's grandmother was uncanny. If it weren't for the woman's coffee-tinted skin, they could've passed for twins—or at least sisters. They even shared the same faded blue eyes.

"Nice to meet you, Harper." Tempted to hold on forever, she gently released the woman's hand.

Cleo walked between them, jarring Briar back to reality. She motioned to the other side of the room. "Your cot and closet are over here." She pointed to another iridescent drape. "The toilet and sink you'll share is in there. Hold your fleshcard to it, as you did when you entered the room. Same applies to all of the drapes in the facility. Your fleshcard will let you into any place you have clearance."

"How will I know if I have clearance?"

"Without clearance, your fleshcard won't light up. And the drape won't dissolve. It will stay firmly in place." She raised her brows, making her large eyes even larger. "I don't suggest attempting to trick the sensor or trying to force your way through a drape." Holding Briar's gaze, she drew in a breath and held it a moment. "It never ends well." She shook her head.

Harper chuckled.

"I guess that's about it," Cleo said. "Any questions, Briar?"

"When will I begin treatment?"

"I'm afraid I can't answer that one. They'll assign you a physician shortly. The doctor will give you an evaluation and go over your treatment options." She stepped toward the door. "Anything else?" She turned her gaze to Harper. "How about you, Ms. Ross? Do you need anything?"

"You'd better narrow that question down, girl. Else I'll be asking you to bring me a King James Bible. Large print."

Briar's heart lodged in her throat as Cleo glanced toward the draped doorway. "Hush, Ms. Ross. Don't say things like that. Haven't you learned your lesson?" Cleo whispered.

"I'll quit learning when I'm dead."

Cleo rolled her eyes.

Briar wished her grandmother would've known Harper Ross. She would've loved her.

"Dinner will be ready in a couple of hours. An orderly will escort you both to the dining room. After dinner, you'll be escorted to the community showers. Have a good evening, ladies." She held her hand to the translucent drape and stepped from the room.

Harper turned her attention to Briar. "I thought she'd never leave." Those faded blue eyes, so much like Granna's, locked on hers. "Are you a Christian?"

Briar swallowed, the dry click echoing through the silent room. She used to be. She'd loved the Lord more than anything and had trusted him above all else. But did she still?

"I—I hope so."

The old woman pointed a shaky finger toward the other chair in the room. "Drag that chair over and sit down. Let me tell you what you've gotten yourself into."

~*~

Briar thought she'd been scared before. Now she

was terrified.

Her trip from Oklahoma to Stone Labs? That was nothing. The flight to the ARC with an exploding bladder and elbow-man breathing down her neck? A child's carnival ride.

But this—this was the stuff sci-fi movies were made of. And horror flicks. What Harper spoke about was the worst of both rolled into one.

"This here's another one." Harper tapped a twisted finger against a small scar below her ear. "Called it a lymph node…something or other. 'Bout six years since that experiment."

Briar closed her eyes for a moment, wondering if she'd blinked for the past hour. Experiments—the kind her mother ranted about—were *real*? At the beginning of the conversation, she'd wondered if Harper might have a touch of dementia. But the woman's sharp wit and even sharper memory squelched the possibility right away. The lady knew what she was talking about.

"They match the old up with the young, like they did with me and you. It works better that way. The young can help the old get around, so the orderlies don't have to work as hard. The old help to calm down the young. Except in this case." She offered Briar a slow wink. "Ouch!" Her hand moved just above her prominent collar bone. "See that tendon jumping around in my neck? Happens every few hours. Been that way since my first treatment—ten years ago." She rubbed the spasm and cringed. "Hurts like a booger."

"We have to find a way out of here," Briar blurted. She grabbed Harper's hand then lightened her grip, afraid of hurting her.

"There's no way out. Best thing to do is hold onto your faith. You have to fight to keep it, but they can't strip you of it. Lord knows they don't show any mercy with your dignity—that's the first thing to go."

A fresh lump joined the others in Briar's throat. "I'm not sure I have faith anymore. I spent a lot of time wishing it away, so that I wouldn't have to deal with anything."

"Maybe you should've spent that time building your faith up, instead. But it's never too late to start. To keep faith, sometimes the person you have to fight is yourself." She patted Briar's hand and then released it. "This old girl's had plenty of faith battles, especially in this place—many times it's been Harper verses Harper. But God gives us the victory, Briar. Even when we are at war with ourselves. Do you understand?"

Briar nodded and wiped a hot tear trailing her face.

"A Christian needs doubt like a bald man needs a hairbrush. It's always there, lurking on the dressing table, hoping the man will forget he doesn't need it and pick it up. That's why every single day I have to take the time to feel the quickening. The Holy Spirit moving inside me is what keeps me going. I rejoice when I feel the Spirit of God move within this body that's worn and dying. Reminds me of the old days, before The Commandment, when I'd read my Bible and those old stories would get my Spirit to dancing. I'd have to shout to the rafters, no matter who was around." Harper raised her hands high and smiled at the ceiling.

Briar squeezed her eyes shut and concentrated on the quickening. It was no use, she couldn't feel anything. If she really tried, she thought she might sense what used to be the Holy Spirit, dried and shriveled inside her. Maybe she didn't need Lukas's abstergent after all. She'd starved the Spirit of God to death all on her own.

~*~

"Granna passed away when I was seven," Briar said, finishing up a brief memoir about her grandmother. "Three days before she was scheduled to have her first SAP injection."

"Sounds like your granny was a wonderful, God fearing woman," Harper said.

Briar wiped her eyes, wondering if she had any tears left. "She was. And even though I've just met you, you already remind me so much of her. I know you'd have been great friends."

"I'm sorry she's gone, but it was such a blessing she passed before her first SAP injection. Praise the Lord your granny never had to feel that venom slithering through her brain. Even after all I've been through, I'm still so very thankful my mind rejected that poison. And you should be, too."

"I am." She smiled. "If I was responsive to SAP, I'd have never met you."

A strange sound, something like a digital wind chime, startled Briar.

"They're here to take us to dinner."

A short-haired orderly in the regulation black smock appeared where the drape had been. "Meal time," she stated.

Briar helped Harper from the chair and helped position her behind her walker.

"Don't get the wrong idea, now." She took a step, pushing the aluminum contraption along before her. "Walkers are for invalids. This here's no walker. It's a four-legged cane."

"Got it." Briar nodded.

The orderly stood outside the doorway, face blank. She led them through the sleek hallways to the dining room.

"Here's our spot." Harper stopped beside a purple, rectangular shaped table and tugged at a matching chair.

The orderly stepped away as Briar moved Harper's walker to the side and helped her sit down.

Briar glanced around at the other tables and chairs of various tint filling the large dining hall. "I take it we're all color coded?"

Harper nodded. "We're amethyst. Amethyst clothing, amethyst living quarters, amethyst furniture, amethyst dining tables and chairs. Everything we touch is purple."

A black-smocked attendant wheeling a cart approached the table, handing each of them a purple cup filled with something cold to drink.

Harper chuckled. "See there? Purple glasses. Plates are purple too. So are the forks and spoons. By now, I'm so saturated, I dream in purple."

"Good thing I like purple," Briar said.

Harper raised her eyebrows. "You won't for long."

"Do the colors serve a purpose?"

Harper sniffed the liquid in her cup and set it back onto the table. "Makes it easier for them to keep track of us. The fleshcards track what's happening on the inside, and the color coding helps them decipher what's happening on the outside."

Harper pointed to a group of women in red clothing seated in the neighboring section. "If one of the rubies falls down in a seizure, they'll know immediately what experimental drug or procedure was performed on her. All of the reds receive the same treatment on the same day. They'll also know to watch the other reds, in case another one has a reaction. That's the way it is with all of the colors."

Briar gazed at the women, some young like her, others elderly like Harper, several in between. Some appeared healthy, others not so much. More than a few displayed obvious handicaps. All seemed to travel by twos—younger with older—as Harper had said.

"So many colors… I feel like I've fallen into a giant bag of fruit chews." Briar widened her eyes at the thickening stream of women flooding the room. "All of those *scrubs*." She shivered. "You'd think the ARC could display a little more imagination."

"Keeping it simple," Harper said. "No buttons or zippers. No specifics for women or men. All the clothing is the same, just different sizes."

"Where are the men?"

"The east wing, in a color-coded nightmare of their own. Experimentation is much harsher for the men. The so called 'treatment' is more aggressive." She pushed her cup to the side, and with a *you'll thank me later* expression, did the same to Briar's. "There are far less men than women at the ARC. Only one quarter of the population is male. And, in case you're wondering, females are *female* here, and males are *male*. Seems to be the only biblical principal the ARC adheres to. No switching genders back and forth and nothing in between. We're segregated by our DNA and sorted by the color of our scrubs."

"Why are the men so outnumbered?"

"The powers that be are trying to figure that out. One theory is that traditional female roles such as motherhood cause women to be more susceptible to the 'god concept.' That believing in an Almighty nurturer is triggered hormonally—a byproduct of the mothering instinct. The hormonal-driven notion of God strengthens the Agathi, enabling them to resist SAP." She narrowed her eyes. "You and I both know that's hogwash."

Briar smiled and thanked the woman who set a purple tray before her, and wondered why. This place was the enemy—a den of the devil. Why was she always so darned nice to everyone? She leaned forward and sniffed the colorless food. "Smells like disinfectant."

"Sodium hypochlorite."

"What's that? Some kind of high-powered preservative?" She poked at a pallid orange wedge that jiggled like gelatin.

"Bleach. They bleach the food, to get out anything that's good for the brain. They're trying to starve our Agathi."

Briar dropped her fork to the tray.

"The only reason they keep this poison in actual food form, is so they can tell the human rights groups and the family members that we're served vegetables, fruit, and protein. They can provide proof of the pantry's inventory and take pre-bleach photographs. Otherwise, we'd be swallowing pills three times daily, and they wouldn't need this kaleidoscope of a dining hall."

The older woman couldn't be serious. Briar leaned closer and raised an eyebrow. "Rumors?"

"Nope. Heard it right from the horse's mouth. One of the cooks developed a conscience and refused to soak the strawberries in the bleach bath. She left the kitchen, marched to the middle of the cafeteria, and climbed on a table there in the blue section—still wearing her hairnet and plastic apron." Harper pointed a crooked finger toward the center of the room. "She stood on that table and said the OLG made the cooks bleach the food to diminish the nutrients, and that she wasn't doing it anymore—told us all about it at the top of her lungs. She warned us not to eat another bite, and promised to have the ARC investigated. Then she announced her resignation."

"Wow." Briar gazed at the blue table, picturing the scenario. "Did she follow through with her threats?"

The older woman shook her head. "The OLG would never let that happen."

Briar frowned. "Where is she now? Does anybody know?"

Harper squinted and craned her neck. "That's her, right over there in the orange section. The one with the buzz cut."

Every cell in Briar's body iced over. "She's—a resident?"

"Yep. Hasn't stepped foot in the kitchen since, that I know of."

"And you're certain that's the same woman—the cook?" It couldn't be true. "No offense, but are you sure you're remembering correctly?"

Harper turned her gaze slowly away and whispered into the ear of the old woman seated next to her.

The woman threw a cautious glance toward the orange section and nodded. "Oh, yes. That's her," she whispered. "The cook that told us there was bleach in the food." She nodded, her eyes bright blue sapphires in a sea of wrinkles. "Doesn't talk much these days. Doesn't climb up on tabletops, either."

A middle-aged woman nudged the older lady's shoulder. "Hush, Maddie. Don't talk about it. You'll get us into trouble," she said in a harsh whisper. "Ms. Ross, please, don't encourage her." She gave Harper a stern glare.

"I apologize," Harper said. She turned to Briar, wearing an *I told you so* smirk. "The dinner roll and butter are safe tonight." She gave the tray a sniff. "But don't touch the fruit or the beans. And definitely don't drink the water."

Briar smeared the small pat of butter on top of her roll. "You can tell the contaminated food from the safe food. You know what goes on in the men's wing. And something tells me that's just the tip of the iceberg." She set the bread down and leaned toward Harper. "How do you know so much?"

Harper's gaze wandered the room then returned to Briar's. "Let's just say I stumbled across a portal that led to a whole lot of secrets. When the opportunity presents itself, I'll show you."

Harper winked, and nostalgia tugged Briar's heart with a thousand strings. She felt as if Granna Grace were seated directly across from her. She nibbled her bread, unable to peel her gaze from those faded blue eyes, now lit with a mischievous sparkle.

"Attention, please. Dinner's over. It's time for showers. You know the drill," an orderly called from a black megaphone with the ARC's bronze lion emblazoned on the side. "Blue table, dump your trays and line up, followed by purple, and so on."

Briar deposited the still-full cups, napkins, and silverware onto her tray, tucked Harper's tray underneath, and made her way to the trashcan. "Let me help you," she said, returning in time to ease

Harper to her feet. She maneuvered the walker in front of her. "Lead on," she said, gesturing for the older lady to take the first step.

"All right, but you'd better keep up." Harper gave an ornery grin and took a slow-motion step toward the line forming in the doorway.

~*~

"...twenty-three, twenty-four. Stop!" an attendant ordered, halting the line at the entryway, behind Briar. Harper, Briar, and the previous twenty-two women were ushered to a long hallway where they were told to remove their scrubs and toss them into a gigantic hamper on wheels.

"You can't be serious." Briar locked eyes with the stocky attendant with the spikey hairdo.

"Dead serious," she answered, narrowing her gaze.

"This is outrageous. You can't possibly expect us to strip naked in public." Briar crossed her arms. "What if we refuse?"

"We? Looks like you're the only one refusing."

Briar glanced quickly to the left and right. With the exception of her and the orderly, everyone was naked. Heat crawled up her neck, catching her cheeks and ears on fire. With rubber arms, she pulled her top over her head then yanked down her pants. She stooped, gathering her apparel from the floor as well as Harper's, then chucked the clothes into the hamper. She'd never been so humiliated. Not even Reid's public thrashing of her at the hot air balloon ball came close.

Two female attendants supervised the naked pilgrimage from the changing hall to the shower area.

"How did you get undressed so fast?" Briar whispered to Harper as she helped scoot her walker along the concrete floor.

Harper shrugged. "Practice. From back in my younger days."

"Don't tell me you were a stripper," Briar frowned and blinked at the same time.

The old woman cackled and shook her head. "Employee at a children's theme park. I played three different characters, and wore three different costumes. Earned the nickname Hurry-up Harper."

Briar grinned from ear to ear. "You're into cosplay! I should've known."

"All on deck!" One of the attendants blared through her megaphone. Briar helped Harper to the center of a huge floor tiled with large black squares containing the ARC lion's outline. She scanned the walls and ceiling, searching for a showerhead, but saw none.

"Choose a tile and stay on it. Soapy water spray will last one minute, rinse water will last two. Ready. One...two...three."

Briar cringed, expecting a cold blast. Instead, warm, sudsy water fell like rain from an invisible water source. She squeezed her eyes shut too late, anticipating the burn that never came. How thoughtful for the ARC to provide tear-free soap to the women they forced to strip naked and cluster-bathe. The people in charge must be absolute angels.

The clear water began to fall, rinsing the soap from Briar's hair and face. She tried not to stare at the other women, but as if by magnet, her gaze was drawn to the scars that puckered the skin of so many. Everywhere she looked, valleys of pink or pale silver ran down spines, trailed over necks, and sliced across abdomens. And Harper...beautiful, sweet, Harper. Hers were the worst.

Briar turned from the scalpel cuts crisscrossing the old woman's spine like mountain switchbacks. Tears hotter than the rinse water stung her eyes. How could this be happening? They were human beings. Flesh, blood, and bone. Their only crime—a predisposed ability to believe in God. Something no one had any control over.

No...something *she* had no control over.

Briar's thoughts ran a marathon back to Stone Labs.

True, there was absolutely nothing she could do about her SAP-resistant Agathi. But *someone* could. Lukas Stone sure as blazes could have. He'd had the power to heal her completely, if he'd wanted to. Yet here she stood, naked and soaking wet in a room full of scarred women, wondering when it would be her turn to go under the knife.

~*~

"Nice outfit," Briar teased as she helped Harper onto her cot.

The older woman clicked her tongue. "Wish I could say the same for yours. That purple leaves something to be desired." She grimaced as Briar lifted her legs onto the thin mattress. "Can you help me onto my side?"

"Sure." She fluffed the flat pillow as best she could and carefully tugged Harper's shoulder and hip, rolling her gently. "That OK?"

"Very nice. Thank you." She nodded her head on

the pillow. "Oh—one more thing, if you don't mind. Pour a little water into that plastic cup and hand it here."

Briar grasped the bottle of water from the nightstand, unscrewed the lid, and filled the purple cup halfway. "Here you are," she said, offering her a sip.

The old woman put her hands to her mouth and plopped something into the cup. "The little tablets are in the nightstand drawer."

Briar peered in the cup as she returned it to the bedside table. Harper's dentures smiled at her. "My, what nice teeth you have," she teased.

"Thank you." Harper gave a wide, toothless grin.

Briar found the effervescent tablets and dropped one into the cup. She spread a blanket that was little more than a sheet over her friend's twisted form, and then slipped into her own cot. It felt too early for bedtime, but she had nothing better to do. She'd barely covered up before the lights switched off. "What happened?" She shot straight up in the bed.

"Automatic timer. It must be nine o'clock," Harper answered from the dark.

"Lights out at nine?" Briar settled her head back on the hard pillow. "Little early, don't you think?"

"You could do what my prior roommate did, and read under the covers by the light of your fleshcard—if you can figure out how. There's a trick to it. She tried to teach me, but I couldn't figure it out. 'Course, there's the problem of having nothing to read—unless you read that anti-Christian garbage they call literature. I wouldn't recommend it."

Roommate? The thought hadn't dawned on Briar. Of course, Harper must've had a roommate before.

Someone younger, to help take care of her.

"Where is your previous roommate?"

Her cot creaked, but she didn't answer. Minutes passed. Briar assumed Harper had fallen asleep.

"They walked her from this room a week ago, and she never returned."

Briar propped herself on an elbow and stared blindly in the direction of Harper's cot. "Maybe she was cured and released. Her Agathi may have finally responded to treatment."

Harper sighed weakly. "I didn't want to tell you, but I don't believe in lying. Residents never go home. I've looked in the files. I've seen the evidence with my own eyes."

"Show me." There must be a logical explanation to where Harper's roommate and the other absent residents had gone.

Briar waited for a response, once again wondering if the old woman had fallen asleep. "Harper?" she whispered.

The old woman sighed, louder than before. "Tomorrow. But you'll have to say whatever I tell you to."

Briar fake-gasped. "Ms. Harper, are you asking me to lie?"

"Don't get smart."

Briar grinned in the darkness.

"Now let's pray together before we go to sleep."

Sincerely, beautifully, Harper prayed to God. She thanked Him for His Son, for His forgiveness, and for bringing Briar into her life. She asked Him to lend His protection to both of them, as well as to the other residents.

Not since childhood had Briar felt such peace—not

since Granna Grace held her hand in prayer.

She was fast asleep before Harper reached Amen.

22

"I was beginning to think you'd moved." Lukas stepped around the wall, into the dark entryway.

Derby yelped and switched on the light. "How'd you get in here?"

"Strangest thing—I slid the key card you gave me years ago into the card reader on your front door, and *presto*. The light turned green." Lukas moved between Derby and the door. "My turn to ask a question."

"I didn't mean to." Derby cut in. His voice shook as his eyes glazed with tears. "I didn't want to do it. I like Miss Briar—I never wanted to hurt her."

"Is she at the ARC?" His blood stopped pumping as he waited for the answer he already knew.

Derby clamped his hands over his eyes and nodded. "I dropped her off at the landing strip outside of town this morning. The ARC reps flew in and took her back to Montana."

Lukas's blood resumed pumping. Hotter and faster than ever, it spewed through his veins. "Filthy, spineless, worm. You used our birthday surprise to hand her over to the enemy." He glared at Derby, his eyes straining against the sockets. "Look at me!"

Derby slid his hands from his eyes. "I had to!" he sobbed. "Reid said she'd come with me if I followed through. I love her Lukas—you know I've always loved her."

"Reid? What are you talking about?" he tore a hand through his hair. "Stop blubbering so I can understand you."

"New Mexico. Caster promised to relocate me there."

Caster. Lukas bristled. He looked forward to scraping that pile of gunk from the bottom of his shoe someday soon. Right in front of Father.

"Reid said she'd come to New Mexico with me, if I delivered Briar to the airport. She said she loves me." Derby's voice cracked as he broke down crying again.

Lukas blinked, unable to believe what he was hearing. Derby was truly insane. He couldn't possibly believe Reid cared for him.

"But it was a lie!" He scuffed a boot over the floor. "I overheard the two of them talking at the lab. They didn't hear me walk in. Reid was asking Caster where you were. He said you were probably at my place, taking a piece of my hide."

"It's on my to-do list."

"Listening to Caster question my whereabouts like that, I almost barged in, thinking they were having an affair. But then Caster began teasing her about how she always keeps tabs on you, and how she follows you around like a teenage groupie." Derby's lip trembled beneath his red nose. "And then Reid said her feelings for you were no secret. She'd loved you since the beginning, and she didn't care if Caster liked it or not. She said Caster had better start treating her nicer because she would one day be his sister-in-law."

Lukas's stomach rolled at the thought.

"Reid started talking about how she wanted to take things into her own hands with Briar. But Caster said no. He'd spoken with Maxwell Brown, the ARC's director of operations. Brown would handle her, and make sure she never came out." Derby's breath hitched. "That's when I got scared—when they talked about what they planned to do to Miss Briar. That's when I knew I'd been tricked. The ARC ain't some kind of resort or a fancy hotel. It's a bad place."

Lukas swatted disturbing images from his mind before they could stick. "What else did they say?" he barked, furious that Derby let this happen. Sure, the man was sorry now, but that didn't change the fact it was his fault the scheme was executed. Of all people to place his trust in—Caster and Reid? How could he be so stupid? Lukas always heard love was blind. Until now, he hadn't realized it had no senses whatsoever—or that it showed up with a big ole heap of crazy strapped to its back.

"Reid said letting someone else handle Briar wasn't good enough. She said if Caster didn't let her use the abstergent on Briar, she would leak everything about his dead wife. She'd tell everyone that Kate wasn't really dead at all—instead, she was being held prisoner at the ARC. Everyone would know he was behind it. She said she'd even tell Gatlin."

The air evaporated from Lukas's lungs. Could Gatlin's mother really be alive?

"Caster said she'd never go through with it. Reid said to try her and see. Then she told him to call Maxwell Brown and tell him she was on the way. I stepped behind a door and watched through a gap between the hinges. She left with an equipment bag over her shoulder."

"What kind of equipment did she take?"

"I don't know." He shook his head. "I'll probably never see her again," he blubbered, cradling his face in his hands. "You're the one she loves, not me."

"Lucky me," Lukas snarled. He'd known Derby

for seemingly a lifetime, but he couldn't feel sorry for the man. Not this time. Not after how he'd betrayed Briar. He started to ask what happened to his hot air balloon, but decided he didn't care. "Come on. We're going to the lab." Lukas wasn't planning on staying, but he needed Derby to keep an eye on things.

"I can't. If Caster finds out I told you, he'll kill me."

"That's a chance I'm willing to take."

~*~

"Hey, girl," Lukas said quietly, stooping to give Roxy a pat before moving down the hallway. The door to the room containing the pharmaceutical closet was cracked a hair, causing his legs to pick up speed. He burst into the room, his stomach swallowing his heart as he gazed at the open medication vault. Both vials of abstergent were gone, as well as both vials of antidote. A pair of sedative vials had been taken as well.

A glance through the implement closet confirmed his worse fear. The retractable cranial drill was missing. His hands shook as he passed them over the other instruments, taking a quick inventory. Not only one drill, but two were missing—the new model as well as the old.

Fighting his no-holds-barred imagination, he scanned the supply cupboard, noting several missing syringes. "No," he growled, the slam of the cabinet door rattling the remaining items. He sped from the room, nearly mowing down Derby who was kneeling and petting Roxy, outside the doorway.

Derby jumped to his feet. "Sorry—"

Lukas stopped suddenly, jerking a finger to his

lips. "Shh! Listen." He narrowed his eyes as he gazed down the hallway. "Someone's here. Hold Roxy still and stay put. Don't move unless I call you." He needed Roxy to keep Derby out of his way, not the other way around.

Ears tuned, he continued down the hall, gaining speed with each step. He rounded the corner in a jog, dodging a small item on the floor. He shuffled to a stop, hoping he was seeing things. Pulse hammering in his brain, he stooped to pick up the obstacle. Gatlin's toy firetruck. Something was horribly wrong. "Caster!" he yelled, saliva hitting the back of his teeth. "What have you done?"

He powered on, kicking open every door. Sweat stung his eyes. Let it burn—he didn't care. "Caster!" the name was bitter on his tongue. He raised his knee, snapped his leg, and drove his heel into the exam room door, blasting it wide open.

His heart melted. He couldn't breathe. The scene was something from a nightmare.

Little Gatlin, lifeless on the exam table wearing only a pair of boxer shorts, his wrists and ankles restrained. Caster, looming over him, gripping a cranial drill.

This couldn't be reality.

"Is he—" Lukas couldn't bear to finish the sentence.

Caster yanked the surgical mask to his chin. "Sedated." He studied the side of Gatlin's head and made an adjustment on the drill.

"You can't do this. The drill could pierce too deeply."

Caster frowned at the tool. "Reid didn't give me a choice. She took the retractable."

Lukas tried not to think of Reid marching into the ARC with the retractable drill tucked under her arm.

"The abstergent hasn't been tested on a human."

Caster turned a hot gaze on Lukas. "And whose fault is that, brother?"

"Gatlin's a child. You could easily dissolve his entire brain."

"Good thing you have that precious antidote. Remember? The antidote you used for an excuse, so you wouldn't have to inject Briar with abstergent. You spent so much time on it, I'm sure it's absolutely perfect."

"Please, Caster. You'll kill him."

Caster's eyes caught fire. "Don't pretend you care for my son. You're the reason he's sedated on this table—you and that...that...freak you're so enamored with. She read to him from the Bible!" His knuckles whitened as he squeezed the drill in his fist.

"It doesn't matter. Gatlin's Agathi are protected by SAP." He'd been over this before with Caster. SAP in the system equaled no religious absorption. It wasn't rocket science—it was medical science. Something his brother knew a thing or two about. So why was it so hard for Caster to understand?

"Gatlin had a flicker." Caster spoke so quietly, Lukas barely heard him. "A single blink. For a fraction of a second, his Agathi lit. It was discovered during his most recent brain scan." He ran a gloved thumb above Gatlin's temple, caressing the small, shaved area. "What if during one of those blinks, some of Briar's biblical debris lodged in his brain? It could fester. I have to get rid of it." Caster pressed the drill to Gatlin's head. "Now." He placed his finger on the trigger.

"No! Wait, Caster. It was probably just a glitch in

the scanner. We can check it again, right now. Right here in the lab."

"SAP isn't enough anymore!" The drill trembled in Caster's hand. "I don't want his Agathi numbed. I want them dissolved. If God gets inside, Gatlin will be aware of sin. Of his inability to measure up. Of the fact he needs a savior." Caster's hands shook harder now, the tip of the drill bobbed against the little boy's temple.

Glued to the trigger, Lukas's eyes widened. "I understand the reason you're doing this. But you must calm down. You can't drill the port with your hands trembling." He kept his voice soft, despite his screaming insides. "Let me do it." Saying the words sickened his stomach.

Caster attempted to steady the drill. "No." Tears flowed down both cheeks, disappearing into the mask still cupping his chin. "It has to be me."

"Please." Lukas said gently. "Let me do it. Your hands aren't steady. You can watch my every move."

He looked at Lukas, perspiration filling the deep furrows on his forehead. "I have to be sure it never works again—not even a flicker. It has to die." He knocked a fist against his own temple. "Die. Die. Die." He knocked again and again, harder each time.

Lukas stared at his brother, a thousand puzzle pieces shifting into place behind his eyes. It all made sense. *Caster had functioning Agathi.* Like Briar, he was immune to SAP.

Something spiritual must've soaked in. The influence could have come years ago, before The Commandment, from anywhere—an unlevel tutor, housekeeper, babysitter—there was no way to be certain. But something triggered Caster's Agathi.

Something specifically Christian. He'd become aware of his sin, and the guilt was killing him. He'd do anything to keep Gatlin from that agony. Even hold a drill to his head.

Had Father known? He must have. He'd kept it hidden to keep Caster from being under house arrest—to keep him from going to the ARC. That was the reason Caster couldn't be in charge of leveling projects, even during his stint at the lab.

Functioning Agathi would leave him vulnerable.

And now, after all Caster had done—sending his wife to the ARC, telling his little boy his mother had died. Remaining silent through Gatlin's pain while Kate was being subjected to the unthinkable. Betraying Lukas by having Briar kidnapped, coercing Derby with lies. The guilt wasn't only weighing Caster down, it was driving him mad.

"I know the truth about Kate." Lukas spoke softly, slowly, keeping his eyes on Caster's trembling hands as he eased forward.

Caster shook his head, as if to deny it. "Kate—" More tears washed down his face. "She's gone."

"But not dead." Lukas inched his foot forward as he spoke.

"She may as well be." Caster's eyes flashed. "She was planning to betray me. Turn me over to the OLG because of my—condition."

To Lukas's relief, Caster removed the drill from Gatlin's temple. He pointed it casually toward Lukas, shifting it up and down, as if it was an extension of his finger. Lukas had to keep him talking.

"Why would she do that?"

"Social justice. Kate was always sympathizing over one group or another—the unlevels were her newest attraction. She insisted people were being treated unfairly because of a trait beyond their control. She even went so far as to compare the ARC to a concentration camp."

"Was Kate unlevel?"

"No." The drill sagged as Caster raised his arms in an exasperated shrug. "Isn't that absurd? Kate was as level as they come. She never once had a problem with her SAP readings or brain scans. She had no issue with Gatlin's leveling, either. Her issue was strictly a social concern. She didn't believe in God, but she didn't want those who did believe to be segregated."

"Kate was a good person."

Caster's jaw ticked. He trained his gaze on Lukas. "Kate was a deserter. A traitor, loyal to scores of people she'd never met but not to her husband."

Lukas regretted the conversation's turn. The look in Caster's eyes made him nervous. He flinched as his brother repositioned the drill near Gatlin's head.

"I shared everything with her. She never judged me. Kate knew of my agony. Day by day she helped me through." He squeezed his eyes shut, wrinkling his brow. "Until she read that post or watched that video—whatever it was that caused her heart to bleed for the unlevels. At that moment, she envisioned me a potential advocate for her new cause—nothing more. Who I was, my career, my position in life, could change the way people perceived the unlevel community. She wanted to turn me into some 'dysfunctional and proud' poster child for the unlevels of the world." He gazed down at his son and shook his head slowly. "She loved those ARC-dwellers so much—well, now she's one of them. Not me. No way. I'd end my life before being locked away in that prison."

Caster would risk Gatlin's life as well, because of a glitch that may or may not exist in the child's Agathi. "What about Gatlin?" Lukas asked. "Kate was a good mother. She loved him, and he loved her. Why do you think he was so drawn to Briar? He saw her as a mother-figure."

"Don't you say that! That freak was no mother to my son. Gatlin doesn't need a mother. He has me. And he has Lira—she's taken care of him since the day he was born."

"A nanny isn't the same as a mother."

"I'm through talking." Caster pressed the drill against the little boy's skull.

Gatlin stirred.

Lukas's heart plummeted to his stomach. "The sedative is wearing off."

"He's still numb." Caster clasped a hand on the boy's forehead and leaned in. "I have to do this." The drill came alive with a sickening whirr.

"You'll kill him!" Lukas shuffled forward. "Your hands are shaking."

"Shut up!" Caster growled.

Gatlin's eyes popped open, then squeezed shut—but not before Lukas saw the fear.

Lukas held out his hand. "Let me do it," he yelled over the screech of the drill.

Caster's gaze flicked to Lukas's.

"My hands are steady." The drill muffled his voice, turning his shouts to whispers. "It's the only way." He stepped to his brother's side.

Caster released the trigger.

"Thank you." Lukas took the drill, his head ringing with the sudden silence.

Caster picked up the syringe from the table. "You drill. I'll administer the abstergent."

Lukas swallowed dryly and nodded. He pulled the trigger, his eyes widening at the sharp rod spinning millimeters from his nephew's skull.

"Do it now," Caster hissed close to Lukas's ear. He clenched the syringe in one hand, tightened his grip on Gatlin's forehead with the other.

Lukas took a deep breath and steadied the drill. For the first time in his life, he whispered what may have been a prayer.

With a movement more like a reflex, Lukas jerked the drill up and around, jabbing the whirring bit into the side of the metal exam table. He let go and the tool stayed put, dangling from its warped bit.

Caster shouted through gritted teeth, the animal-like sound echoing through the silent room. Like a Hollywood rendition of a mad scientist, he held the abstergent-filled syringe above his head, while keeping his eyes trained on the soft area above Gatlin's ear.

Lukas's heart stilled. Caster would jam the needle in the boy's temple. He lunged for the vial, careful not to bang against Gatlin's small body.

Caster stumbled out of his reach and laughed. "You're the one with the brains, remember? Not the brawn." He shoved Lukas out of his way and repositioned his hand on Gatlin's brow.

The boy squirmed against the restraints. Gatlin couldn't open his eyes in the middle of this. It would scar him for life.

Lukas backed away, his blood running cold. He stood with his back to the door now, his feet longing to turn and run, to carry him far away from this nightmare.

Lukas bowed his head.

Like a cartoon bull, he ran full force across the room, dodging the exam table, ramming the top of his head into Caster's sternum, not stopping until Caster was pinned against the wall. Air whooshed out of his brother's lungs, accompanied by the pop of a dislocated rib.

Caster held tight to the syringe as Lukas struggled to twist it from his grip.

He grimaced. "You can't stop me," the words hitched from Caster's throat.

A soft groan snapped Lukas's head around. He cut his gaze to the exam table.

Gatlin shivered.

Whatever Lukas was going to do—he had to do now.

"Roxy!" Lukas shouted.

Two barks rang out, followed by what sounded like a stampede of cattle.

Caster's gaze shot to the door.

Lukas clamped a hand around his brother's fist, and with a quick jerk, drove the syringe into the wall.

Roxy leapt into the room, rattling shelves and crashing glass bins to the floor. The antidote shattered on the tile. Through a blizzard of cotton balls, swabs and gauze, the dog closed in, baring her teeth at Caster.

"Keep him there, girl." Lukas inched to the counter and filled a syringe with sedative.

"Get away from me, you mangy beast." Caster darted to the right as Roxy sank her teeth into his left buttock.

Screaming in pain, he didn't notice Lukas plunge the hypodermic needle into his thigh.

Derby ran into the room.

"Help me with him," Lukas yelled, struggling to slide his brother to the floor so he wouldn't crack his stupid head on the tile.

Derby shuffled over.

"Uncle?"

Leaving Derby to wrestle Caster's limp body, Lukas rushed to Gatlin's side. "Everything's OK," he soothed, removing the restraints from the boy's wrists and ankles. He eased him into a sitting position and covered his bare limbs with a paper blanket. "I'll carry you to the chair in the corner, so that your daddy can rest on the table, OK? One, two, three." He picked up Gatlin, settled him gently in the chair, and covered him with more paper blankets. He then stepped across the room and knelt beside his brother's head. "Let's move him to the table," he said to Derby.

Lukas at his brother's head, Derby at his feet, the two men hefted Caster onto the exam table. Fighting a smirk, Lukas dabbed at Roxy's bite with an alcohol pad and covered the superficial wound with an adhesive bandage. He removed his brother's surgical mask, cuffphone, keys, and wallet, stuffing the items into his pockets before fastening Caster's wrists and ankles in the restraints.

"You forgot his gloves," Gatlin said, pointing to his father.

"You're right." Lukas pulled the rubber gloves from Caster's hands and tossed them into the trash. "Your daddy isn't hurt, he's just taking a little nap."

Gatlin nodded. "I know." He clicked his tongue and patted his lap, calling to Roxy. The dog dashed over to him, thumped her big front paws onto his thighs and licked his face. He giggled.

"Derby, get them out of here." Lukas tapped

Gatlin on the nose and patted Roxy's head. "And make sure you take good care of my nephew until I get back." He stopped at the doorway. "On second thought, let Roxy take care of Gatlin."

23

"That orderly over there, named Cleo. You've met her." Harper rested against her walker and pointed a crooked finger to a caramel-skinned woman with braided hair. "She's the only one in this godforsaken place that has a heart. I'm amazed she's still around."

Briar nodded. "I get a good feeling from her."

Harper stepped slowly forward, scooting her walker. "The others are watching her. She has a God-zone. Somehow she slipped under the radar."

"She told you that?"

"Her eyes told me."

Briar glanced at Cleo. The woman caught her gaze and offered a warm smile. Maybe Harper was right.

"Listen up," Harper said, pausing her steps in the dining hall doorway. "What we are about to do is not right. Not by any means."

"Oh-K?" Briar frowned and grinned at the same time.

"It's not honest. Think of it as being in the same vein as Rahab and the spies. A little dishonesty for the sake of the common good."

Briar's mouth fell open as Harper popped out her dentures and slipped them into her waistband. Glancing around to make sure no one had seen, Briar stepped into the dining area behind Harper.

"Follow my lead." The old woman winked.

Having no idea where things were going, Briar nodded.

They chose a table in the purple section and sat

down. Immediately, an orderly slid a tray of food before each of them.

"I don't have my teeth!" Harper yelled at the purple tray. "How can a person eat breakfast without her dentures?"

The blank-faced orderly stared.

"How am I supposed to eat this—" She leaned over the tray, inspecting the food. "What are we having?"

"Diced peaches, toast, and a protein similar to eggs."

Harper frowned and resumed her complaint. "How am I supposed to eat peaches, toast, and scrambled-up protein without my teeth?"

The orderly motioned to Cleo, who was kneeling, speaking with an elderly woman in a wheel chair. She gazed in Harper's direction and gave the woman a pat on the shoulder before leaving her side.

"Is there a problem Ms. Ross?" she asked as she approached.

"Not if you want me to starve to death. Which is exactly what I'll do without my dentures."

"You'll have to wait a few minutes, until everyone is seated. Then I'll get someone to escort you to your room to get your dentures. We're short staffed this morning."

"My food will be cold by then. I can't eat cold food. Freezes up my insides. Makes me sluggish."

"I'm sorry, Ms. Harper. It's against the rules to let you go back to your room before breakfast is over without an orderly to escort you. You already know this. We can't have people wandering around the facility unattended."

Harper's chin trembled. Tears slipped down her

wrinkled cheeks. "I just want my teeth."

Briar's heart tugged for the old woman. For a second she almost forgot the dentures were tucked snugly in Harper's waistband.

"Ouch!" her thoughts were jolted by a sharp pain in her thigh. Harper had pinched her, and was now staring at her intently. She cleared her throat. "I'll walk her back to the room," she offered, no longer captivated by Harper's award-winning performance.

Cleo shook her head. "I'm sorry, that's against regulations," she said loudly. She then leaned close to Briar, rearranging the silverware on her tray. "Straight to the room, and straight back," she whispered. "Make it quick."

"Yes, ma'am." Briar helped Harper to her feet. "Thank you."

They walked through the crowded dining hall and through the doorway without seeing another orderly.

"How did you know they were shorthanded?"

"I didn't." Harper shrugged. "Must be a God-thing." She pulled her dentures from her waistband and slipped them into her mouth. "Now hurry up, before we're spotted."

Briar bit back a giggle as Harper scooted her walker forward at a snail's pace. She hoped she could hurry fast enough to keep up with the old woman.

After creeping down the hallway for what seemed like hours, Harper paused her walker. "This doorway, right here. The nurse's station." She pointed to a sign above the iridescent drape.

Anxiety inched up Briar's spine. "How will we get in without clearance?"

Harper held up the back of her hand. "All taken care of. I've been to the nurse's station a thousand times. Nicks, cuts, scrapes, cramps, backdoor trots. Name the affliction, and odds are I've suffered it." She glanced around. "Eventually, the nurse that worked in here got so sick of letting me in, she gave me clearance. Apparently, she never told anyone." She shrugged one bony shoulder. "These days, there's no nurse in this wing. The orderlies just roll around a medication cart all day in case someone needs a cough drop or an adhesive bandage. The more serious conditions are sent to the infirmary ward. Is it my fault no one reprogrammed my fleshcard after the nurse disappeared? That's how I discovered what all they keep inside this room."

Briar felt her eyeballs expand. "What did you discover?" she whispered.

"A computer. In the back, behind the supply room." Harper took a step toward the drape. "There's lots of information in there—the kind they don't want anyone to see. The top-secret kind." She braced against her walker and held the back of her hand to the curtain. Under her papery skin, the fleshcard glowed.

The automatic light switched on as Briar followed Harper into the space. She glanced over her shoulder as the drape reappeared in the doorway.

"This way," the old woman said, pushing her walker toward the back of the room.

Briar glanced at the cardboard boxes of medical supplies as they made their way to an area the size of a large closet. Harper snapped on the light. On a small, dust-laden desk, sat an old-fashioned laptop that had definitely seen better days. "So, this is where they keep all the top-secret info?" Briar asked, trying to mask her disappointment. There was no iridescent drape, just a regular door standing wide open, to set the room apart.

How top secret could the information really be?

"Yep." Harper crept to the desk, creaked open the laptop, and wiggled her finger on the touchpad. A password bar appeared beneath the golden image of a roaring lion. "*Chocolate*," she recited, clacking the keys. "Figured that out all on my own. 'Course, it wasn't too much of a feat. Nurse Brumble never skipped dessert, if you get my drift."

Briar stepped closer as the screen blinked to life. Probably just an old inventory file or a bunch of outdated order forms.

"Hold on a second. Ah—here we are. The main portal." Harper tapped a lion icon on the desktop then removed her fingers from the keyboard. She scooted her walker to the side. "The ARC's entire computer system is at your fingertips. Click on any tab you want to read."

"Warning: Classified Information. Credentialed Employees Only," Briar read from the top of the page. "Unbelievable. Why would the ARC leave confidential information unguarded?"

"They forgot. That's my theory. Best I can figure, Nurse Brumble handled some of the data entry. Light stuff, such as how many people visited the station for antibiotic ointment and ear swabs, that type of thing. Boring, low profile information no one cared about or paid much attention to. Once she left, that kind of data was no longer needed. No one thought twice about checking this dusty little cubbyhole for secrets. Even if they did, what use would they have for an obsolete computer that can't handle much more than standard Internet? For all practical purposes, this workstation is invisible."

Briar squeezed closer to Harper's side, squinting

as she scanned the tabs of endless options. "Mission statement, policy and procedure, schematics, logistics. I don't even know where to start."

"May I suggest, Inactive Patients?"

Briar clicked the tab above Harper's fingernail. A list of names and ages appeared on the screen. "Who are they?" she asked, scrolling continuously without reaching the end.

"Those who have died here."

Briar's finger froze on the touchpad. Her heartbeat rang in her ears. "No. That can't be accurate. You've misinterpreted the information—"

"Fifteen hundred people were sent to the ARC ten years ago. And the numbers continue to increase. Tally up the names on that list, and you'll find well over two thousand people—close to twenty-six hundred. But how many are actually here?"

"I-I don't know. No one ever told me."

"Six hundred. That's how many. A total of six hundred patients reside here. So where are the other two-thousand?"

"They must've been cured and reunited with their families—which actually lifts a weight off my shoulders. Such a high number of rehabilitated unlevels gives me hope."

Harper gently removed Briar's hand from the pad and continued scrolling. "No one is rehabilitated, Briar. No one leaves. Not ever. Over two hundred people per year have disappeared since the opening of the ARC ten years ago. These people are casualties. Over two thousand human beings, dead. They're all listed here." The never-ending list of names rolled down the screen. "Some were young, some were old. All of them suffered."

Briar shook her head. "I hate to say this, but you're delusional. I believe there are surgical procedures—I can't argue with your scars. But extermination? Harper, I just can't accept—"

"More than two hundred people per year. Hacked to pieces by scalpels. Burned to a crisp by lasers. Skulls cracked against the tile to quiet their own diced up brains."

"Stop it!" Briar clamped a hand over Harper's, stilling her fingers. "It's not true."

"Look at the dates." Harper pointed her gaze to the screen.

Briar whispered a name and the date beside it. "There's a mistake. This can't be right. According to the date, this person would be a four-year-old child. Everyone at the ARC is at least eighteen." She traced her finger down the alphabetical listing, choosing another name. "This one would be even younger—just over the age of two. And this one, only six."

Harper nodded. "Yes, you would be correct, if those were their *birth* dates."

Briar looked again, her heart leaping into her throat, choking her, squeezing tears from her eyes. "No," she mouthed silently.

"Those are the dates their lives ended." Harper patted the younger woman's back.

Briar clicked on a woman's name, her insides curling into a tight ball. Harper was right. The woman's cause of death appeared, along with the types of experiments she was subjected to.

"Why didn't you tell me before, when you told me about the surgeries? When you explained what they'd done to you? You never mentioned murder."

"I tried to, but your brain couldn't process it. You

had to see for yourself."

"But—the bodies. What do they do with the...remains?"

"Cremation. No graves. No memorials. Just gone." Her eyes gleamed. "But if they accepted Christ, we know where their spirits are, don't we?" She wiped a tear. "That's the important part."

Briar returned to the main menu and chose a tab labeled *Photos*. Horrified, she closed the tab, wishing she could un-see the empty-eyed woman with the shaved head and sutured scalp.

"So, the reunion videos and smiling family photographs, all of the heartwarming stories shared in the brochures and on commercials—those are all fake."

"Fabricated. Every single one of them. No one leaves. Families of young victims are told their loved one is still undergoing treatment. Families of the old are told their loved one has passed peacefully away of natural causes."

Briar drew a shaky breath. Her mother had been right.

"Someone's coming." Harper scooted her walker toward the open door.

Briar listened, but heard nothing.

"The footsteps in the hallway stopped outside the drape. Stay in here. Don't come out for any reason—do you understand?"

Briar had no intention of abandoning Harper, but nodded anyway.

"Promise me."

That complicated things. A promise was for real. The swish of the dematerializing drape rushed her response. "I promise."

"All along, I've been waiting for you. God has sent

you here for such a time as this." Harper snapped off the light and hobbled from the closet, pulling the door closed behind her.

Esther. Briar's mind reeled at the old woman's biblical reference. She felt Granna Grace was watching over her.

Briar held her breath and pressed her ear to the door, recognizing the stern voice of an orderly.

"What are you doing in here, Ms. Ross?"

"Looking for the dining hall. Guess I got turned around."

"Where's your friend?"

Briar's stomach dropped.

"Some friend." Harper sniffed. "Is a friend someone who runs down a maze of hallways to the cafeteria, leaving a toothless old woman with a walker to fend for herself?"

"Briar returned to the dining hall?"

"Didn't even have my teeth in yet. Girl took off like a shot, muttering about not having time to wait. She was afraid they'd dump her tray before she got back. Has a thing for peaches."

"Is that so?"

Hearing footsteps, Briar backed from the door.

"It won't do you any good to open that door—the traitor ain't in there. I told you, she's in the cafeteria stuffing her face with peaches—probably eating mine, too!"

Frantically, Briar stretched out her arms and felt around the room. Her fingers skittered across the small desk. She ducked under it, wrapping her arms around her knees, squishing into the space like a human stress ball.

The door creaked open, illuminating the closet.

Briar squeezed her eyes shut in silent prayer.

Footfalls neared, then stopped.

Briar pried open an eye to see the orderly's ugly shoe touching her own. Her heartbeat thumped like a stereo with too much bass.

Please, God, don't let her hear it.

The shoe moved away.

"Come with me, Ross. I have to report you for breaking protocol."

The closet door slammed shut.

In the darkness, Briar rolled from under the desk and lay shaking on the floor.

24

Briar sat up in her cot and gasped for breath. She ran a hand over her slick forehead, into her sweat drenched hair. People died here. Thousands of them. Perhaps some had taken their last breath in this very room—in this very bed.

She wanted to get up, but it would do no good—just as it hadn't the three other times she'd awakened. The lights were still off and the drape was still locked. And Harper's bed was still empty.

Why had she made that promise? And why hadn't she broken it? Sure, there would have been a struggle, but she could've kept Harper from being taken away. Maybe even saved her life.

Briar fell back on her pillow and closed her eyes. "Take a deep breath. Calm down," she said aloud. Who said anything about Harper being dead? The old woman was probably sleeping soundly in a private room down the hall. Or perhaps they'd paired her off with a new partner—someone more responsible who wouldn't let her wander off alone.

Harper was fine. She'd see her in the dining hall a few hours from now, at breakfast.

"She's fine," Briar told the darkness, before drifting immediately into another nightmare.

~*~

Briar scanned the dining hall for Harper. Maybe she'd been forced to change colors, and was wearing something other than purple. Earlier, she thought she'd spotted her in the blue section and rushed to the other side of the room. It wasn't Harper. Beside the silver-haired woman sat a younger woman with familiar dark eyes. She could've sworn she'd seen her before.

Briar could feel it in her gut, something was terribly wrong. She had to report Harper missing. But what good would it do to report a kidnapping to the kidnappers?

Cleo. Harper said she was unlevel. Surely, she would help her. Briar stood and scanned the crowd, searching for the woman's intricate braids. She was nowhere to be found.

"Residents, I need your attention, please." A blonde woman in a golden smock entered the doorway as she addressed the crowd. "Every color of the rainbow—put down your eating utensils and focus your eyes upon me, Vanessa, your pot of gold." She gestured to her shimmering jacket and chuckled, her maroon smile pulling downward, instead of up. "It's time for our weekly session." She clapped her hands. "Lights out!"

The room turned black. In the center of the space, a flicker of light appeared and grew, becoming an enormous, three-dimensional profile of a roaring lion. Then the lion was gone, replaced by a plethora of images changing so rapidly, Briar could barely tell one from the other.

"We are level," the woman's voice boomed. "There are no lines."

In the blur of images, Briar caught sight of a woman dancing with a Great Dane.

"To be level is to be human."

The image of a shrouded man with red eyes blinked briefly on the screen, followed by a quick glimpse of tattooed children.

"There is no right or wrong. To be level is to be free."

Women writhing in cages, men biting one another, horned beasts sitting on thrones.

"Level equals love. Level equals life."

Briar turned from the visuals and held her ears, muffling the woman's malevolent chant. She squinted at the throng of people surrounding her, each face coated by the ethereal glow of the images. She glanced over her shoulder, and the outline of a woman in a wheelchair caught her attention. "Harper!" she cried, unable to stop herself. She pushed through the crowd toward the old woman. "Harper, you're OK!" She threw her arms around her friend and cried.

Harper sat unmoving in her wheelchair, glacial and rigid as a stone slab.

Briar stepped back. "No." She stared into the woman's vacant, faded blue eyes and shook her head. "No, no, no," she cried, taking her friend's cold cheeks into her hands.

"Sin is a lie. To be level is to be free!"

The devil's mantra thundered from Vanessa's maroon lips and drowned out Briar's sobs.

~*~

"You all right, man?" A concerned frown creased the brow of the young man seated beside Lukas.

Lukas attempted a smile. "Fine, thanks," he choked.

The man stared a moment longer before

reinserting his left earbud and turning back to the window.

Lukas coughed and tugged at the nonexistent collar of his t-shirt. His tongue was too large for his mouth. He opened his fist, shook out the damp paper napkin, and mopped his brow. Nausea washed over him in a wave. He'd never been so sick in his life.

Funny thing was, if he died, the airline would identify him as Caster Stone. He'd used his brother's credit card and I.D. to book the flight. The thought of Caster's irritation over being dead made him feel better—momentarily.

He pressed a hand to his chest. He was having a heart attack—that had to be it. That figured. He'd finally taken his eyes from himself long enough to focus on someone else, and now he was dying. What kind of hero flies a thousand miles to rescue the girl, only to die on the plane?

Not that he fancied himself a hero. Non-hero was more like it—or whatever the term was for opposite of hero. He wasn't doing this to be heroic, anyway. That wasn't the reason he was thirty thousand feet in the air, facing his worst fear—maybe even getting killed by it. He'd boarded the plane because he'd realized flying wasn't his worst fear. His worst fear was losing Briar.

What if he was too late? His throat clogged, making it hard to swallow. He wished he had something to hold onto at this moment—hope, faith—whatever it was that Briar held to so easily. Maybe he needed God.

"And maybe you just need to man-up," he exhaled in a whisper.

"Good afternoon, passengers. This is your pilot."

Lukas jumped at the sound of the intercom.

"We would like to welcome you to Idaho. We have begun our descent to Mandrell Memorial Airport, where the current weather is mild and sixty-two degrees. At this time, please return your seats to the upright position, buckle your seatbelts, and turn off all electronic devices. We will be landing shortly. Thank you for flying with us today."

Layover. And he was less than halfway to Montana.

His stomach cartwheeled as the nose of the plane lowered, causing his seat to lean slightly forward. He ran a hand nervously over his chin, dully aware of his stubble. He didn't have his shaving kit—or anything else. With luck, he could pick up a razor and a few other toiletries at the airport. Caster wouldn't be caught dead with five o'clock shadow.

~*~

"Lunch?" Briar threw her legs over the side of the cot. She'd been asleep since right after breakfast.

"Yes, lunch," the stone-faced orderly repeated from the doorway. "Make your way to the dining hall."

Briar rubbed her eyes, sticky from crying herself to sleep, and slid from the bed. She glanced at Harper's cot, a fresh wash of tears overtaking her. "What did they do to her?" she asked, turning to find the orderly gone.

She stepped through the doorway, the drape reappearing behind her. It seemed she'd just left the dining hall. It wasn't as if she could eat, anyway. Not without Harper there to tell her which foods were safe. She shivered. After being subjected to Satan's pitchwoman at breakfast, the dining hall was the last place she wanted to be.

At the end of the long hallway, Briar paused before turning the corner. Light shone through the normally dark windows of an enclosed space labeled The Meeting Room. Muffled voices trailed from inside. What was going on in there?

She glanced around. Behind her, women wordlessly continued their march to the dining hall. She knelt and waited, pretending to have an issue with her slipper, and then popped up when the hall cleared. Cupping her eyes, she pressed her nose against the window. Through a thin gap between old-fashioned lace curtains, she made out a couch, recliner draped with a knitted afghan, and coffee table. A large orange cat curled on a braided rug next to a stone hearth. She imagined the space smelled of lilacs and fresh baked cookies.

Her heart squeezed. She could almost picture Granna Grace sitting in the cherry wood rocking chair beside the fireplace. The room looked like home. But no, that wasn't right. It looked nothing like her home. It looked the way home *felt*. Inside. Within the soul. The sensation was hard to explain.

From nowhere, a man entered the room carrying a camera and microphone stand, spoiling the ambiance. Another man placed a lamp and large umbrella beside the loveseat. Suddenly, everything in the room dematerialized. The furniture, fireplace, even the cat vanished. The lace curtains disappeared, prompting Briar to duck to the side and peek around the edge of the window. A man dragged two folding chairs to the center of the empty space and clicked a remote, filling the room with entirely different decor. The area took on a lavish feel as upscale furnishings emerged atop a marble floor and expensive looking paintings materialized on the walls. The folding chairs became a sleek, white leather sofa.

Vanessa, minus the pot of gold jacket, appeared with an expressionless young woman in tow, and directed her to the computer-generated couch. Briar recognized the girl as one of the stone-faced orderlies, wearing a blue dress in place of the black smock. A fiftyish, motherly woman Briar had seen wiping the dining hall tables sat down beside the orderly.

Briar squinted through the sliver of windowpane, confused by what she saw. Nothing added up…then, suddenly, it did. What she was seeing made perfect sense. The women were role playing, pretending to be mother and daughter. She was witnessing a farce. A charade. One of the infamous, staged reunions her mother and Harper warned her of. A cruel device used to exploit families of ARC residents who waited, indefinitely, for their own reunion to take place.

She turned from the window, despair filling her stomach like hot rocks. She would never leave this place. Never see her mother again. She'd be as gone as her father, without the luxury of scrawling a soap message across the bathroom mirror.

Would Lukas even care?

The stocky attendant with spikey hair lumbered up the hallway. "Keep moving," she barked, skittering Briar around the corner to the dining hall entrance.

Food smells mingled with the scent of chemicals as she stepped into the crowded room. She made her way toward the purple section, her gaze combing the area for an empty chair.

Abruptly, she stopped, the breath knocked from

her body by an invisible wall. In front of her stood the familiar woman with the dark eyes. *Charcoal* eyes.

Kate Stone.

Realization hit Briar, strong and sure as the stench of bleach in the dining hall air. Kate never had cancer, nor had she ever checked into a cancer treatment hospital. She'd resided within the cancerous walls of the ARC all along. A prisoner abducted and held against her will, same as Briar. And Caster was undoubtedly behind it all.

The woman readjusted her tray of food and snaked through the crowd, headed toward the blue section. Heart thundering, Briar followed close behind. She had to talk to her, let her know Gatlin was OK.

"The purple section is over there." A black-smocked orderly pointed Briar in the opposite direction. "Move along."

She nodded, keeping her gaze on Kate—so close she could reach out and touch her. But not for long. The blue table was just steps away. Briar faked a yelp and lunged, driving her body into Kate's, propelling the woman and her tray of food to the floor.

"I'm so sorry!" she cried, kneeling beside the woman. "I tripped. Are you all right?"

"I'm OK," she answered, blinking those unmistakable eyes.

No doubt about it, the woman she'd tackled was Gatlin's mother.

Briar picked up the scattered silverware. "Kate," she whispered, keeping her head near the woman's. "You don't know me, but I know who you are, and I know your little boy. Gatlin is safe."

The woman's eyes widened, then misted with tears.

"He remembers you. He carries your picture in his pocket."

"Get up." The attendant clamped a hand above Briar's elbow and yanked her to her feet. "Next time watch where you're going. You could hurt someone."

Briar glanced over her shoulder as the orderly ushered her roughly to the purple section.

"Thank you," Kate mouthed from the food strewn floor. She covered her face with her hands.

25

Lukas reached for the cup of coffee and thanked the ponytailed cashier who eyed his trembling hands. Did she know?

Know what? That the thought of boarding another plane turned his guts inside out? That, at this very moment, he was impersonating his older brother, whom he'd drugged, restrained, and abandoned five hundred miles away at a scientific lab? Of course, that part sounded worse than it actually was. Caster deserved every bit of it—plus an unfeasible amount more. And Lukas would be around to make sure his brother got what was coming to him. That's what he'd continue to tell himself, anyway. It kept him going.

Focusing to put one foot in front of the other, walking in what he hoped passed for a natural gait, he returned to the seat in his airline's section of the airport. He shifted in the chair, pulled Caster's wallet from his back pocket, and removed the cards from the slots. Grimacing at the cold glare of his brother's driver's license picture, he sifted through the cards.

What would happen when Caster woke? Had Derby taken Gatlin to a safe place far from the lab, as Lukas had asked? When it came down to it, could he really trust Derby, after all he'd done? Lukas sighed. He had to trust Derby. There was no other choice.

He glanced at the wall clock. Reid would be at the ARC by now. The thought stood his neck hairs on end. His plan to reach the ARC as fast as possible was in motion—after that, his strategy screeched to a halt. He had no idea what to do once he got there. He knew he had to stop Reid from injecting Briar with the abstergent. But he didn't know how.

Slowly, he examined the cards, stopping to retrieve one he'd accidentally dropped. A black business card emblazoned with the metallic bronze profile of a roaring lion. "Maxwell Brown," Lukas read. "Alternative Research Center, Director of Operations." In Lukas's head, a thousand bells sounded. Caster's inside man, according to Derby. The guy who would make sure Briar never left the ARC. He had to talk to this weasel.

He slid Caster's flattened cuffphone from his pocket and dialed Maxwell Brown's office number. How well did Caster know the man—did he call him Max? Maxwell? Mr. Brown?

Voicemail.

"Hello, Mr. Brown." He decided on the formal, as the guy's recorded greeting sounded no nonsense. "This is Caster Stone of Stone Labs. It is imperative I speak with you."

Lukas paused, formulating what he would say next. He wished the guy would pick up.

"This is Max. Go ahead, Caster."

Relieved, Lukas cleared his throat and mimicked his brother's voice. "Max. There's been a sudden turn of events. Under no circumstances, is Reid Laughlin to enter the ARC."

"What are you trying to pull, Stone?" It sounded as though Max's teeth were clenched. "I put my neck in a noose for you by altering your wife's SAP readings to have her institutionalized—and this is how you compensate me? For months I've risked my career, trusting you'd keep your end of the bargain. The OLG would have me locked up because of the things I've done for you. Lining your pockets with ARC funding. Kidnapping your brother's test subject for who knows what reason. All for what? Bad deals and broken promises? That doesn't work for me. The plan—a plan *you* called to arrange—was for Reid Laughlin to deliver the abstergent. You can bet your designer haircut I'm letting her in."

Lukas couldn't believe it. What Derby said was true—Kate was still alive. Caster planned to sell the abstergent to Brown to keep her in the ARC.

"If Reid enters your facility—specifically, if she comes near Briar Lee—all agreements are off."

"You won't get another cent until I get the abstergent."

"I don't care about the money."

Max laughed. "Are you sure you're Caster Stone? If I wasn't staring at your number on the screen, I wouldn't believe it."

Lukas swallowed hard. "I'm on my way. Detain Reid until I arrive or watch me pour your millionaire dreams down the drain."

Lukas ended the call. He pressed his brother's phone between his palms and rested his chin on top. Reflected in the airport's plate glass window, he appeared to be praying.

~*~

Briar pushed away her untouched food, and widened her eyes at her glowing tattoo. On the back of her hand, the bronze lion blazed like the sun.

Other women in her section glanced down at their hands, along with several orderlies scattered throughout the dining hall. Whatever was going on, the pit of her stomach didn't like it.

"Come with me, please." Cleo smiled at Briar and offered her hand. "It's time for therapy."

Harper's twisted scars flashed through her brain. "Please. I don't want to go." She couldn't hold her voice steady.

"Honey, don't be afraid." Cleo smiled, though lines creased her brow. "It's nothing to worry about. It'll be over before you know it." She helped Briar to her feet.

Heart climbing to her throat, Briar walked with Cleo to the hallway where they joined five other women and their escorts. Together, they strode to the laboratory wing, and into a white, sterile looking room with six chairs.

"Please be seated," Cleo said, patting Briar on the back.

When all six women were seated, a lab technician with a handheld wand scanned each of their fleshcards, while another drew and labeled their blood, carefully setting each vial into a compartmentalized tray.

"Thank you, ladies. Please follow your escort to an individual examination room and wait for your therapist to arrive."

"Here we are," Cleo said. With her tattoo, she dissolved the iridescent drape, revealing a purple exam room. "I'll be right out here if you need anything." She patted Briar's shoulder and gently nudged her inside.

The drape rematerialized, along with Briar's fear. If she could only see Cleo, she wouldn't be as frightened. Right away the curtain flickered, filling her with relief. She smiled. Cleo was letting her know she was still there.

"Good afternoon, Miss Lee."

Beneath her skin, Briar's muscles jumped. The smile slid from her face as the drape disappeared.

Reid stepped through the opening, medical case in one manicured hand. An identification card hung from her neck.

"Cleo!" Briar yelled.

Cleo stepped in. "Miss Briar would be more comfortable if I stayed."

"That won't be necessary." Reid thumped her case to the countertop.

"Don't leave me alone with her. She's insane."

Reid raised an eyebrow. "I'm not the one confined to a facility." She tapped a few times on the medical kit's keypad, solving the combination. The case popped open. She cut her gaze to Cleo.

"Braids, if you insist on being here, hold her still."

Cleo jammed a hand to her hip. "Braids?" She glanced at Briar.

"Show me your credentials."

Reid rolled her eyes and lifted her badge.

Cleo scrutinized the card.

Reid snatched it back. "It's legit. Question me and I'll complain to your supervisor."

"Don't believe her, Cleo. She's lying."

Reid stretched on a pair of gloves, filled one syringe, and then another.

Cleo turned her gaze to the open case on the counter, her eyes bulging as she spied the cranial drill. "Lady, if you think you're going to touch my girl with that thing, you've got another thing coming." She stepped in front of Briar.

"Then I suggest you find some other place to be."

Reid's heels clicked the tile as she stepped toward Cleo.

"I'm calling security."

Reid lunged as Cleo turned toward the drape.

Briar caught hold of Cleo as her legs melted out from under her.

"What did you do?" Briar screamed, cradling Cleo's head on the floor. A bomb detonated behind her eyes. "You're a monster," she yelled, rising to her feet. Like a machine, she marched forward, chopping the air as Reid backed away, blocking with her arms.

"Relax." Reid held up a syringe. "It's a sedative. It'll wear off." Reid's pink lips twisted into a sarcastic smirk. "Braids will be just fine."

Briar drew her fingers into a fist and punched, hoping to make Reid's surgically fattened lips even fatter.

Quick as a snake's strike, Reid grabbed Briar's wrist. "Gotcha!" She smiled and backed away, letting Briar's wrist drop.

Briar winced. Something was pinching her. Her gaze swam to the syringe jutting from her arm.

The purple room swirled to black.

26

"I agree, you probably are exactly who you say you are. But that's not the point. The point is, you don't have clearance to enter the ARC. Therefore, if I let you in, I lose my job." The man shook his head. "It's out of my hands."

Lukas glanced away from the security booth's barred window and squinted at the iron gates in the distance. The place was a fortress.

"I'm sorry to keep repeating myself, but it's very important I gain entrance to the facility. You say Mr. Brown never called to inform you I was coming, but what's hindering you from calling him? A little inconvenient, perhaps, but I'm being a little inconvenient as well—correct? And I'm not going anywhere. I'll stand right here, continuing to be inconvenient, until you reach my friend, Max Brown."

The man flared his nostrils and knocked his fingertips against the screen that encircled his forearm.

Lukas enjoyed watching the irritated tick in the man's jaw, and was a tad ashamed of himself. But being an annoying jerk was actually kind of interesting when he was flashing someone else's I.D. And since his brother was, indeed, an annoying jerk, Lukas was simply keeping it real by playing the part.

"Maxwell Brown," a man's curt voice sounded from the guard's cuffphone.

The guard uncurled the device from his arm and snapped it flat. Glaring at Lukas, he placed it against his ear. "Mr. Brown, this is Samuel Dupree at the security booth. There's a—" He stopped to read the identification card Lukas had given to him. "Caster Stone requesting admittance. Says he spoke with you by phone earlier."

The guy frowned. "A picture? Yes, sir."

Lukas held his breath. Max wanted the guard to text a photograph. Could he pass for Caster in full sunlight?

The guard took the phone from his ear and snapped a picture of Caster's I.D. "Sent the photo to you just now, sir."

Lukas exhaled, relief washing through him.

Finally, the guard spoke into the phone. "Right away, sir. Thank you."

Lukas grinned, anxious to hear Samuel Dupree's affirmative verdict.

Instead, the guard made another call. "Joe. Bring the car. A guy at the booth needs a ride in." He tossed an irritated look at Lukas. "He's clear. Got the word straight from Brown."

~*~

"Special?" Briar mumbled. Someone had glued her eyelids together. She didn't really mind. She could use the rest—if not for that annoying nibble at the edge of her brain telling her to wake up, that something wasn't right.

"No. Not special. Are you deaf?"

The voice battered her ears. Harsh. Mean. Not a nice voice at all.

"I said Lukas won't think you're special—won't believe you're some kind of princess. Not anymore."

Briar felt her forehead crease. She lifted her

eyebrows, but her lids wouldn't budge. They were too heavy. Made of solid concrete.

"Lukas is so far out of your league." The voice gave a bitter little chuckle. "Personally, I can't figure out his attraction to you. Pity is the only thing I can come up with. He feels sorry for you. The way Dr. Frankenstein ended up feeling sorry for the monster."

A motor whined, jarring Briar's eyes open. Was she in the dentist's office? Through a haze, she saw—Reid? Holding something. What was it? She tried to rub her eyes, but her wrists wouldn't move. Neither would her neck—her head, turned to one side, was clamped to the table. Her brain roused enough for her to panic. She struggled to bend her knees, but her ankles were restrained. "Help," the scream came out a whisper.

The whirring motor died. Reid's footsteps clicked across the floor toward Briar. She kicked something out of her way. "That'll teach you to wear such ugly shoes."

Briar tried to move her head, but could only cut her gaze to the floor. A loafer slid to a stop against the baseboard. Cleo! She flicked her gaze over the tile, heart sagging as she spied her friend's hand beside the wheel of the exam table.

"I love him, you know," Reid said. "I've loved him for years. He never seemed to notice. Then you bounce into Stone Labs like some puppy without tags, and he's head over heels."

Hot tears slid over the bridge of Briar's nose.

"I'm not so sure he'll like your new haircut, though." Reid stepped to the side of the table and slid a gloved hand over Briar scalp. "I decided to take it all off. Smooth as a baby's bottom."

Briar's eye sockets stretched as she recognized the tool in Reid's hands.

Tracing her terrified gaze, Reid tapped the drill with her finger. "This?" She smiled. "Oh, yes. It's exactly what you think it is. I'm going to rid you of those pesky—and oh-so-special—God-zones, once and for all. Once they're gone, you'll be unremarkable. Then the playing field will be level." She poked a wad of gauze into Briar's mouth. "And Lukas will be mine." She leaned over Briar and pressed the drill to the side of her head.

The drill whirred to life, humming like a thousand bees inside her skull.

Please, God...please, God...please.

Briar bucked against the restraints. She strained her neck, but her head wouldn't budge. This time, the scream came out a scream, blasting from her lungs like a foghorn, matching the intensity of the spinning icepick sinking into her skull. Bolts of thin red lightning zipped behind her eyelids. Her senses exploded, perceiving the crunch of bone.

Her skull was punctured. Somehow, her lungs were too—she couldn't breathe. Nausea punched her stomach like angry fists.

The bees silenced. The icepick slid from her skull. Relief shuttled through Briar, so intensely she nearly thanked Reid for showing mercy. Her eyes misted. Around the gauze she whispered a prayer of gratitude.

"Don't thank Him yet." Reid placed the drill on the implement tray and held up a hypodermic with an extra-long needle. "That was only the access port." She turned the syringe in her fingers, giving Briar a good look at the milky serum. "On second thought, go ahead and give thanks now. After I inject the abstergent, you'll never talk to your God again."

"No," Briar mumbled. Her neck popped and cracked as she strained against the head restraint.

"Don't worry. There are no pain receptors in the brain." Reid tapped the syringe and leaned in. "Although," she whispered, "there might be a few in the surrounding tissue."

Briar's eyelids jumped and fluttered as her eyes rolled back. Her brain searched frantically for something with which to compare the pain, but her memory banks came up dry. No past suffering paralleled this white-hot agony.

All at once, the pain was gone. In its place, something slithered. Some foreign thing, squirming deep within her brain, as if the hypodermic needle had come to life. She squeezed her eyes, frantic to block the sensation.

"There." Reid's voice barely out-sounded the ringing in Briar's ears. "Halfway done."

Maybe she'd fainted. Perhaps Reid had given her another sedative. All Briar knew was that suddenly her head was clamped down in the opposite direction—and someone was yelling.

"Put the syringe down, now!"

Briar opened her eyes. The guy was red as a cactus flower. He would keel over of a heart attack before he could stop Reid. "Caster is on his way."

"It's too late, Max."

Reid lunged for the table, plunging the needle into the side of Briar's head, blinding her with agony.

The pain was unbearable. Briar hoped she wouldn't live through it—prayed to God she'd open her eyes to find her grandmother there beside her, smiling, ready to escort her through the pearly gates of heaven. Granna Grace would hold her hand and take her to meet…to meet…

Something was fading deep inside her. Something significant—the most important thing she'd ever known. A loss so great, her heart ached for its return. Tears drenched her face and pooled beside her on the table. Someone had died. The One she loved above all others. But she couldn't remember His name.

~*~

A black vehicle pulled up, and Lukas climbed in.

"You look different in person." The guard behind the wheel held up his cuffphone, allowing Lukas to glimpse the photo onscreen. In red, the word "clearance" blinked above the I.D. picture.

Lukas shrugged. "That was taken on a bad hair day."

"Armed guards and EMTs to laboratory wing B, immediately!" The command blasted through the guard's cuffphone.

Lukas's pulse revved along with the security vehicle's motor. "Can't this thing go any faster?" he yelled at the driver.

"Sure, and we can crash right into the front entrance and explode in flames." The guard screeched to a stop in front of the building.

Lukas leapt from the car.

"Stay here," the guard yelled, holding his fleshcard to the front sensor, disabling the locks.

"Not on your life." Lukas bolted past him in a dead run. Inside, armed guards shouted for him to stop as he tore down the hallway. "Caster Stone! I have clearance from Brown. Check your cuffs," he puffed over his shoulder.

Lukas ran the same direction as the guards. He had no idea where he was going. He only hoped the chaotic parade would come to an abrupt halt with Briar standing safely at the end.

Lukas burst through the double doors of the laboratory wing. He rushed to an open doorway surrounded by guards with weapons drawn.

"Move back, before you get hurt," A harsh voice whispered from behind. He turned to find a half a dozen more guards rushing into the area.

Lukas ignored the man and pushed against the throng of uniforms in the doorway. He lifted to his toes, straining to see over the shoulders of the guards. His heart seized as he glimpsed Briar strapped to the table, and Reid holding an empty syringe.

Five minutes, maybe less, before Briar's soul was lost forever.

"Brown," he shouted hoarsely. "Caster Stone. Let me through."

The guards tightened their barricade, some elbowing him, others ramming him with their shoulders.

"Let him in."

Lukas shoved a hand in his pocket, grabbing Caster's surgical mask.

The guards parted at Brown's command. Lukas tied the mask behind his head as he rushed to Briar's bedside.

"No!" Reid screamed, lunging for Lukas. Her shouts became a shrill operatic scream as the electric current of a stun weapon arrested her vocal chords. Two guards maneuvered her to the floor while another secured her in handcuffs.

Lukas searched the implement tray for the antidote vial. It wasn't there. His blood chilled. What if Reid had destroyed it?

The medical kit—where was it? Maybe the vial was still in the case. He dashed around an unconscious woman and two medical technicians to reach the counter, where the kit lied open on the surface. Relief flooded him. The antidote was there, loaded in a syringe.

He snapped on a pair of gloves from the box on the countertop, wove around the EMTs and security guards, and returned to Briar's side. She was unconscious. From a sedative? From the pain? He didn't know. Willing his hands not to shake, he inserted the needle into Briar's cranium, injecting the antidote.

She didn't move. He wondered if something had gone wrong—even more terribly wrong than he'd assumed. Had Reid done something more heinous than he'd anticipated? Had she injected Briar with something other than abstergent? Something lethal? Lukas immediately crushed the thought to dust.

From the implement table, he retrieved the preloaded inserter, and quickly implanted the tiny collagen plug into Briar's skull. He unfastened the head restraint and gently turned her head, clasping the other side to the table.

He positioned the needle above the hole as Reid's laughter raked over his spine. He glanced up as two guards yanked her to her feet.

"Max, you idiot. That's not Caster Stone. It's his brother, Lukas."

Brown glared at Lukas. "Seize him," he ordered.

The guards moved toward him.

Lukas lowered the syringe to Briar's skull, concealing the needle behind his palm. "The needle is in her brain. One wrong move could kill her."

"And this death will have witnesses." Aided by emergency techs, the woman with braided hair rose from the floor. "Unlike the hundreds of others you've covered up."

A vein in Brown's neck bulged.

"The ARC's going down, Max," Lukas said. "So are you. Briar Lee's death will be the nail in your coffin."

A guard turned to Max. "Sir?"

Max shook his head.

Lukas nearly collapsed with relief. He inserted the needle, draining the antidote into Briar's brain.

"Come back to me," he breathed, implanting the second plug. He returned the inserter to the tray and unfastened each of her restraints. "Come back to me." He removed the surgical mask, snapped off his gloves, and took her face in his hands, his vision blurring as he willed her eyes to open.

There must have been sound in the room—the technicians helping their patient to the door. The anguished cries of Reid, restrained in handcuffs. The incessant ring of Maxwell Brown's cuffphone. Lukas heard nothing. Activity took place silently around him. Life was on mute. The only sound, the thickening air pushing and pulling from his lungs.

"Briar," he whispered, caressing her cheek with his thumb. "I'm so sorry. Please stay." His tears fell to her face—that beautiful face he'd hoped to wake up to every single day, for the rest of his life. Only God could have fashioned something so perfect. A priceless gift. A woman custom created for him. He knew that now.

And he didn't need functioning Agathi to recognize it. "I love you."

He closed his eyes. "God—please forgive me. Please bring her back to me. I believe in her. And I believe in You."

"Lukas? You're here?"

His eyes snapped open. "I'm here."

Briar's brow furrowed. "Did you fly?"

"I flew. Can you believe it?"

"You must really love me a lot." Her eyes crinkled as she grinned.

Lukas laughed and cried at the same time.

The noise level returned. Guards struggled to escort Reid from the room as she thrashed violently and called them names.

A nurse approached Briar's bedside. "I'll take your vitals."

"Is Cleo all right?" Briar asked.

"She's fine," the nurse said, tapping Briar's fleshcard. "Resting in the next room."

"Thank God," she whispered, closing her eyes.

Lukas leaned down to kiss her forehead.

Her eyes flew open, shining like stars "Lukas! He's here," she said, pressing a hand to her chest.

"Who?" Lukas asked.

"God," she breathed.

"Yes." Lukas nodded. "I know."

27

Briar glanced around the beige hospital room. "I don't know why I'm still here. I feel good, physically." She wished she could say the same for her emotions. But wounds of that nature mended slower than a couple of jabs to the brain. She doubted they ever truly mended at all.

"Relax," Lukas said from her bedside. "Your evaluation will be finished soon, and you'll be free." He gave her hand a gentle kiss.

You'll be free. She couldn't imagine three more beautiful words. She gazed up at Lukas. Then again, maybe she could.

Lukas aimed his cuffphone at the wall, filling the space with images and sound.

"Ugh, turn it off." Briar covered her head—her *bald* head—with the thin hospital pillow.

"Off?" Don't you want to see Maxwell Brown and his wife, Vanessa, forced into the police car for the zillionth time?"

"No!" Briar peeked from under the pillow. "They've been showing that clip for days."

Lukas grinned and flipped through the channels.

"Stop!" Briar shouted. "Go back one." She sat straight up in the bed.

Lukas switched to the previous channel. An African-American woman with silver curls sat in a softly lit room, conversing with a brunette anchor from a nightly news program.

"Harper!" Tears fell from Briar's eyes as she gazed

at the screen.

"Experimentation?" Harper asked the reporter. "Oh, yes, ma'am. The scars on my back are the worst. But this is the only mark I'm willing to show on television." Harper lifted the back of her hand to the camera.

Briar rubbed a thumb over her matching emblem.

"My lion. The ARC symbol. They branded us so we could be identified." Harper lowered her hand to her lap. "Always made me think of that Scripture in First Peter about how the enemy is a roaring lion, seeking to devour." She caressed the tattoo. "Today it makes me think of the Lion of Judah. A mighty conqueror." She gave a little grin. "Most folks have no idea what I'm talking about. But now—praise be to God—they'll have the opportunity to find out."

The reporter offered a somber smile. "As a society, what can we learn from this horrific event in American history?"

The camera closed in on Harper's lined face. "The mind governed by the flesh is death, but the mind governed by the Spirit is life and peace. Romans, chapter eight, verse six. And a mind governed by the government ain't worth two cents. I made that part up." She winked. "People can destroy our bodies, but they can't destroy our souls. God is faithful. His commandments are the only ones that endure."

Briar wiped a tear and applauded. Granna Grace wasn't here to see the fall of The Commandment, but Harper Ross was.

Epilogue

Ten years later

Briar watched her husband from the doorway, loving the way his hair fell across his brow as he worked. She walked to his stool and kissed his cheek. "What's cooking, Dr. Stone?"

He glanced up. "Well, *Prettier Dr. Stone,* we've received another large order for SAP antidote, and have once again run out. I'm preparing to make more."

"Ran out since yesterday?"

"Impossible, right?"

Briar perked an eyebrow. "Caster Stone is an ordained prison minister. Nothing is impossible."

Lukas grinned. "You left off the important part—nothing is impossible *with God.* Running out of SAP antidote is definitely a God thing."

Briar agreed. Since the fall of The Commandment, the demand for anti-SAP was never ending. All three Stone Labs locations were preparing antidote around the clock, and still couldn't catch up. People were taking back their Agathi—and their God.

"Dr. Stone?"

Lukas and Briar both turned to see Derby in the doorway, wearing his "Holy Floats" ball cap and t-shirt with hot air balloon graphics.

"*Mrs.* Doctor Stone." He motioned to Briar. "Someone's here to see you."

Briar squeezed her husband's shoulder and

walked to the door.

"Derby, remind me later, I have a permission slip to give you from one of my patients. I recommended your hot air balloon ministry to his mother as part of his therapy plan."

Derby gave a wide grin.

As Briar entered the waiting room, a young man jumped to his feet and stuck out a hand. "Michael Owens."

Briar shook the man's hand. He was tall and handsome with a few boyish freckles. She'd seen him before…hadn't she? But where? Her eyes went wide. "Mouse!" She yanked him in for a tight hug.

Mouse chuckled. "It's good to see you, too, Briar."

"I'm so glad you're all right." Briar released him and stepped back. "What happened? I tried to contact you. It was as though you'd vanished."

"I know. I'm sorry. After the whole thing with the ARC, my mom went a little nuts. Took herself—and me—completely offline. I'm still convincing her to wire back in, a little at a time. These days, I buy my own technology. He glanced at his cuffphone. "Find me online—under Michael Owens, not Mouse."

"I'll do that."

"Anyway," His eyes turned serious. "I saw your picture on the Stone Labs advertisement—you haven't changed much, by the way—and looked you up. I had to come. To say thanks. For helping a sad little kid find some happiness."

"I enjoyed our online visits. I'm sure you helped me as much as I helped you—maybe more."

"You're still helping me. When I saw you on that ad, I clicked onto the website. I watched the video about everything you'd experienced, heard you talk about how God brought you through it." Mouse took a deep breath. "I did some research on anti-SAP, and had an injection a week ago. My grandmother's taking me to church next Sunday."

Briar hugged him again. "I'm so proud of you."

He gave her a tight squeeze. "Me, too." He released her and stepped toward the door. "I'll stop by again sometime."

"You'd better." Briar waved. "See you later, Michael."

"You can call me Mouse."

Briar watched him go, her grandmother's voice filling her ears. She closed her eyes and spoke Granna Grace's words aloud. "Who knows whether you have come here—"

"—for such a time as this." Lukas finished the sentence.

She opened her eyes to find him by her side. Forever.

Thank you…

for purchasing this Watershed Books title. For other inspirational stories, please visit our on-line bookstore at www.pelicanbookgroup.com.

For questions or more information, contact us at customer@pelicanbookgroup.com.

Watershed Books
Make a Splash!™
an imprint of Pelican Book Group
www.PelicanBookGroup.com

Connect with Us
www.facebook.com/Pelicanbookgroup
www.twitter.com/pelicanbookgrp

To receive news and specials, subscribe to our bulletin
http://pelink.us/bulletin

May God's glory shine through
this inspirational work of fiction.

AMDG

You Can Help!

At Pelican Book Group it is our mission to entertain readers with fiction that uplifts the Gospel. It is our privilege to spend time with you awhile as you read our stories.

We believe you can help us to bring Christ into the lives of people across the globe. And you don't have to open your wallet or even leave your house!

Here are 3 simple things you can do to help us bring illuminating fiction™ to people everywhere.

1) If you enjoyed this book, write a positive review. Post it at online retailers and websites where readers gather. And share your review with us at reviews@pelicanbookgroup.com (this does give us permission to reprint your review in whole or in part.)

2) If you enjoyed this book, recommend it to a friend in person, at a book club or on social media.

3) If you have suggestions on how we can improve or expand our selection, let us know. We value your opinion. Use the contact form on our web site or e-mail us at customer@pelicanbookgroup.com

God Can Help!

Are you in need? The Almighty can do great things for you. Holy is His Name! He has mercy in every generation. He can lift up the lowly and accomplish all things. Reach out today.

Do not fear: I am with you; do not be anxious: I am your God. I will strengthen you, I will help you, I will uphold you with my victorious right hand.

~Isaiah 41:10 (NAB)

We pray daily, and we especially pray for everyone connected to Pelican Book Group—that includes you! If you have a specific need, we welcome the opportunity to pray for you. Share your needs or praise reports at http://pelink.us/pray4us

Free Book Offer

We're looking for booklovers like you to partner with us! Join our team of influencers today and periodically receive free eBooks and exclusive offers.

For more information
Visit http://pelicanbookgroup.com/booklovers

www.ingramcontent.com/pod-product-compliance
Lightning Source LLC
Chambersburg PA
CBHW020418260626
47156CB00007B/2441
* 9 7 8 1 5 2 2 3 9 7 8 2 3 *